CONTENTS

THE MOST HERETICAL LAST BOSS QUEEN

FROM VILLAINESS TO SAVIOR

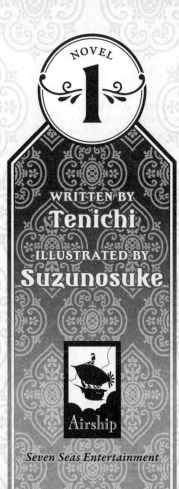

NOVEL

1

WRITTEN BY
Tenichi

ILLUSTRATED BY
Suzunosuke

Airship

Seven Seas Entertainment

Higeki no Genkyoutonaru Saikyou Gedou Rasubosu
Joou wa Taminotameni Tsukushimasu. Vol. 1
© 2019 Tenichi. All rights reserved.
First published in Japan in 2019 by Ichijinsha Inc.
Publication rights for this English edition arranged
through Kodansha Ltd., Tokyo.

Seven Seas press and purchase enquiries can be sent to
Marketing Manager Lianne Sentar at press@gomanga.com.
Information regarding the distribution and purchase of
digital editions is available from Digital Manager CK Russell
at digital@gomanga.com.

Seven Seas and the Seven Seas logo are trademarks of
Seven Seas Entertainment. All rights reserved.

Follow Seven Seas Entertainment online at
sevenseasentertainment.com.

TRANSLATION: Emma Schumacker
ADAPTATION: Michelle McGuinness
COVER DESIGN: H. Qi
INTERIOR LAYOUT & DESIGN: Clay Gardner
COPY EDITOR: Meg van Huygen
LIGHT NOVEL EDITOR: T. Anne
PREPRESS TECHNICIAN: Melanie Ujimori
PRINT MANAGER: Rhiannon Rasmussen-Silverstein
PRODUCTION MANAGER: Lissa Pattillo
EDITOR-IN-CHIEF: Julie Davis
ASSOCIATE PUBLISHER: Adam Arnold
PUBLISHER: Jason DeAngelis

ISBN: 978-1-64827-842-6
Printed in Canada
First Printing: April 2022
10 9 8 7 6 5 4 3 2 1

1
The Selfish Princess Awakens

WHEN MY LIFE flashed before my eyes, I found it remarkably...normal. That isn't to say it was all smooth sailing, but compared to most, it was pretty darn ordinary.

After getting accepted to a junior college in my senior year of high school, my only real dilemma was how I'd enjoy my break to the fullest. I skipped right along through life, daydreaming about replaying my favorite otome series from the beginning. I was humming to myself, fantasizing about all the routes and romances, when I stepped out onto the crosswalk just as a car barreled through the intersection.

That was how life as I knew it ended.

"Your Highness! Can you hear me?!"

"Princess Pride!"

Servants frantically called my name. I cradled my head and sank to the floor as the world faded to darkness around me.

"Someone call the doctor! We must tell the queen and prince consort what's happened!"

"The princess is hurt!"

My name was Pride Royal Ivy. I was the eight-year-old daughter of the queen—the firstborn princess of my country. At least, that's who I was here in the world of *Our Ray of Light*, the otome game I'd planned on replaying. But why did I have to end up as Pride, of all people? She wasn't just evil and devious. She was the final boss!

I awoke in a plush bed. I forced my eyes open, staring at the ceiling as maids flitted by, rushing in and out of the lavish room, arguing over details that my reeling mind couldn't quite grasp.

I only have ten years left... I can't believe I'm going to die at the same age in two different lives.

My head spun, trying to sort the memories of my past life from the reality before me. Incredible as it sounded, I'd really woken up in a video game world. I knew the protagonists, the background characters, even the setting itself. I recognized every detail.

And I knew I wouldn't live long.

As Pride, I would destroy the kingdom in ten years' time and terrorize this world as its final boss. Destiny decreed that I scar the hearts of the love interests—and pay for my crimes with my life.

Indeed, this was the world of *Our Ray of Light*. It was a longer series than most, and from what I could tell, I was in the very first game. People of all ages enjoyed "ORL," as we called it. I got hooked on the anime version of the third game, and that infatuation grew until I played through every single installment, from oldest to newest. Whenever they released a new one, I jumped right on it. I was *obsessed*.

"Pride!"

My father flung the door open with a bang, charging right past the flustered guards.

"Father..."

The prince consort scowled—or, at least, he seemed to. Everyone else mistook his wrinkled forehead and serious expression for sternness, but I knew just how kind he was beneath the surface. Sure, he could be strict, but he loved his daughter with all his heart. He shooed the maids and guards out of the room to speak with me privately.

"Are you all right?" he asked me.

"Yes. My head started to hurt all of a sudden..."

"The doctor says your life isn't in any danger, but Rosa was worried about you too."

As queen, Rosa Royal Ivy, my mother, was the highest authority in the kingdom. Needless to say, she outranked Father in that regard. It was no surprise she was too busy to come see me herself even under these circumstances. While Father always told me she would visit me if she could, I now knew the true reason for her absence.

"Father."

"What is it?" he said, watching me anxiously.

"I have a little sister who will soon turn six, don't I?"

He blinked, taken aback, which only confirmed what I already knew. If this really was the world of my otome game, then I had a younger sister—Tiara Royal Ivy, the protagonist of this whole story.

"How do you know that?" Father said.

It was the first time I'd ever seen such shock on my father's face. Something about my question threw him off, but I'd only just regained my memories, so I wasn't sure what.

Wait, this all seems familiar somehow...

"Could it be?" he said. "Do you share the same precognition as your mother? Is that what made you collapse?"

Father stared down at me, his gaze never wavering, and gently brushed my hair off my brow. I'd inherited my father's crimson locks, but my mother's soft waves.

"Yes," he mused. "My congratulations, Pride. This proves you are the true heir to the throne."

Father beamed at me, tears forming in his eyes. I, meanwhile, tried not to cry for a wholly different reason. With a few simple words, I'd royally messed up. Now, all I could do was try not to scream as the gravity of the whole situation sank in.

That's right! I was thinking of Pride's childhood in the game!

You see, with that one simple line about my sister, I'd just marched beat for beat toward my own doom.

Our Ray of Light was set in the sprawling kingdom of "Freesia," a mysterious land and the only place in the world where humans were born with special powers. Naturally, that included my precognition. While one out of every couple hundred people would inherit some kind of power, precognition was the rarest. It belonged solely to those in line for the Freesian throne and existed only among members of the royal family, especially women, manifesting once every few decades. Many viewed precognition as a divine message anointing our next ruler. In the game, Pride fainted when she was eight years old. When she awoke, she mentioned a younger sister who had been kept secret from her. She said all this to her father on the very day he planned to reveal the secret himself. It was the moment her precognition awakened and she earned the title of the future queen of Freesia.

But that's exactly what just happened to me!

When the love interests talked about this scene, they called it "The moment that would lead to unimaginable tragedy for our kingdom."

Even as dread sank cold into my gut, my father's face lit up with joy. But I knew things were playing out exactly the same way as they had in the game. Guilty as it made me feel, I needed a way to make this seem like anything *but* precognition. However, when I opened my mouth, no words escaped.

Father noticed my confused expression, but he apparently took it for exhaustion. "Get some rest for now, Pride," he said. "I know you're still confused, so we'll talk about your sister Tiara some other time."

He offered a smile before he rose and left, surely on his way to tell Mother of this momentous development. The instant he exited, the guards and maids swept back in.

"My sister..." I muttered. I turned to the window, staring out at the gardens below as though I could escape that way. "But...I already know everything about her."

For example, I knew my younger sister, Tiara Royal Ivy, inherited our parents' compassion and grace. My mother carried herself with poise and wisdom, while my kindhearted father served as her assistant. Frail, delicate little Tiara was the protagonist of this game, a sweet princess who had to be kept a secret to protect her from kidnapping and assassination attempts.

Tiara... Even her name was cute, unlike "Pride," a rough, overbearing name suited for the villain of the story. I teared up just thinking about her, but that was wrong, so very wrong. My little heart simply couldn't take the waves of emotion, and soon I was desperately sniffling, trying to keep the snot and tears inside me. I would become the wicked final boss—and Tiara would become the heroine.

During every single route in the game, Pride died at the hands of the main characters. Even the "bad" endings simply had Tiara or a love interest take Pride's place. No matter how I looked at it, I was doomed. Moreover, I *deserved* it. Tiara and her love interests were good, honest people. I wouldn't dare cheat my way to a bad ending with my past-life memories. By the end, Pride was so completely evil, she deserved nothing better than death. As much as I loved the game, I certainly wasn't a fan of Pride when I played ORL in real life. Fans of the love interests especially hated Pride, and some of that hatred seeped into me now.

I lashed out at the table beside my bed, frustrated to find myself in the body of someone I detested. A maid jerked at the sound of the kick and the table rattling.

"Oh... I'm sorry," I said.

Shoot! It's things like this that'll add up to make me the wicked queen...

The wide-eyed maid simply straightened out the table. "There's no need to apologize," she said stiffly, shooting me nervous glances out of the side of her eyes.

Well, no surprise there. Pride—or, I suppose, *I*—didn't hold back at all with the maids. I'd fired many and even threatened some with death if they displeased me. Of course, Father intercepted all my attempts to punish them. The normal Pride would have sent the table flying across the room and screamed at the maids to fix it at once, but I couldn't act out like that, not while retaining my memories of my previous life. I didn't want to be like that Pride. I *couldn't* be like that Pride. In the game, Pride used precognition to torment the love interests and allow tragedies to unfold, but I wanted to take a different course. If only I knew more than just the existence of my sister. If only I knew about my father's—

"Ah!"

I leapt out of bed with a gasp. The maids all spun toward me. Even the guards outside the door rushed into my room. A flurry of voices asked me what was wrong, but I brushed them all aside.

"Where's Father?!" I said.

"His Royal Highness just left to inform Her Majesty of today's events," a maid informed me.

This is bad! At this rate, he'll...

"Stop him right now!" I ordered. "He can't get on that carriage!"

"But Her Majesty is here at the residence, so I don't believe he'll need to take a carriage."

It was no use. The maid, stuck here at my bedside, didn't realize the queen's plans might have changed.

I rushed to the window, sticking my head out to view the sprawling garden below. A single carriage sat parked before the house. My father approached it alone, preparing to go see my mother. Contrary to the maid's assertion, Mother was back at the main castle attending to urgent business, and that was precisely where Father planned to go.

No! He can't take that carriage!

"Father!" I screamed.

He froze, but then he simply waved up at me.

No, I'm not saying goodbye!

I'd intended to warn him, but he carried on, blissfully unaware. I couldn't just go on yelling for him not to board the carriage. He'd think I was a kid throwing a tantrum.

In that case...

I placed my foot on the windowsill and leaned out past the frame. Father's pleasant smile melted into raw fear. My room, the room of a firstborn princess, easily rose higher than an average house. A fall would be fatal.

"Your Highness?!" the maid behind me blurted. "Stop that at on—"

"Stay back!" I said. "It'll be your head if you stop me!"

I lifted myself up to stand on the windowsill. If I lost my footing, I'd plummet to the ground. The wind gusted against me, sending my long hair streaming behind me. I could hardly breathe aside from panicked sips of air.

"Get down from there, Pride!" Father shouted far below, his face twisted with terror.

Well, I definitely got his attention. Thank goodness.

I steadied myself by clutching the posts and forced down a deep breath.

"Father!" I yelled down to him. "You can't board that carriage! It has a broken wheel, and you'll get into an accident before you can speak to Mother!"

Even from a distance, I could see him blinking in confusion. For the second time today, I'd shocked him with one of my pronouncements.

I hardly got the words out before one of the guards grabbed me and yanked me back into the room. But back outside, my father's voice rose as he demanded someone inspect the carriage's wheels.

Crisis averted. Now I can relax a little.

This time, at least, I thwarted the events of the game. In ORL, Pride's father boarded the carriage to rush to the queen and inform her of Pride's newly awakened precognition. But the carriage collapsed, gravely injuring him. He survived only long enough to tell the queen of Pride's gift with his dying breaths. Somehow, Pride never foresaw her father's accident. Not in the game, at least. Here, where I knew the whole story, I could save him. It was truly a blessing.

The guard loosened his grip when he realized I wasn't resisting. I turned, relieved, but yelped when I saw a maid curled up on the floor in tears. Everyone else stood frozen around her, their faces pale and bloodless. Only that one guard seemed capable of speaking.

"Are you hurt, Your Highness?" he asked me.

Before I could answer, an older maid stepped in front of the one crying on the ground. She fell to her knees at my feet.

"P-please, Your Highness, forgive her. She has nowhere else to go, so I beg of you, please show her mercy." She trembled as she apologized over and over before me.

Whoops. Might've overdone it there.

I should have known better than to throw around threats, even in the heat of the moment. The maid apparently believed I really would have her executed for trying to stop me in the window. I was the crown princess, after all. Everyone around me was at the mercy of my whims. Once again, Pride's selfish whims, *my* selfish whims, had caused so much pain.

"I'm..."

I wanted to apologize, but the more I thought about it, the more my head spun. Even the guard who'd pulled me away from the window must have been bracing for some sort of punishment, yet he'd reached out to protect the precious daughter of the queen anyway.

"I'm...I'm sorry," I said.

Perhaps the emotions were just too much for an eight-year-old's body. Something reached into my chest and squeezed all the air out of my lungs. I burst into tears before I could stop myself. The guard and maids all looked on in bewilderment as I sobbed before them, babbling out tear-thickened apologies.

From the eighteen years of experience I'd gained in my past life, I knew just how much fear power could instill in others and just how much grief could come from having that power used against you. More than anything, I wanted to engrave these facts into my mind for the ten remaining years of my life, so that I would never forget or abuse this authority I'd woken up into.

After all, I was the crown princess of this kingdom.

Father eventually came back up to my room. He consoled me while I cried until I calmed enough to speak, and he made me swear never to do anything so reckless again. Though he did confess that the attendants found one cracked wheel and one defective one when they inspected the carriage.

"I owe you my life. Thank you, Pride," he said, wrapping me in his arms.

Almost as quickly as I'd managed to stop crying, the tears flowed again.

Later that day, when Mother returned to the castle, Father recounted the day's events to her. I became the official heir to the throne at that point, and the news of my awakened powers spread to the people of the kingdom. When Father tried to ask my guards and maids what exactly happened, I placed myself between him and the servants.

"It was all my fault," I said. "These people were only looking out for me, so if anyone deserves punishment, it's me." But Father just smiled and shook his head, and I realized he'd never intended to punish anyone in the first place.

That night, Father stayed by my side until I fell asleep. He hadn't done that for me in ages. He spoke softly and soothingly, telling me about my younger sister Tiara like it was a bedtime story. He said he'd planned to tell me about her that very day before I blurted it out myself. I would get to meet her in one month on her birthday, but until then I wouldn't see her or Mother much. It turned out the queen had to spend a lot of time looking after sickly little Tiara on top of all her other duties.

He stroked my hair, so like his and my mother's, as he described Tiara more. "You and Tiara are both our precious daughters. Nothing could ever change that," he said, his gaze brimming with affection.

I had to wonder if the Pride in the game would turn into a corrupted, evil queen if her father had gotten to live and say such lovely things to her all the time. It was still possible, of course, but maybe his kindness would have changed the course of events for her.

Father warned that the pace of my studies would pick up now that I was officially recognized as the heir to the throne. He rattled off a list of subjects—governing, local history, etiquette, procedures—and my eyelids grew heavy as lead. I drifted off to the sound of his voice, the deep rumble of his soothing tone as he debated adopting a little brother to serve as my assistant now.

Wait... A brother?!

꧁❀꧂

"I won't forgive you... I'll never forgive you! I'm going to kill you!"

A boy was crying, his tearful eyes ablaze with pure hatred. He stared straight ahead at a girl who cackled right back at him, a girl too young to soften her laugh to be more ladylike. She clutched her sides as she laughed down at the boy.

"Ah ha ha! How foolish can you be? You could never kill me. After all..."

I knew both of these people. No, it was more than that...

That girl was me.

Pride Royal Ivy. She...or rather, *I* was the girl who irreparably scarred the hearts of all the game's love interests. My younger sister, Tiara, would sweep in to heal their wounds. After I received my punishment at the end of the game, Tiara would take my seat as the queen and set the kingdom back on the path to harmony alongside her love interest.

I remembered this scene from the game. From what I could recall, it was the memory of one of the love interests.

"Why did you trick me?!" the boy said. "I-I just... I wanted to see her, that's all..."

The boy gritted his teeth, tears tracking down his cheeks while I pointed at him and howled with laughter. That laugh was too big, too cruel, too evil to fit inside one little girl, yet there I was. Meanwhile, the boy kept calling out for someone.

"I missed her. I missed her so much," the boy said.

"Ah ha ha ha! Oh, that's right. You'd better keep this a secret," I said. "Not that anyone would listen to a dirty former commoner like you."

I kept up my laughter, and the boy howled until his voice went hoarse. Over and over again, he cried out that he would kill me.

His name was...Stale. Stale Royal Ivy—Pride's adopted younger brother-in-law.

Someone... Someone save him.

He hadn't done anything wrong, but I couldn't do anything for him. After all, I was the one who hurt him.

The one who could help him, the one who was his only salvation from the life he lived at the castle, was his adopted younger sister-in-law.

"Tiara..."

I opened my eyes with a gasp. Just a dream. But I recognized the events from the game.

The moment I awoke, my maids launched into my morning routine, starting with grooming. I glared back into my own dark eyes in the mirror, watching one of the women comb through my hair. Those eyes were so much like Father's, just like the bright red of my hair, even if the waves came from Mother. Father beamed with pride to have a daughter who'd inherited so much of him, but I couldn't help thinking the combination of purple eyes and bright red hair made me look like a witch—or a final boss. I struggled not to wince at the reflection of the wicked enemy of

ORL staring right back at me. No one wanted to look at such a thing early in the morning.

In the game, Pride took the throne quickly thanks to her newly awakened precognition, seizing the opportunity after her father died in the accident and her mother followed after him from grief. Still, she was spiteful about her mother's disproportionate attention toward her younger sister. Thus, Pride sent Tiara away to live in a distant castle, creating a life of luxury for herself as she ruled over the country with an iron fist. The surrounding countries grew increasingly worried as Pride turned into a dictator.

But all of that wouldn't happen for ten more years, on the day of Tiara's sixteenth birthday. In the meantime, Tiara met her many love interests, healed the trauma they carried in their hearts, and stood up to Pride, deepening the rift between them. Eventually, Tiara's own powers of precognition emerged, bestowing upon her the same divine mark of leadership.

"Princess Pride... Your Highness?"

"Huh?"

The maid's voice finally dragged me back to the present. It was the same woman who'd been so overcome with terror that she'd cried on the floor the other day. Now, she gently set my hair down, having finished brushing it. Remarkably, she didn't seem to hate me for the incident. If anything, she'd become kinder, more tender as she chuckled and told me my hair was all combed through.

How did I never notice until now? I have such a wonderful maid working for me. She's very... Wait...

I cocked my head in confusion. Now that I thought about it, I hardly knew anything about this woman.

"What's your name?" I asked.

The maid raised her eyebrows before she could compose herself and smiled sweetly. "Lotte."

I made a point of asking the names of other servants as I made my way through the castle that morning. The older maid who'd defended Lotte was Mary. The guard who'd pulled me out of the window was Jack. I committed these three names to memory—Lotte, Mary, and Jack. Such a simple thing, yet it was like opening the curtains and letting the sun shine into this dreary castle. This was the first time anyone apart from Father had added vibrance to my world.

I spent much of the day that way. It wasn't long before I noticed the staff looking at me a little differently. I was still the firstborn princess, of course, and the official heir to the throne, but that wasn't the only change. Rumors swirled about how I'd saved my father from that carriage ride.

"That spoiled little princess finally learned how to behave?"

"The bratty princess must've been possessed by a goddess."

Some people seemed to believe that developing precognition was the reason my personality changed so drastically. I bit my tongue and let them believe whatever they liked, even though I wanted nothing more than to tell them they were all wrong. I wasn't possessed by a goddess or anything like that—I'd simply regained the memories of my past life. Certainly, in the game, precognition did little to improve Pride's sinister personality.

If anything, she became more vile. But now, I appeared to them much more competent to rule the kingdom in the future.

By afternoon, I couldn't remember that morning's dream anymore, even though something about it seemed so important. The more I thought about it, the more I realized the names of the love interests weren't coming to me either. I knew there were five total in the series, including certain hidden characters. Also, I could still recall the plot of the game from replaying it over and over to get all the endings. However, I didn't remember many details about the love interests themselves. My favorite was the third game in the series, which I'd replayed now and again, but I only ever fully cleared the first and second games. Once each at that. How could I forget games I'd played so obsessively in life? Even on the day I died, I'd been daydreaming about replaying the series all over again from the first game.

It's fine. I'm sure I'll remember the details when I meet everyone, since my life follows the same plot as the game.

Except that all depended on this life being the same as the plot of the game and, well, I'd already gone and changed that. The mere fact that both my parents were alive proved deviation was possible.

Can I actually change the story of the game?!

It was a little late for me to make that realization, but it struck me like a slap to the face. What else could I change? How much could I change?

I didn't have much time to think it over. At dinner the next day, Father said my adopted brother-in-law, one of the game's love interests, would be arriving at the castle in two weeks.

The Wicked Princess and the Adopted Brother-in-Law

*H*OW *UTTERLY depressing.*

Stale, my little brother, was finally due to arrive at the castle.

I still couldn't wrap my head around having a brother-in-law, even an adopted one. I mean, I was only eight years old, a bit young for that kind of thing. I even tried to convince Father to drop it, but he insisted we adhere to the tradition. In Freesia, custom demanded the heir to the throne have a special assistant or servant, a boy adopted into the family precisely for this purpose. He had to be younger than the heir, which, combined with his gender, would make him ineligible for the title, even once he became a member of the royal family. It shielded him from assassination attempts so he could perform his function.

"Stale..."

I sighed. I still found the whole thing weird. Stale probably suffered so much after being ripped away from his own family to serve mine.

Stale Royal Ivy had lost his father to illness at a young age and spent his childhood with only his mother. While a commoner, he too possessed a special power. Stale could transport anything he touched, including himself, like a sort of teleportation.

In the game, Pride took advantage of Stale's desire to return to his mother to lock him into a "fealty contract," a horrible deal that forced him to obey Pride's every order without fail. He wasn't even an assistant at that point—he was just a puppet.

Of course, I had no plan of putting him through anything like that. But I couldn't help worrying that my good intentions would mean little. For one thing, why would Stale listen to his new sister-in-law at all? And what would I do if he didn't? Would I become like that other Pride, the Pride from the game? Part of me feared she was the one making me think such ugly thoughts in the first place. In the game, she savored Stale's rage, his hatred. Ultimately, she forced him to commit an act he never recovered from.

"Your new brother-in-law has arrived at the castle, Your Highness," Lotte said, jolting me out of my anxious thoughts. "Your father would like to introduce him to you."

I had no choice but to follow her to where my father awaited, his hand resting on the shoulder of a boy with glossy black hair and dark eyes. Stale looked just the way I remembered from the game, from his pale skin to the high bridge of his nose. Though youthful now, I knew he would grow into a quiet, intriguing, bespectacled, intelligent man. It seemed the glasses would come in to the picture later.

"Pride," Father said. "This is Stale. He's to be your younger brother-in-law. He's one year younger than you, and he'll be serving as your steward and assistant. Once you rule, he will be your seneschal. Though he's a commoner, his power of teleportation is quite impressive. I expect the two of you will get along splendidly."

At first, I saw nothing but the character from the game, the Stale I expected. Then I noticed something I never saw in the game and jerked back a step.

Everything about his appearance was ordinary enough—aside from the handcuffs binding his wrists. His hands weren't completely constricted, but it was still a shocking sight. Stale glared at the floor with a grim expression. Even a child could easily tell that these weren't normal handcuffs. They were made of some kind of shiny material and decorated with jewels.

"Ah, did the handcuffs startle you?" Father said. "While I pity the boy, this is necessary for now. He kept escaping via teleportation while we were traveling here. He even injured a guard at one point. He seems to have settled down for now, but we can't have him disappearing on us again. These shackles will prevent him from using his power until he can enter a subordination contract with you tomorrow. Then there'll be no point in keeping the chains on any longer." He stroked Stale's hair as he spoke, an oddly tender gesture when contrasted with his words.

I had to remind myself that all of this was normal in this world, regardless of what my morals and ethics from my previous life dictated. Even the "subordination contract" was just an ordinary part of what my younger brother-in-law could expect. That contract existed so he could never betray me. It was a kind of bond found only in our kingdom and backed up by enchantments so neither signer could break the conditions of the contract.

My brother-in-law would need to remain within a certain physical distance of me at all times and remain loyal to my commands.

The Pride of the game took it a step further, forcing Stale to sign a bond of "fealty." That was a stricter bond that tacked on compulsory obedience to every command. In ORL, Pride stole that contract from her dead father's study, switching it for the supposed "subordination contract."

"Once you sign this, I'll let you see your mother again," she told him.

From that moment on, Stale was doomed. Even if he signed a subordination contract, the stricter fealty contract always took precedence. Stale, the seven-year-old commoner who could read and write no more than his own name, only realized the horror of what he'd done after the contract was complete.

But I'd never do anything like that!

Stale was still studying his feet. I rushed to his side and took his shackled hands in mine, giving them a gentle squeeze.

"I'm Pride Royal Ivy," I said. "It's so nice to meet you, Stale. We'll be family from here out, so let's get along, okay?"

Stale looked up, blinking in surprise before his head wilted right back down.

"Okay..." he murmured.

What?! Hold on, I think I've seen this before...

My smile withered. I backed away from Stale as realization crept over me. Pride said those exact same lines during this scene in the game. Later, Stale spoke of his past and mentioned how kindly Pride had been when she approached him, acting like a compassionate older sister the very same night she forced him to sign that fealty contract.

I knew it. I'm stuck in the same script from the game, no matter what I do...

I froze, despair welling up inside me, and Father stepped in front of Stale. "You must be exhausted from the day's events," he said. "Rest up so you're prepared for tomorrow."

Then Father led Stale away toward his new room in the castle. But something about this felt off. In the game, an assistant introduced Pride to Stale.

So are things different because Father's alive now? Wait, and didn't something happen with that assistant?

I dug through my memory to dredge up Father's assistant, but I couldn't recall the man. Father visited me alone most of the time, meaning I'd probably met this assistant a few brief times at most.

But what about Stale?!

I broke into a run, chasing after Father and Stale. I had to know which room he'd be in, or else my plan would fall through!

As I rushed after them, I realized I was headed right for the room below mine. Father stopped me outside the door.

"Let him rest for today. Understand?" he said. He waved for Lotte and Mary to escort me back to my own room.

But that wasn't good enough! I had to talk to Stale before he signed the subordination contract tomorrow. It was late in the evening when Pride coerced Stale into falling for her trap, which meant I might get a chance to talk to Stale sometime tonight.

Lotte and Mary got me to my room, but I didn't stay long, claiming I wanted to see Father. They let me go, but rather than heading directly to him, I veered off toward his study. Just like in the game, I found guards in my path. And just like the Pride in the game, I managed to tiptoe past them and break into the study. I made quick work of rummaging through the room, stashing my prize inside my dress before I snuck back out.

That wouldn't be the end of my clandestine activities that night. Stale didn't appear at dinner, eating in his room instead due to fatigue. Later, I would sneak into that room, just as Pride did in the game.

I briefly considered a rope of bedsheets to clamber straight down out of the window, but the maids and guards had already seen me throw myself out of it before. Probably better not to make them think I was leaping out of it all over again. Plus, a princess couldn't behave in such an undignified manner.

Then what exactly did Pride do? How do I get to Stale like in the game?! I'd have to...

Realization hit me, and a smile spread across my face. It faded just as quickly; I was truly becoming just like Pride, the same devious queen I loathed in the game. However, I couldn't linger on the thought. Once night fell, I picked a random book from my room and headed to Stale's room. The two guards stationed outside it raised their eyebrows at me.

"Your Highness."

I smiled at them sweetly. "Stale doesn't know how to read,"

I said, "so I'd like to read this book to him. Father said that was a nice idea."

I'd given the guards outside my own room the same story. It was a lie, certainly, but using my father's name meant that they couldn't stop me. They hesitated only a moment before stepping aside.

"Stale? I'm coming in."

The room lay cloaked in pitch-black darkness when I entered. Once the door closed behind me, I strained to make out anything around me. Only the faint moonlight filtering in through the window provided any help.

"Princess Pride?" Stale said. "Is there something you need from me?"

I'd found him. Stale was sitting on his bed, hugging his knees to his chest. When he looked up at me, he seemed even more worn and weary than he had this afternoon when he'd first arrived.

"I'm sorry to bother you so late," I said. "I simply had to speak with you before you signed the contract tomorrow."

I took step by careful step toward Stale, slowly, trying not to scare him. It was like approaching a wild animal without them spooking and dashing off.

"The crown princess wants to speak with me?" he said, cocking his head.

"Tell me, Stale. You want to see your mother, don't you?"

His eyes widened. All the weariness fled, replaced by sharp focus.

Wait, that's the exact same line from the game! It's how Pride introduces the contract to Stale. Shoot.

It seemed that any time I followed the plot of the game more closely, I could also remember it more clearly. Like now. I retrieved the item hidden in my dress and showed it to Stale.

"What's that?" His eyes went even wider.

"It's the key for those handcuffs. I snuck into Father's study and borrowed it. Now you'll be able to run away."

Without those shackles, Stale could teleport again. In the game, Pride forced him to use that talent for assassinations. He once even used it to transport himself and the heroine outside the palace. Now, hopefully, it would take him to his mother. With the money she'd surely gotten from giving up her son, she and Stale could escape to the countryside.

"I can't do that."

I didn't even breathe for a moment, stunned into silence. "Why not?" I finally asked.

"Mom said I can't go see her anymore," he said. "I'm supposed to serve Your Highness, live a happy life here at the castle, and forget all about her. If I run away, my family will face terrible punishment. That's what the person from the castle told me before I came here. I don't want Mom to be punished."

His knuckles turned white as he gripped his pants and stared at the floor. His eyes shone with suppressed tears.

I see. So that's why he bought it when Pride said she'd let him see his mother. With Pride's official permission, his mother wouldn't face punishment.

Unfortunately, that too was a lie. I couldn't do anything about the threat hanging over Stale's family. A boy adopted into the royal family would never be allowed to visit commoners. He had to be protected from assassinations and kidnappings while also exemplifying upstanding royalty to the kingdom's citizens. I'd heard the adults saying as much, and even my eight-year-old mind could understand it. If the order came from the castle, it was set in stone.

"When the man from the castle first came, he wanted me to leave the next day, but I just couldn't do it," Stale said. "I ran away and put up a fight. But His Royal Highness granted me two weeks before I had to leave, so I spent that time talking to Mom, and when we finally said goodbye, I didn't have any regrets. She told me how much she loved me." Stale stopped, head hanging even heavier. In a hushed voice, he added, "She cried so much..."

He went on, "I know they'll just pick another kid if I manage to run away. I have a friend whose only family is his little sister, and he has a special power like me. I don't want him to end up here instead."

I could hardly believe my ears. Stale was only seven years old, and he already had such compassion for the well-being of others. Shame burned my cheeks, his words searing my heart. I'd encouraged him to act selfishly, and he'd outright refused. I definitely didn't remember this from the game. *Pride is...no, I'm such a terrible person. How could I be so cruel to this child? How could I make him kill his own mother?*

Once he learned that Pride's promise of reuniting him with his mother was just a trick to get him to sign the fealty contract, Stale came to hate Pride for what she'd done, and yet, due to the binding contract, he had to obey her every order. Then, on the day before Tiara's birthday, Pride kept her word in the most horrible way possible.

"Stale, remember my promise? I'll let you see your mother now," she said. Then she handed him the knife. "Use this to kill her, and be sure no one sees you."

Stale's eyes went wide, mouth falling open as all the blood drained from his face.

Pride cackled. "Ah, there it is! That's the face I wanted to see."

Unable to disobey her orders, Stale murdered his mother, and in so doing wounded his heart in a way that would never heal.

Is that what I'm going to do to him too?

Without the memories of my past life, perhaps. Maybe I would have been just as cruel as Pride, seeking to torture a new reaction out of Stale every day, using him like a toy, an amusement. Could those memories save me from becoming that sort of monster?

I observed the boy curled up before me, and guilt stabbed into my gut. How could I apologize? He didn't even know what horrible things I was capable of. I just stood there with the key to the handcuffs, feeling useless and ridiculous.

"Thank you very much for thinking of someone like me," Stale said, presumably noticing I was at a loss for words. "I'm glad you'll be my elder sister, Princess Pride. It's an honor. But I don't need that key you have, so please go back to your room. I'll see you tomo—"

I lunged forward, wrapping my arms around Stale before he could finish. He was slender for a boy, even if he *was* a year younger than me. I felt like I might break him if I used any more force. Just how much strength and how much kindness did Stale carry in those fragile bones?

I wouldn't be the one to save him, though. That role belonged to Tiara.

Only her compassion and pure love could heal his scars. The more Stale found ways to protect her (unbeknownst to Pride, of course), the more her happiness became his hope in the world. He didn't lose his way, even when Pride ordered him to interfere in political matters or carry out assassinations using his power. Around Tiara, he was always the kind older brother—a human and never a monster.

I couldn't save Stale. I couldn't help him escape. All I could do was bind him to me for the rest of our lives. In that case, at the very least...

"I promise I won't cause you any more suffering," I said. "I'll make it so everyone in this kingdom, including you and your mother, can spend each day with a smile on their faces! I swear it, for as long as I live."

The tears flowed free before I even finished speaking. How shameful. Especially in front of Stale, who must have held back so many tears in my presence. I swiped at my eyes with my arm and sniffled, still holding him tightly.

Some dependable big sister I'm being right now, crying at a time like this.

Stale stayed silent in my arms for a while. Then a knock sounded on the door, probably the guards here to usher me away.

Glad I managed to stop crying.

I gently detached myself from him. Stale kept his head up, meeting my gaze. The moonlight glistened in the wetness on his cheeks. It looked like neither of us had escaped this conversation without waterworks, but I was supposed to be the one here to comfort him, not the opposite. I wiped the tears from his face with my fingertips.

"I'm sorry to keep you up so late," I said. "Goodnight, Stale. I hope you get a good night's sleep."

I forced a smile.

Stale's lips trembled, as if he was trying to offer me parting words of his own, but I couldn't make out anything he said.

Ten more years. At the very least, I could use this time to do everything in my power as the crown princess to improve things for people like Stale. I steeled my heart around that solemn resolution and left the room with that vow in my soul.

The next day, the day we were supposed to sign the subordination contract, Stale didn't show up for breakfast. A knot of anxiety tightened in my stomach, but a bit later, at a time of my Father's choosing, Stale finally appeared. Not only that, but

I swore he looked...almost relaxed. He even greeted me with a "Good morning, Princess Pride" as he arrived.

Later, we had to sign the contract before Father and a few other witnesses. The language was dry and devoid of sentiment, but I still cringed as I watched Stale write his name so earnestly with shackled hands.

Father's assistant stood at his side during the signing. He looked quite a bit younger than Father with his light blue hair tied back in a ponytail and spilling over one shoulder. Keen, slender blue eyes observed the proceedings.

It took me a moment to recall the man, but when I did, I nearly gasped. Of course he looked young. That was his power— the power of eternal youth. He could alter his age at will, though I suspected his current form represented his actual age. Father seemed rough around the edges by comparison, even though he wasn't yet thirty. I'd heard the man was five years younger than my father, but I felt their gap was even wider.

Wait a minute. Neither one of them looks his age at all!

I was still reeling from that when the ceremony finished. I'd assumed it would be a lot more complicated; the minister called to the ceremony certainly made it seem that way. But in the end, all we had to do was sign the contract and that was it. No magical light pouring out. No booming ethereal voice. No physical change at all, aside from my heart hammering a bit harder and Stale pressing his hand over his chest. He must've felt the same way.

With that, Father removed Stale's handcuffs using the key I'd stolen last night and replaced this morning. Stale clenched and unclenched his fists, finally free of that extra weight.

"Let's be a happy family together from now on, my son," Father said. He set his hands on Stale's shoulders, and Stale offered a wavering smile and tiny nod.

In the game, if Tiara wound up with Stale he became the prince consort. That might not be a bad outcome for this kingdom. In ORL, Stale became a scheming, bitter man due to Pride's abuse and manipulation, but perhaps we could avoid that here if I continued to show the boy some kindness.

"Princess Pride!"

Stale scampered up to me, full of energy. It was like that heartbroken boy I'd seen the night before never existed at all.

"I hope the two of us do well together. I promise to protect you, as well as our younger sister," he said. He placed his hand on his chest like a knight and smiled as he spoke, while Father stood behind him with a relieved grin on his face.

Wait. A knight?! Something was bugging me about the resemblance, but I chose to focus on the boy before me instead.

"Thank you, Stale," I replied. "But since we're family now, you don't have to call me 'Princess.' Can you call me 'Pride' instead? Mother's assistant, my uncle, addresses her without any title."

In the game, everyone called Pride "Her Majesty" or "Queen Pride," but I didn't want to be addressed like a stranger. However, Stale hesitated, some of his exuberance fading.

"Oh, but I... No, I don't..." he stammered.

"Your Highness." Father's assistant stared down at Stale and me with a stern expression.

Whoa. He's handsome, even from a lower angle. Wait. I think I saw this face in the game before... Or was that later in the series?

"Prince Vest, the seneschal, may refer to Her Majesty by her first name, but before commoners, he addresses her as 'Your Majesty' or 'Elder Sister.'"

Prince Vest was my uncle—Mother's younger brother-in-law. As Mother's right-hand man, he possessed an equal amount of power as my father, the prince consort, making him a man of high authority in the kingdom.

I see. I've hardly ever seen Mother around commoners, so I didn't know that.

"In that case, please call me 'Elder Sister' around others and 'Pride' when we're alone," I told Stale. "We're family, after all, so that makes us equals."

With that, I reached out to shake Stale's hand. Father, his assistant, and all the witnesses gaped at the gesture. The witnesses, who'd known me for a long time, all cried out in shock. "Is that really Her Highness?!"

"Okay, Elder Sister," Stale said, accepting my handshake.

"Well, well. It appears that Her Highness has grown into a wonderful young lady since I last saw her," Father's assistant said. "But I would expect nothing less now that she's gained her precognition at such a young age. When I first heard your powers had awakened, I wasn't sure what to expect."

"Is that supposed to be praise, Prime Minister Gilbert?" Father said, a warning in his voice. I wasn't particularly put off, however. After all, Pride grew up to become a heinous, evil queen in ORL.

Father's assistant, Prime Minister Gilbert, just shrugged.

"My apologies," he said, bowing his head. "That was an inappropriate comment for the prime minister to make. What a shame that Her Majesty could not be here to see you today. It's quite a big day for her dearest daughter, the crown princess. Well, we all know how busy she's been since the international discussions were decided over a month ago. Not to mention Tiara's—"

Father smacked him on the head before he could continue.

Yes. Now I remembered Gilbert, Father's assistant. That speech of his jogged my memory and not in the best way. I was still musing it all over when Father called for Lotte, Mary, and the other maids, as well as Jack and the rest of the guards so we could return to the castle residence. The whole way back, I held my new brother's hand, the hand of the heroine's brother as well.

In the three days since we signed the contract, Stale spent nearly every moment at my side, the perfect doting brother. Since he was originally a commoner, he still had quite a lot of reading, writing, and etiquette to learn, which had to be exhausting all of a sudden. But despite that, whenever he had free time he'd rush to my side with a smile if I called his name. We did just about everything together, from reading to meandering through the castle gardens.

I wanted to help teach Stale too, if I could. My own education was thorough, of course, but I felt bad taking up even more of his time for tutoring. Plus, I didn't want to burden him with the memories of his mother. Whenever we were together, I tried to avoid the topic of mothers altogether. I really just wanted to do whatever I could to help him, but I had no idea how to accomplish that.

"Hey, Stale, let's play tag together. I'll race you to the garden!"

I took off at a dash, trying to outrun the melancholy weighing me down when I thought about his plight.

"Ah, wait a minute, Pride! That's not fair!" Stale called after me.

I was pretty fast, but when he wasn't holding back, Stale was always faster, probably from playing tag with other kids, an activity I rarely got to enjoy.

But after only a short way, I glanced behind me and couldn't find Stale anywhere. I slowed, looking around in confusion.

"Stale?!"

Then I spotted him sprawled out on the ground and rushed back to his side to help him sit up. He was flushed red and gasping for breath, but he seemed okay otherwise. Still, something was obviously wrong.

"Somebody, help!" I cried. "Stale's hurt!"

Guards rushed over while I called Stale's name over and over, but he merely mumbled and slurred incoherently. Jack scooped the boy into his arms and rushed him back to the castle. I hurried to follow, Lotte and the other maids fast on my heels.

Stale had caught a cold.

Fortunately, it was nothing major, probably just fatigue, but I wondered if he'd been hiding it all day while overexerting himself for my sake. How had I failed to notice anything was even wrong until he collapsed right there before me?

With Mother and Father busy with their work, only Uncle Vest, the seneschal, could come to check on Stale. It was the first time he ever met Stale, yet he looked at him so kindly, perhaps because they had the same position, the same lot in life. Uncle Vest swiped his blue hair out of his eyes and straightened, marching toward where I waited outside the sickroom. He was dressed impeccably, as always, yet he crouched down to meet me on my level.

"I'm sure he was tired after leaving his mother to come live at a faraway castle," Uncle Vest said, reaching out to stroke my hair. "I remember that feeling well. But don't worry, he'll get better once he spends a few days resting."

Uncle Vest, only in his late twenties—two years younger than Mother—and dressed like a handsome gentleman, was truly a wonderful man. I almost wished he'd been a love interest in the game... Well, no, the game didn't actually start for another ten years or so.

"I won't forbid it outright, but you shouldn't go into his room. You could catch his cold, and we definitely don't want that," he said.

He left me with those words and a concerned smile before returning to Mother.

Only after he left did I realize how dark the castle had gotten. The sun hung low in a sky rapidly deepening to blue and purple. In all the commotion, I'd completely lost track of time.

I asked the guard to tell Lotte to come get me when dinner was ready, then returned to Stale's sickroom. He slept peacefully, perhaps thanks to the medicine the doctor gave him. His face wasn't so pale anymore either. I sighed as I sat beside the bed, watching his face, relieved but still alert. This was really the love interest Stale that I knew. He had the exact same beautiful face as he did in the game.

I took out my handkerchief and dabbed at the sweat on his brow, trying not to wake him. Stale tensed, eyebrows knotting together as though he was in pain or having a nightmare. In fact, it looked exactly like one of the cutscenes featuring the older Stale that I remembered from the game. He was unconscious and groaning in his sleep as Tiara nursed him back to health... *Oh...*

I gasped as the scene came back to me. In it, Stale, ten years from now, had a nightmare about his past. Then, as now, he suffered from some sort of cold. Pride snuck into the sleeping boy's room.

"Hmph. My slave sure has some nerve, catching a cold without my permission," she said as she stared down at Stale, just as I was doing now.

"Have you no shame, being the commoner son of some commoner woman? You know, I wonder...if I ordered you to run laps around the garden until you dropped dead, would you do it?" Pride laughed as she wiped his brow with her handkerchief.

"Hey, you'll go back to normal, right? Your life belongs to me, you know. Hurry up and get better so I can play with you again, got it? My adorable little slave."

Stale gasped for breath, even in his sleep. He muttered to himself, but I couldn't remember what he said to himself in that scene. All I knew was that it sent Pride into a fit of laughter.

"Ah ha ha ha! Such a pathetic man. You're just like a little baby. You shameful, embarrassing, ugly little toy. You're my slave, you baby. No one needs someone like you. Mother and Father, if they were still alive, even Uncle Vest—none of them need you at all. Your own mother probably wouldn't even have any use for you. All you ever do is make trouble for everyone."

She continued to whisper into Stale's ear while he was lost in his nightmare.

"But because I pity you, I'll do you the favor of needing you. You're my slave, right? So we'll be together forever and ever and ever..."

In the game, that was when Stale awakened and for the first time revealed a bit of his painful past to Tiara, who had been taking care of him while he was ill.

Ah, I did it again. I recreated another scene from the game.

Here in the present, outside the game, Stale groaned just like in that scene. I was busy wondering if my deepening forehead wrinkles would make me look more like Father when he began muttering to himself.

"M-Mom... Mmph... Mom..."

Tears glimmered at the corners of his eyes. I froze, chest going tight as I watched him cry out for his mother.

How could Pride... How could I torture Stale when he's like this?!

I couldn't comprehend it. Yet I knew that other side of me lurked somewhere in my heart.

What seven-year-old boy wouldn't miss his mother in circumstances like this? They'd only been apart for a few days. When I was in elementary school during my other life, there were always homesick kids who cried on the first night of a field trip. But it was worse for Stale; he would never get to see his mother again. He had no choice, no option but to sign the contract and dedicate himself to his new life. He must have been holding back so much these past several days. Even though he studied hard and carved out the best life he could at this castle, the grief suppressed within him was still enough to make him ill. He was just a child, but strangers had taken his whole life from him, and he had no choice but to endure it.

Yet in the time we'd been together, I hadn't once seen Stale complain, cry, or even scowl. The more I thought about it, the tighter my chest felt, until I couldn't stand it anymore.

I can't do this again. Stale's keeping everything inside him. I can't be the one who starts crying so easily.

I could rationalize like an adult, but I was in the body of a child. The emotions overwhelmed me. I hung my head, but I couldn't tear my eyes away, and the tears spilled out before I could stop them, dropping right onto Stale's face.

The more I tried to force myself to move, to bear all the sadness, to keep the tears inside, the more the emotions poured out, until the tears turned to outright sobs. Stale squeezed his eyes tight, then started to open them. I gasped and tried to jerk away, but it was already too late—Stale was blinking up at me.

"Pride?" He didn't push or demand answers, but I knew he was confused and curious about the sight before him.

"I'm...I'm sorry," I said. "I'm so...sorry! I'm...sorry... I'm sorry... I'm sorry, I'm sorry, I'm sorry..."

I'm sorry you had to see me breaking down like this, and I'm sorry I made you play tag, and I'm sorry I didn't notice you were sick, and I'm sorry I took you from your mom, and I'm sorry I couldn't save the two of you... I'm sorry I can't do anything to fill the hole in your heart.

The more I thought about it, the less I knew where to start with my apologies. All I could do was desperately force out one "I'm sorry" after another in a voice that had gone hoarse from sobs. Stale just lay there watching me, fully awake now. A combination of his own sweat and my tears dampened his face.

"What do you mean?" he asked.

The question he finally landed on made my heart ache in my chest. *What do* you *mean?* I thought. Anything I said then would only hurt him. Besides, I wasn't seeking his forgiveness. How could I? But when I thought about how things would be if I didn't remember my past life, when I thought about all the horrible things I would have done to Stale, I just couldn't hold the tears back.

"Ngh! I'm...I'm sorry...I can't be...a source of strength in your life...and that I didn't notice how you felt... I'm so sorry!"

I managed to get that much out before I completely broke down again. I folded my arms atop him and leaned all the way forward, hiding my face. He must have been burning up from his cold; the warmth radiated through the sheets when I rested on him. I shifted to bury my face against Stale's shoulder, then continued my sobbing there.

He flinched at first, then gently set his hands on my back. It was hard to tell which of us was the older sibling in this state. Stale was the one who needed comforting and yet here he was comforting me instead. The shame of my failings, both as an older sister-in-law and as the crown princess, burned hot inside me. Stale said nothing, just held me. Maybe he was trying to think of what to say to a pathetic older sister who'd caused him so much worry.

Ten years from now, I would become the evil, nefarious queen and bring this kingdom to ruin. I didn't yet know if the person to stop me would be Stale or Tiara or one of the other love interests.

As helpless and pathetic as I was, there was only one thing to say in that moment...

"If I become a wicked queen...then I want you to...I want you to kill me..."

Kill me, before you and your mother and both of my parents and Tiara and everyone else in this kingdom...before even a single one of them falls into misery.

That was all I managed to say, then my voice gave out from all the crying. I slipped into an exhausted sleep against him. By the time Lotte and Jack came to fetch me, Stale was asleep too. It must have been a shock to Lotte and Jack to find the princess in bed with a boy I had no blood relation to, even if we *were* both children. Half-asleep, I muttered and mumbled as Jack scooped me out of the bed and into his arms. I roused a bit as he carried me back toward my room, enough to feel embarrassed by the whole ordeal. Voice thick with sleep, I begged him and Lotte not to mention any of this to my parents.

"Of course, Your Highness," they both replied with small chuckles.

All the more, I realized just how foolish I'd been to never notice the kind people I had all around me this whole time—not before I regained the memories of my past life, anyway.

⚜

Stale made a full recovery a few days later. With his doctor's permission, he returned to his vigorous school studies and etiquette lessons. However, whenever it was time for his breaks, he would come visit me. Neither of us ever spoke about the night I visited him while he was sick. Perhaps, sick as he'd been, Stale didn't even remember it.

The reason didn't matter to me; I knew he wouldn't have a clue how to respond to my apology. Plus, I definitely preferred it if he just forgot how shameful his older sister had acted in front of him. I mean, I'd asked a seven-year-old to kill me. The Pride I knew from the game was clearly still a part of me. I could never bring myself to go back to Stale's bedroom to see him after that. I tried to just keep myself busy instead.

One day, after finishing lunch, I took Stale to visit Father between lessons. Apparently, Father had something to give him.

"These are special circumstances. You can't mention this to anyone, even in the castle," Father warned us, then handed Stale a single sealed envelope.

When Stale opened the envelope and scanned the contents, he choked back a shout of surprise. His eyes went wide, mouth falling open as he gazed at a letter from his mother.

"Pride's the one who asked for this," Father said. "We already promised to send your mother compensation from the castle coffers, but now she'll receive a lump sum once a month. When the delivery is made, she'll be able to send a letter back to the castle. But you'll only be able to write back to her once a year on your birthday."

Father and other castle officials would review Stale's letters, of course, and he could never speak about any kind of royal affairs to his mother. Stale's mother agreed to these conditions, Father told us, although he would probably have to repeat that part again.

Stale had burst into tears before he could even finish. He clutched his mother's letter against his chest and wailed. Even I, standing behind him with my hands on his shoulders, flinched back. I never imagined him being the type of kid who could cry so loudly. He must have been trying to hold back so much still.

I had asked Father if he would let Stale visit his mother, but he rejected the idea, which came as little surprise. But that led me to the idea of letters. I had things like the internet and social media in my past life that allowed me to stay connected with faraway family members, even if we weren't meeting in person or exchanging phone calls. I hoped letters could do the same for Stale in this world.

Their correspondence couldn't become a regular thing, but at the very least, they could hear from each other and perhaps even connect, if only a little. I'd begged Father over and over to allow it. Once I framed the idea in a political context—mentioning how important it was for the ruling family to be exposed to unfiltered voices from the commoner classes—he finally considered my idea. Prime Minister Gilbert seemed a bit troubled by the proposal, but once we received permission from Mother, he laughed and said, "Such great character it takes to be queen. The two of you are both very open-minded."

It seemed like Father bit his tongue at that little quip, but I couldn't tell. Anyway, everything worked out in the end, so that was all that mattered, right?

I stroked Stale's hair as he cried. He turned suddenly, pulling me into a tight hug. Stale had always accepted my displays of emotion, but this was the first time he ever initiated contact like this himself. Maybe he'd truly accepted me as his sister. He stifled his hitching sobs, letting out only little grunts now and then. I hugged him back, but the warmth spreading through me had nothing to do with physical contact and everything to do with Stale finally seeming happy.

"Mother and Father and I, and your other mother too, we all love you very much," I said.

He cried even louder, his face still buried in my dress. Father just smiled at the two of us. Stale...my younger brother-in-law. I could only hope that he would love Tiara in the same way. While I held him, I stared out the window and let my thoughts drift to the sister I had not yet seen.

Stale never let go of that letter, even when he calmed and returned to his room. I feared the gesture would only make him ache to return home even more so, but he appeared promptly when called for dinner and seemed in good spirits.

However...that look on his face was something new—neither melancholy like when we first met nor the bright and happy smile I saw after he first arrived. He looked more like the Stale of the game: calm, quiet, somewhat calculating. But I had to be imagining that, right?

After that, Stale also stopped calling me "Elder Sister" and "Pride" as often when we were in public, and instead chose to address me as "Your Highness." The idea that he would grow more distant or even come to despise me like in the game burned as it sank in and a cold dread seeped through my blood.

In ten more years, I would receive my punishment.

Stale Royal Ivy.

I repeated that name in my head over and over again, making sure that I had it memorized.

Never in my life had I so despised the special power I was born with. Mom was all I had left after Dad died, but she was a kind woman, so I lived a happy life with her and my friends in town. Mom would always brag that my special power was an extremely rare one, but all I really wanted it for was to help her. We weren't wealthy, so the only words I could read and write were the ones my mom taught me—my own name. Things weren't easy, but with my power, I could find work someday and maybe improve our lot in life. Mom and the neighbors even told me how I'd grow up to be someone important, since I was such a fast learner.

Their words filled me with pride. But I never could have imagined the course my life would take—and how I'd have to leave home to become someone "important."

When the castle's messenger said I'd be the next generation's steward, I had no idea what he meant. It sounded amazing, and for an instant, hope bloomed in my chest. Then I turned to Mom and saw all the color drain from her face. Dread dropped heavy into my stomach as the man told me I would be adopted and never see my family again, never see Mom again.

No, I don't want to leave Mom. She's the only family I have. She only has me, and I only have her.

Immediately, I wanted to use my power to teleport me and Mom away from here, but she stopped me before I could act. There was no disobeying an order from the castle. My refusal would be a serious crime, and my whole family would pay the price.

I didn't have a choice. Still, when they told me I only had one day before I would report to the castle, I couldn't think of anything but escaping together with my mom. Then we received a two-week postponement from the prince consort himself.

Mom took time off work. We spent every moment of every day together over those two weeks. She managed to keep smiling during the day, but at night, after I went to bed, I heard her stifled sobs coming from the other room.

"I don't want any money," she said. "Just please don't take Stale away from me."

She covered her mouth with both hands so that she could cry without waking me, but I knew, and I'd never forget it for the rest of my life.

When it was time for me to leave, neither Mom nor I shed a single tear. I soaked up her parting words, doing my best to keep a smile on my face like she always did. Then I told her to take care of herself and her health and that I'd always love her no matter how much time passed.

As the carriage rolled away, Mom faded to a faint shadow in the distance. Then she shrank even more, as though she'd collapsed to the ground.

"I'm sorry you had to say goodbye to your only son while he was in handcuffs," I wanted to tell her, but I never got the chance.

I couldn't get that image of Mom out of my head, even once I arrived at the castle, and I couldn't bring myself to properly greet His Royal Highness either. Even the threat of death that loomed over me for disrespecting the prince consort wasn't enough to snap me out of my stupor. Trapped in the storm of my turbulent emotions, all I could do was try to stay standing.

Even before all this, I was never very good when it came to things like how to express myself. I never really bothered trying to show my emotions on my face. It felt like too much effort just for the sake of other people. But Mom always knew exactly how

I was feeling, and my friends didn't seem to care either way. Of course, in certain circumstances I would smile like anyone else— like when I got to be with someone I liked or when someone gave Mom work or something. Smiling in that kind of circumstance would make life easier for Mom and me, I knew. But here, in front of the prince consort, I just couldn't muster the energy to force a smile.

Then there was Princess Pride. There were rumors in town that the crown princess had grown up spoiled. They said that unlike the queen and prince consort, she was quite the selfish young princess.

But my first impression when His Royal Highness introduced me to Princess Pride was simply that she was beautiful. Red waves of hair framed her face. Her skin was so smooth, her lips bright pink. She stood so elegantly, so poised, that I could hardly believe she was only a year older than me. Only the sharp, upturned corners of her eyes gave any impression of cruelty.

His Royal Highness explained who I was and why I was in handcuffs, but Princess Pride was clearly disturbed by the shackles. I just kept my eyes on my feet the entire time, avoiding her judgmental gaze. If I would be spending the rest of my life in her service, I didn't want her thinking I was glaring at her or something. The idea of the princess hating me was too terrifying to risk. But then Her Highness reached out and took my hand, introducing herself so kindly. It didn't stop me from worrying that the friendliness was just an act, though, and the more I thought it over, the more the distrust inside me grew.

They led me to a room, and I lay curled up in a bed much too big for me, though I certainly had no hope of sleeping. When I closed my eyes, I saw Mom's tearstained face, and my heart ached.

"Stale? I'm coming in."

I jolted up when Princess Pride entered the room. I couldn't imagine what she'd want with me. Honestly, I would have preferred to be left alone, but I couldn't offend the princess like that.

"Princess Pride?" I said. "Is there something you need from me?"

What could she want from me right now? Starting tomorrow, I'll be forced to serve by her side for the rest of my life. Why does she want to steal the little time I have left to myself?

The longer those thoughts swirled through my head, the angrier I became. But I swallowed my irritation down; I could never let her see those feelings. I wouldn't dare offend the princess now.

"I'm sorry to bother you so late," she said. "I simply had to speak with you before you signed the contract tomorrow."

She approached me slowly, like an animal she feared startling. Why wasn't she just barging in, as was her right? None of this made any sense. The crown princess didn't need to be nice to someone like me, she didn't need to talk to me at all. She could simply wait a day and command me as she willed. I just couldn't figure it out.

"The crown princess wants to speak with me?" I said, cocking my head.

"Tell me, Stale," she said. "You want to see your mother, don't you?"

What?!

My heart leapt into my throat. I stared at Her Highness, choking down a cry of "Yes!"

I do want to see her. I want to see her more than anything.

I'd do anything for a chance to see my mother again. All I wanted was to see how she was doing and tell her I was okay.

Her Highness wore a strange, strained kind of smile as she looked at me. Then she reached into her dress, and in the darkness, I could just make out the shape of a key clutched in her hand.

"What's that?"

No, it can't be... Why would the crown princess have such a thing? If she truly held the key to my handcuffs, why would she show that to me? Surely she realized that I could take it by force and escape any moment. Yet every time she spoke, she only added to my confusion.

"It's the key for those handcuffs," she said. "I snuck into Father's study and borrowed it. Now you'll be able to run away."

She's helping me escape?! But why?! For a moment, I wondered if this was all just some cruel prank. She must have known I couldn't just leave.

"I can't do that," I told her.

It was Princess Pride whose mouth fell open in surprise this time. It seemed she really did mean to help me run away.

"Why not?"

Was she dumb or something? Was the royal family completely oblivious to what they put people like me through? Anger threatened to well up inside me at the thought, but I stuffed it down and instead told Her Highness about my mother and why

I couldn't just leave. Still, it was hard laying it all out so plainly. I kept seeing that image of Mom crying in the back of my mind, and tears stung my eyes the longer I spoke.

No, I mustn't cry. I have to be strong, just like Mom. She always managed to keep smiling no matter what. I can't let any of the royal family see me acting so weak.

I was sitting up and gripping my pants. My hands curled tighter into the fabric as I continued speaking and holding back the tears.

"And I know they'll just pick another kid if I manage to run away," I said. "I have a friend whose only family is his little sister, and he has a special power like me. I don't want him to end up here instead of me."

That would only make things all the more painful for Mom and me. Instead, maybe I could just act more and more helpless until Her Highness gave in and let me see Mom.

What if I just stop holding back and cry as loudly as I want?

If she really was just a dumb but nice person, there was a chance she'd grant my wish. Rumor had it she used that sweetness to convince her father to dote on her. Maybe I could turn it around and use it against her. A wicked plan began to take shape in my mind. I snuck a glance at the princess, trying not to get caught as I did. The moment I saw her face, I abandoned my scheme entirely.

Princess Pride looked absolutely stricken with grief. I flashed back to how Mom looked when we'd said goodbye. That caged-in grief, the strength it took for her to hold back what she was feeling. I saw that in Princess Pride now, that painful concern for someone else.

For someone else? For me?

I was more shocked by the sight than anything else, but I instantly knew I wouldn't be going through with any plans to manipulate her. How could I trick someone like her into helping me?

"Thank you very much for thinking of someone like me," I said. "I'm glad you'll be my elder sister, Princess Pride. It's an honor. But I don't need that key you have, so please go back to your room. I'll see you tomo—"

Just leave me alone already. What can you do for me? Nothing. There's nothing you can do to help me. Absolutely noth—

Suddenly, Princess Pride pulled me into a hug.

At first, I simply froze. Why would the princess hug me, and why would she do it with such force, and why was this country's crown princess so close to me in the first place?

Why was this girl crying so hard?

Part of me still believed it was all a joke or prank of some sort. Yet I heard her sniffling and wiping at her tears. If this was an act, it was a very convincing one.

"I promise I won't cause you any more suffering," she said mid-sob. "I'll make it so everyone in this kingdom, including you and your mother, can spend each day with a smile on their faces! I swear it, for as long as I live."

My head felt light. None of this matched anything I'd ever heard about the princess. In town, everyone said she was spoiled and foolish, a brat unfit to serve as the next queen. Yet here she was talking about the well-being of all her citizens, even me.

She couldn't possibly be the self-absorbed, empty-headed princess everyone described. The Princess Pride before me seemed so dedicated to working for the citizens of Freesia—a true crown princess indeed.

Something warm welled up in my chest. My vision blurred. I hadn't even felt this way when I had to say goodbye to Mom.

A knock rapped against the door, and Princess Pride, her eyes now puffy from crying, stepped away from me. Only when she wiped the tears from my cheeks did I realize I'd been crying too.

"I'm sorry to keep you up so late," she said. "Goodnight, Stale. I hope you get a good night's sleep." She looked like she could start crying again any instant, yet she smiled at me as she spoke.

Why? Why are you being so kind to me?

I wanted to ask, but I just couldn't get the words out. All I managed to do was watch her as she left my room and disappeared down the hall.

The next day, I was supposed to sign the subordination contract, but I was still reeling from the previous night.

I hid in my bedroom all morning. I couldn't see the princess again, not after that moment last night. It should have scared me to skip two meals in a row like that and possibly anger the royal family, but I felt more confident today that they would forgive me for something like that.

I used the time to gather my thoughts. The despair that overwhelmed me just yesterday wasn't such a heavy burden today. Maybe I'd simply accepted my fate; maybe it was that late night talk with the princess and the revelation that she was far kinder than the rumors suggested. Maybe it was simply the tears of relief I shed the night before. Whatever the cause, I felt lighter, even with those shackles still binding my wrists. When I attempted to smile, it emerged easily and naturally.

Her Highness was nothing like the princess I'd heard about in town. Incredibly enough, she cared about people like me, people like my friends and family. Her compassion was nearly a liability, but at least I felt like I understood her now. We were nearly the same age, and my older friends were a lot like her. Strange as it was to comprehend, she would be the next queen—and I would be her seneschal, the second highest authority in the kingdom.

Perhaps someday, if I stayed in the princess's good graces, the two of us could change Freesia when we ruled it. At the very least, I might just be allowed to see Mom on my own, since there would be no one left who could tell me no—so long as Princess Pride allowed it, of course. Becoming queen could still change her. It could turn her into a selfish, authoritarian ruler. But if I kept on her good side, maybe I could influence her to change some of the laws and rules around here. Toward that end, I also needed to keep Her Majesty, His Royal Highness, and Princess Tiara on my side as well. I couldn't possibly predict who Princess Tiara might marry and what the prince consort would feel about me, but if I had all those others as allies I could still make this work.

Princess Pride, the future queen of Freesia, was the most important ally of all. I would use my position as her assistant in whatever ways I could, stay by her side, and ensure I earned her highest favor. It didn't seem like it would be hard; I liked her already. She'd gone and stolen the key for those handcuffs for me and even cried when I explained why I couldn't use it. Not to mention those things she'd said to me...

"I promise I won't cause you any more suffering. I'll make it so everyone in this kingdom, including you and your mother, can spend each day with a smile on their faces! I swear it, for as long as I live."

I really believed she meant those words.

Okay, I've made up my mind. I'll work hard to stay on Princess Pride's good side.

I believed I could do it too. As vain as it might sound, I was pretty popular back when I lived in town. Both the boys and girls took a liking to me. Since I knew Princess Pride wasn't the selfish person of rumor, I knew I could win her over by playing the role of the good boy, deserving of all her praise. All for the day that I could see Mom again.

Someone knocked on the door, interrupting my musing. It was almost time to sign the contract. Princess Pride was waiting for me when I arrived in the chamber set up for the signing. Her worried expression eased when I greeted her.

The minister began the contract procedures. The shackles made it awkward when it came time to sign my name. But we all made it through the ceremony. By the end, my heart was racing. I could physically sense the new bond between Princess Pride and me. Someone removed my shackles, and I rubbed my wrists, which felt lighter than ever before. Then the prince consort...or rather, "Father," placed his hands on my shoulders.

"Let's be a happy family together from now on, my son," he said.

I paused for a moment as those words sank in. I was a member of the royal family. Me. I smiled back at Father, careful not to seem rude like yesterday.

"Starting today, you're to live as royalty, doing everything in your power to assist Pride and the governance of this country," he told me.

Father beamed, and I tried to return the smile. The moment he let me, I ran over to Princess Pride.

Smile. Make her proud of you. I'll be the perfect assistant and the perfect brother-in-law.

"I hope the two of us do well together. I promise to protect you, as well as our younger sister," I said.

Just as I expected, the princess responded with a smile. *Yes, I can do this*, I thought. But the next words out of her mouth caught me completely off guard.

"Thank you, Stale," she said. "But since we're family now, you don't have to call me 'Princess.' Can you call me 'Pride' instead? Mother's assistant, my uncle, addresses her without any title."

What? Don't address her formally? Even though we only became family just now?!

Sure, the seneschal—or steward, as I was now—could address the queen informally, but that came from years of mutual trust. An assistant should call the crown princess "Your Highness" or "Princess Pride." As her younger brother-in-law, I should have called her "Elder Sister." But if Princess Pride was against all of that, I had to follow her wishes, even if it felt strange being so familiar with the princess. Especially considering all that happened the night before...

I stumbled over my words, tripping over the strangeness of the whole idea and feeling ever so shy. I supposed I'd called older girls by their first names before, but none of them were princesses. Not to mention that she was so beautiful and kind and compassionate...

"Your Highness."

The prime minister, who was there as a witness to the ceremony, turned his sharp gaze on the two of us. Ostensibly, he smiled at us, but his eyes were strangely cold in comparison. I shifted under his attention.

"Prince Vest, the seneschal, may refer to Her Majesty by her first name, but before commoners, he addresses her as 'Your Majesty' or 'Elder Sister.'"

To be honest, the prime minister's words came as a relief.

He was right. Though I'd never heard Her Majesty...never heard Mother speak with the seneschal before, I knew that was the proper way for him to address her. I was glad the prime minister was the one clearing up the confusion here before I blundered into some sort of mistake. My relief lasted only an instant before Princess Pride once again made a pronouncement that left me bewildered.

"In that case, please call me 'Elder Sister' around others, and 'Pride' when we're alone. We're family, after all, so that makes us equals."

You still want me to call you Pride?! And what do you mean by "equals"?!

To the whole world, we were master and servant now with the contract signed. Yet Pride went on insisting I could address her like we were on equal footing.

I stuffed down my surprise in time to shake Pride's hand. I even managed to call her "Elder Sister" as I did. But inside I felt just as perplexed as the adults around us looked. While Father and the prime minister were speaking to each other, I was busy trying to figure out whether I'd really be able to call my sister "Pride" when we were alone.

However...I had a little trouble getting through it the first time.

Right after we signed the contract, Her Highness gave me a tour of the castle library. I tried my best, but ended up adding a quiet "Your Highness," to the end of my sentence, though I wasn't sure if she heard it or not.

The second time, I accidentally blurted out "Your Highness" without thinking. The princess just smiled and said, "You can call me Pride." Then she added, "It's nearly time for dinner, so let's go back now, Stale."

On the fifth time, I made it as far as "Pri—" and the princess smiled shyly. "Pride," she corrected me. The time after that, I managed to say her name correctly as we exchanged our "goodnights" and headed to our separate rooms.

Then there was the eighth time. "Pri...de," I stammered. It was a bit clumsy, but the princess still smiled and invited me to join her in enjoying the nice weather out in the garden.

And then came the fifteenth time.

"Pride," I said, without any hesitation or faltering. Even I was surprised to hear it, but it seemed I really did see this girl, my sister, as simply "Pride."

Of course, I did things other than try to learn her name after signing the contract. I also had to start learning reading, writing, and etiquette, before moving on to math and Freesian history. I absorbed an onslaught of information, but I enjoyed working through all these new ideas.

Plus, Pride and I often had our lessons at the same time, though we had different teachers. I asked mine about what she was studying; it gave me a little more insight into her. The teachers seemed to have a high regard for Pride's intelligence. Apparently, she picked up new subjects pretty quickly, even compared to other nobles.

"Your own memorization skills are quite impressive, considering you started with no education at all, Stale," the teacher said.

I wasn't sure how I should respond to that. No one would be surprised if someone like me, Pride's assistant and younger brother, wasn't as smart as the crown princess. But some part of me wanted to catch up with and possibly surpass her. Better that than having her tutor me. I shuddered at the mere thought.

Life at the castle kept my days and my mind busy. I did my lessons, tried to address Pride by her first name, memorized all the things I needed to learn to serve as her assistant. But at the same time, I was always calculating—was I saying the right thing? Was I doing the right thing? If Pride offered me help, how could I turn her down without getting into trouble? And more loomed on the horizon, such as the fencing lessons I knew they'd want me to take someday.

But whenever I paused long enough to wonder how Mom was doing, my chest clenched around an old, familiar pain.

Three days into my lessons, I woke up with my head pounding from all these conflicting thoughts.

No, I still have so many things I need to focus on. I can't just stay in bed. I'll study a lot today so that I can see Mom as soon as possible. I just have to tell everyone I feel fine.

It took all of my energy to act normal during my lessons that day. Most of the information just went in one ear and out the other. *I'll have to repeat all this on my own later,* I realized, but there wasn't much I could do about it except keep trudging onward.

I headed out to the gardens, where I'd promised Pride I would meet her, trying my best to keep my legs steady as I walked. Being around her always eased my mind a bit. She would greet me with a smile, laugh at the silliest little things, and say how much she enjoyed just being with me. It almost reminded me of being with Mom. I knew once I was with her, I'd feel a little better.

I ran into Pride before I even made it to the garden. She'd finished her lessons for the day too. She greeted me with her usual bright smile. Even in my exhausted state, I couldn't help reciprocating the gesture.

"Hey, Stale, let's play tag," she said. "I'll race you to the garden!"

Without another word, Pride broke out into a run. I chased after her, but quickly lagged behind.

I have to catch up. I have to be faster. Faster at tag, faster at studying, faster at growing up, faster at everything...

"Stale?!"

Suddenly, my vision blurred to white. I couldn't seem to open my eyes at all.

Somewhere outside me, Pride was screaming. I could hear her, but I couldn't make out the words as I swam through hazy incoherence.

What...am I...supposed to be thinking about?

M-Mom...

I was dreaming.

Mom and I were together. She had her back to me while she made dinner, just like always.

Hey, forget about dinner. We're finally together, so let's talk.

How have you been, Mom?

I've learned so many new things, Mom.

Mom, the prince consort is actually a nice man.

And Pride's nothing like all the rumors, Mom.

Mom, are the townspeople treating you well?

Mom, you have enough to get by, right?

Mom, you're not still crying, are you?

I grabbed at the bottom of her shirt, and she finally turned to look at me. "Just wait, dinner will be ready soon," she said with a smile.

Oh, thank goodness. She's smiling. But even as the thought hit me, Mom stopped her cooking and sank to the floor, breaking down into sobbing. I reached out for her. *Don't cry. I'll come see you again, Mom. I'll work really hard. Mom, are you listening to me? Hey, Mom? Mom...*

"Ngh... Hng..."

She was still crying.

Mom was still standing there crying.

Something trailed down my face, one heavy drop at a time. My eyes were still closed, but consciousness returned slowly and Mom faded away, just a figure in a dream. For some reason, the sound of crying didn't fade away with her, as though I'd used my power to teleport back home.

Don't cry, Mom. I'm right here with you. But when I opened my eyes, it was Pride and not Mom crying atop me.

"Pride?"

Am I still dreaming? So that wasn't Mom crying? Why am I here now? Why is she crying?

I struggled to steady my swirling thoughts, let alone speak. All I could do was stare up at Pride, who seemed nearly overcome with emotion as she watched over me. And when she finally spoke, she offered...deep remorse. I couldn't make any sense of it at all. Why was she crying so hard again? That question stuck in my mind as I pieced together my thoughts.

"What do you mean?" I asked her.

At this innocuous question, Pride pressed her lips tightly together and sobbed anew.

Why does she look like she's holding so much back?

"Ngh! I'm...I'm sorry...I can't be a source of strength in your life...and that I didn't notice how you felt... I'm so sorry!" Her lips trembled as she forced the words out.

Pride collapsed on top of me and pulled me into a hug. Her body, scent, and gentle weight washed over my senses, leaving me too embarrassed and nervous to move. I froze as heat flushed through me and the princess cried against my shoulder.

But why? She already cried so much for me that one night. Pride's the reason I went from hating life at the castle to enjoying every day here. She'd always tell me about how good the food was, so I started looking forward to every meal with her. If it weren't for her, I'd have been terrified of the subordination contract. She's the reason why I have any hope for the future. She accepts me for who I am, smiles at me, needs me. If that isn't a source of strength, what is it? She knew I was in pain and understood my feelings without a word.

When Pride brought me the key for the handcuffs that night, I wasn't just heartbroken over the fact that I would never see my mom again. I was lonely there without my mother, worried that she was lonely too, and devastated that there was nothing I could do for her now that she was all alone. I felt that I was going to be alone forever, that everything in my life would only bring me more pain.

But Pride said that she would never hurt me again. She promised that she'd make sure me, Mom, and all the people of the kingdom had reasons to smile. And then she hugged me.

Pride knew before I even did just how lonely and hurt I was. She'd seen right through me. She must have been holding back her tears all that time, and that was why they came flooding out that night.

Ever since, she stayed by my side, prayed for my happiness, called us equals, spoke to me by name, and encouraged me to use her name as well. She greeted me in the mornings and offered a fond goodnight when it was time to part ways. Around her, I had moments of true peace and comfort in this place, moments when my heart didn't feel so heavy. She'd lead me through the library or the gardens, and for a little while, I truly wouldn't feel alone.

Pride filled the hole that had consumed my heart.

So why was she apologizing? She was the one who'd saved me.

I didn't even realize for a moment that I was hugging her back. There was so much I wanted to say, but all the words stuck in my throat. None seemed quite right. All I could do was sit there and hold her and hope that conveyed what I felt.

Eventually, she calmed enough to speak, breath brushing against my ear.

"If I become a wicked queen...then I want you to...I want you to kill me..."

Her words chilled me to my core. My mind went completely blank. For a while, I didn't even believe I'd heard her correctly. But something about those words pierced me right to my heart.

Kill her? I would never. No, I couldn't possibly kill her. I could never kill such a kind, wonderful person.

I sat there trying to sort through my thoughts for so long that Pride actually fell asleep in my arms.

"Pride?" I tried, squeezing her gently. She didn't respond.

What in the world had the poor girl so scared? How could someone so caring and intelligent possibly think she would grow up into a wicked, cruel queen? I just couldn't believe it. But if the person who'd shown me so much kindness truly feared this fate, if it truly burdened her, then...

"I'll protect you."

I whispered it into her shoulder, knowing I'd get no response. Still, that quiet declaration filled me with determination. I hugged her a little closer, pressing that vow between us.

By the time I woke up the next morning, Pride was already gone. The doctor came to check on me and recommended I rest for a few days just to be safe. That was fine with me; I was still processing the previous night. Part of me didn't even believe it was real. Yet Pride's words and warmth, and my own determination, all still rang fresh and clear in my mind.

Pride didn't come to check on me any more after that. Impatient to see her again, I asked the maid—who bowed and introduced herself as Lotte—about her when she visited my room.

Lotte said Pride felt too awkward about falling asleep in my bed that night to come see me again.

"The princess ordered us not to inform Her Majesty or His Royal Highness so as not to upset them. There's nothing to worry about," she said with a teasing smile.

That was the first moment I really believed that everything that happened that night was real and not a dream. And that it was... Well, I wasn't sure what to call it. But every time I thought back to that night, my chest got warm all over again, like my fever was coming back. I sure was glad it wasn't, though. Despite that, it felt so strange not seeing Pride for several days. The moment I got permission from the doctor, I went back to my etiquette and other lessons.

I returned to my training refreshed. Memorizing all the information they gave me felt even easier than before. And it meant I could see Pride again. Butterflies battered at my stomach. Pride herself wore an embarrassed smile. But she quickly gave me her usual grin, and all the nerves and strangeness dissipated.

"I'm so glad you're better now," she said. Instantly, a weight lifted off my shoulders.

Pride didn't bring up that night. I thought better of mentioning it too. If she wasn't inclined to talk about it, that was fine by me. It didn't diminish my determination whatsoever.

After lunch that day, Pride and I went to see Father. She kept her hands on my shoulders as we approached him, as though bracing or supporting me.

"These are special circumstances," Father said. "You can't mention this to anyone, even in the castle."

With that, he handed me a single envelope. I broke the seal, but I had no idea what could be inside. Perhaps an invitation of some sort? Why would I need to keep something like that secret?

I slipped a letter free of the envelope and began to read, eyes widening with every word. I read it over and over, not believing my eyes. It was a letter, a letter from someone I was sure I'd never see again—my mom.

"Dear Stale."

I knew her handwriting immediately. It was the same hand that had taught me how to write my name. The only education I got back in town came in this very handwriting.

How can this be happening? They told me I could never see her or write to her again. I really thought it was impossible, at least for now. That's why I... That's why I...

Father explained that this letter was Pride's idea, but I hardly even heard him. A torrent of clashing emotions crashed over me.

Once every month? I can find out how Mom's doing once every month? I can know for sure that she's okay? And I even get to write back to her on my birthday?!

This went so far beyond my tenuous little plot to serve as Pride's assistant in the hopes of some sort of good grace far in the future. Even if that plan worked, it would be years before I'd have any kind of hope, but I'd given up on any other possibility. My hands trembled as I held the letter, the implications of the words on that paper sinking in. My gratitude toward Pride and Father, my love for Mom, and the joy that surged in my heart were too much to contain, and soon they came pouring back out.

I never cried so loudly in my life.

Tears tracked down my cheeks. I couldn't stop the loud, indecent sobs, but in that moment, I didn't even care. Someone stroked my hair, trying to soothe me as I went on crying. I turned and found Pride smiling back at me. Instantly, I pulled her into a hug.

Just how many times is this person going to change my life for the better?

I was still embarrassed to have Pride and Father see me in such a state, but I was long past the point of bottling any of this up.

"Mother and Father and I, and your other mother too, we all love you very much," Pride said.

I couldn't take any more kindness. I buried my face against her chest as the last strands of control snapped and all of my emotions flooded out. My voice echoed around the high ceilings of the castle, but all I could think about was how much I owed this person. Just protecting her wouldn't be enough. I had to repay her for everything she'd done for me, even if it took a whole life's worth of work.

When I could, I thanked Father, though my voice emerged raw and ragged. Then I shuffled out of the room with Pride at my back. As we exited, she whispered a reminder to hide the letter in my pocket before the guards and maids on the other side of the door could see it. Even when I made it all the way back to my room, I couldn't quite stop crying. The moment I was alone, the tears threatened to well back up, so I pressed my arm over my mouth to contain the sobs.

I took out Mom's letter and read it all yet again.

"Dear Stale." Those words alone were enough to have tears prickling my eyes anew.

I was so glad I'd studied reading and writing at the castle. What I knew before coming here wouldn't have gotten me much further than my own name. Now, I could read how Mom was doing and how the townspeople were helping her. She said she was so happy to be able to write to me, and she'd be counting the days until she got to hear from me again. She wrote of her gratitude to His Royal Highness for allowing this and asked me to stay happy and healthy. Between every other line, the words "I love you" appeared over and over again.

I read that letter what felt like dozens of times, wiping my eyes with the bottom of my shirt and sniffling as I went. When I held the paper close to my face, I could even catch faint traces of Mom's scent on the sheet. *It really is Mom,* I thought as the reality hit me once more.

It took a long time before I could finally tear myself away from the letter, but I knew I had to hide it eventually. No one else could see it, or I'd lose this precious point of contact. As I searched, voices drifted into my room.

"Whatever are we supposed to do? The princess's selfishness is maddening."

The voices were coming from the window. My room sat one floor below Pride's. From my window, I could look down at the path that led out from the gardens and stretched to the front door. Now, I perched beside that window, covering my mouth with my hands to keep extra quiet.

"Are you sure we should be discussing this outside of the castle?"

"The instructor told me that neither Her Highness nor her younger brother are studying in their bedrooms, so there's no need to worry. But do keep your voice down. If you speak so loudly, you'll be overheard by someone."

I could just barely pick up the hushed conversation. One of them called Pride selfish again, then their voices lowered. As much as I strained my ears, I couldn't hear them after that.

Something about the situation didn't sit right, though. With my handcuffs gone, an idea sprang to mind. For the first time in a long time, I called on my power, teleporting to a bush out in the garden that I hoped was closer to the speakers.

As soon as I landed, the conversation sharpened. Someone remarked confidently that no guard would ever be foolish enough to turn them in even if they did overhear something. Apparently, a small group had gathered, including the two louder voices I just overheard. Only one of the voices sounded at all familiar, but I clung to that one, searching my memory.

"I strongly opposed those special measures. Yet the princess and His Royal Highness gave me orders, so I must keep it all a secret."

"I'm sure you made every effort, Prime Minister Gilbert. However, should we take this as a sign that the crown princess is still unable to resist indulging her every whim?"

"Yes. It's truly unfortunate. I had heard rumors of her new-found maturity ever since her power manifested, but it sounds as if she's been dragging Prince Stale all around the castle since his arrival, and she even forced him to run when he was unwell. Perhaps she's jealous of her younger brother's already apparent prowess in his studies."

Gilbert!

It was the prime minister. I'd seen him with Father just the other day. It took all my self-control not to leap out of that bush and confront his lies right there and then.

"His Royal Highness struggles to refuse requests from the princess. In this instance, he didn't hesitate to agree to her special request. I just regret that I was unable to convince him of my concerns."

"Prime Minister, there's no need for you to blame yourself."

"He's right! Though she's the daughter of the prince consort, this raises concerns for her eventual ascension to the throne."

"Well, that's why it's our job to protect and assist the members of the royal family. Princess Pride is still so young. I'm sure she will grow into the role along the way."

"You're certainly open-minded, Prime Minister Gilbert. It's no mystery why you were chosen for your title at such a young age."

"Please, you flatter me. However, the royal family must serve the people of the kingdom. For the prince consort to bend to his daughter's every whim and impulse, well, it makes it seem as though the monarchy has nothing better to do than indulge a little girl, wouldn't you agree? This must stay a secret, but Prince Stale is also facing rather disgraceful treatment. The boy is a commoner, yes, but the princess looks down on him and has been quietly finding ways to harass him almost every day."

My hands trembled with rage. I couldn't believe how he just kept going with these blatant lies. Pride had never once harassed me, yet he spoke with such authority that everyone seemed to believe him.

"However, even Prince Stale's teacher has recognized the boy's extreme wisdom for his age. He won't accept what we have to say uncritically, though he already appears to harbor concerns over Princess Pride's future as the queen. It pains me to see such a smart boy trapped in a situation like that."

"Unbelievable. Even young Prince Stale can see it."

"If only His Royal Highness and Her Majesty would take notice as well. If my proposed national special power registration became law, we would finally have a way to know what powers the people of this kingdom possess. Just locating Prince Stale for his rumored teleportation power took the work of many soldiers and quite a considerable amount of taxpayer money. Such expenses could be avoided if this kingdom had a system of organization."

Murmurs of agreement sounded all around.

"But I'm still the prime minister. Even if Her Majesty can't say no to her beloved husband, and even if that husband can't help but spoil his eldest daughter, who doesn't yet have the character required of a crown princess, I intend to support them all until the end. Oh, and of course, this conversation must remain between us, for the good of the kingdom."

I peeked between the bushes then and caught a glimpse of Gilbert's face. The people around him nodded, but I saw the cunning smirk beneath his smile.

With those final words, Gilbert and the others dispersed in different directions. I teleported back to my room, then snuck back to the window to get a look at the group. A few of them looked familiar, but I didn't have many names. They were just people I'd seen around the castle here and there.

I can't let this go.

I yearned to dash out of my room and tell Mother and Father everything I'd just heard. Gilbert and the group who shared his ideals would all be sentenced to death for defamation of the monarchy, or so I hoped. Otherwise, they might get away with continuing to spread their horrible lies. But what could I do? No one would believe me, no matter what I told them. Mother and Father would definitely trust Gilbert over me.

But still!

The "special measures" he'd mentioned had to be the letters I was exchanging with Mom. Gilbert didn't seem to mind flagrantly disobeying the order to keep quiet about those—and lying on top of that to make it sound like something nefarious. Worst of all, that whole group seemed to believe him. Despite Gilbert's decree to keep the information secret, rumors would surely swirl. They might even make it out of the castle and into the town.

Pride had given me everything. Now those gossips wanted to make it sound like she was the villain. From both inside the castle and outside, Pride, Father, and even Mother would take a hit to their reputations. I hadn't yet met Mother, but Father was such a kind man, and Gilbert intended to tarnish both of them, along with Pride. My blood boiled at the mere suggestion.

"If I become a wicked queen..." Why had she suggested that? Who could possibly make a better queen than her? No matter what people like Gilbert peddled, I refused to believe it.

But again, what could I do? The adults wouldn't listen to anything Pride or I had to say. They'd surely listen to Gilbert over two kids. Then the kind, intelligent girl who cried in anguish over the grief of others, the girl who was victim of awful rumors, would get crushed by wicked adults like Gilbert with his eloquent words and good reputation. Neither me nor Pride could do much against that, especially with me being newly adopted into this family. I didn't have a reputation or social standing or fancy words. I didn't have anything. I could study, but that wouldn't be enough. I could build up my reputation, learn to read and write, hone my understanding of others, but that wouldn't do it either. Even if I ensured Pride, Father, Mother, and Princess Tiara all loved me and saw me as a good and dutiful son and brother, that wouldn't stop Gilbert's plan.

No, I had to do more than that. I had to become the most cunning, calculating person in the entire kingdom. I had to learn to manipulate people's hearts to earn their trust. I had to make the whole castle, the whole *kingdom*, love the version of me I sold them. Potentially, I had to become someone I wasn't, but it would all be worth it if I thwarted Gilbert.

Pride didn't need to follow in my footsteps. She was perfect as she already was—innocent and warmhearted. As long as she stayed like that, the kingdom would someday flourish under her rule. I just had to learn to be conniving enough for the both of us...and then some.

I had heard Gilbert possessed the power of eternal youth, which meant he would always be around, even once Pride and I had grown. That meant I needed to enact my scheme before Pride took the throne. As the steward, I'd have the power to chase him out of the kingdom no matter what his lackeys said. Raising my reputation would not only remove Gilbert, but it would raise Pride's status as well once I served beside her in earnest.

I wish Mom knew what Pride was like too, I thought as I took out her letter again. I skimmed through it once more, searching for the section where she wrote about the prince consort. *So, Mom knows that Father was the one who gave her permission to write a letter, but she doesn't know that Pride orchestrated the entire thing. I need to include that in my birthday letter. I'll tell her all sorts of things about Pride too.*

Then I scanned a little farther along, and my eyes caught on the words "I love you."

"Mother and Father and I, and your mother too, we all love you very much." That was what Pride had said to me, but now it was my turn to return that love.

Don't worry. I'll make sure you're safe, I swore. *I'll protect your gentle voice, your smile, your heart, every wonderful thing about you.* Pride promised that as queen she'd ensure all the people of the kingdom—including me and Mom—were happy. But I would ensure she was happy too. Whether she was my crown princess, my older sister, or just a girl I knew, I'd protect her from adults like Gilbert no matter what. If I had to corrupt myself to do that, so be it, but I would never allow her pure heart to be tainted the same way.

It wasn't just a promise—it was a vow.

My name was Stale Royal Ivy.

I was the crown princess's younger brother-in-law, and the steward of the next generation. I existed to fulfill those duties and serve at Pride Royal Ivy's side.

Starting right then, I existed only for her.

The Heinous Princess
and Her Family

"NGH... WAAAAAAAH..."

Who is that? I hear someone crying.

Wails rose inside a pitch-black room. It was... It was me.

"Oh, Stale? You're back already? That sure was quick."

Someone was approaching. I couldn't see much through that heavy darkness, but I knew it was a girl.

That's right. She's the one who ordered me to kill Mom and come back here.

Mom looked so happy, but so surprised when she first saw me. I begged her to run, but she didn't understand. She just stood there and died on my knife.

"Stale... Why?"

Her voice still rang in my ears. She sank to the floor, bleeding profusely, tears shining in her eyes.

I turned away, unable to look at her, and left her there on the floor. Then I...then I...then I...then I...!

"You came right back so you wouldn't be spotted, just as I ordered. What a good boy you are."

Her hands stroking through my hair left me nauseated. The mirth in her voice ignited a surge of murderous rage inside me. I howled like an animal, scooping up the knife I'd stabbed Mom with and swinging it straight at the girl.

She didn't even have time to move out of the way before my blade reached her throat...and stopped. I had no hesitance, no reluctance about killing the wretched creature, yet my body was frozen and out of my control.

"Ah ha ha! How stupid can you be? You can't kill your master once you've signed a fealty contract," she said.

Just hearing her voice makes me want to puke.

"Why?!" I asked. "Why did you make me kill Mom?! What did I... What did Mom ever do to you?!"

She merely shrugged, unmoved by my shouting. "Nothing, of course. I did it because it's just so entertaining. Ahhh, Stale, my adorable little slave. Thanks to you, I'm having the time of my life lately." She looked like a mere child, but that laugh held a cruelty that clashed with her innocent image.

"Then kill me," I said. "If making me suffer is so much fun, then why don't you just kill me?!" At this point, death would be a mercy. How could I go on living in this world without Mom?

"What're you talking about? I thought you said you'd kill me when you signed the fealty contract, no? But now you want to die? You want to be with your dead mom?!"

My hands trembled around the knife. If I could just move it even a little, I could kill her. It would be so very easy to drag the blade across her throat.

"Okay, then here's an order for you," she said. "From here out, you can never take your own life. You can never tell anyone about what you did today or about this new promise either."

"What...?"

She wouldn't even let me die.

"Oh, yes, that's the look," she said. "Why don't you keep that look on your face for a while? Goodnight, Stale. Be sure to clean off all that woman's disgusting commoner blood before the birthday celebration tomorrow." She turned on her heel, nearly skipping out of the room.

I collapsed right where I stood, falling to the ground and slamming my fists against the floor. I lay there raging like a wounded beast, nearly incoherent, howling with all my might. I longed to plunge that horrible knife into my own chest and end my pain.

Unfortunately, all I could do was curl in on myself and go on weeping. Anger and sadness and grief clenched around my heart. My breathing turned ragged, small sips of air squeezing into lungs crushed by agony.

This is the end. I don't want to live anymore. Nothing good will ever happen to me again in this life. Mom was gone and, with her, my entire world. Plus, the contract chained me to the girl who'd forced me to kill her. I had no one left, no one but the person responsible for Mom's death.

If only I was never born with this power, then I'd get to be with Mom forever. Why did I have to be born with teleportation? I can't take it anymore. I want to die, I want to die, I want to die, I want to die, I want to die, I can't take it, I can't take it, I can't take it, I can't take it, I can't take it anymore! There's nothing left for me in this life. Nothing. Nothing at all, because...

Because I'll be alone for the rest of my life.

If I could just die, I might get to be with Mom and Dad. Yet my orders forced me to keep on living.

"Mom... I'm s-sorry... I just..."

I just wanted to see you. That's all I wanted.

I hadn't even gotten an opportunity to tell her I loved her. The moment I signed that contract, both our fates were sealed. I would never forgive that girl for what she did.

No, she wasn't a girl. She was a demon in human skin. Whatever it took, I would get revenge for Mom's death. I would destroy that wicked creature. That would be my only hope...

"Good morning, Your Highness."

A maid drew the curtains back and light flooded into the room.

"Good morning," I said, groggy and disoriented.

Sunlight poured in through the window. I nestled deeper under the blankets and rubbed at my eyes. *What was that just now? I think I had some kind of dream.*

I tried to dredge up the details, but all I got were hazy snatches.

"You were groaning in your sleep. Are you feeling well?" the maid said, but I couldn't even remember if it was a good dream or a bad one. When I rubbed at my eyes, however, I found faint traces of tears.

I don't think I've ever once cried in my sleep since I came here. I was still wondering at the dampness around my eyes when I dragged myself out of bed. Well, I'd definitely cried at things other than dreams.

My face grew hot when I thought back on what had happened with Pride a few days earlier. The more I remembered, the more embarrassed I became, yet something softer and warmer filled my chest at the same time. I tried to shake it off as the maids helped me dress and go over the day's schedule.

Oh, that's right. Today is...

"We'll also be making the final preparations for Princess Tiara's birthday party tomorrow," the maid said.

Princess Tiara, Pride's younger sister. I hadn't even managed to meet her yet. I'd get my introduction at the same time as the rest of the kingdom.

"Thank you very much," I said. "Elder Sister is looking forward to it, and so am I."

Tiara Royal Ivy was the second-born princess. I'd heard she was sickly. Even as Mother, Father, Pride, and the rest of Freesia celebrated her birthday, I resolved to look out for the girl.

Although...

I finished my morning preparations and left the room. I was still musing over who Tiara was and what this party would be like as I hurried down the hall and came to a staircase.

"Good morning, Stale," a voice called up the stairs.

I gazed down at the girl destined to be queen, the girl who already meant so much to me, the girl who might change this whole kingdom someday.

"Good morning, Pride."

Even if I wanted to protect Tiara, my first priority would always be Pride. It was her happiness and success that I truly needed to cherish and bolster.

Tomorrow was Princess Tiara's birthday party. It would also be my first time meeting Mother since I was adopted into the family, and Pride's first time seeing Mother since she became the official successor. Both of those things far eclipsed Tiara for me.

After all, everything I did, I did for Pride.

In the days since Stale joined the family, he proved himself a shockingly fast learner. He was developing a keen interest in reading books, so we spent less time playing in the gardens and more time studying in the library. Even collapsing during that game of tag didn't staunch his voracious appetite for more knowledge.

When I asked him about it, he simply said, "There are more things than ever that I want to learn."

But I just couldn't shake the feeling that something about Stale was different ever since he got over his cold. He was calmer, cooler, as though there was something lurking under the surface. In fact, he felt just like the scheming boy I remembered from his route in the otome game. Just the other day, when I asked him what he wanted to do when he became the seneschal, a sinister smile curled his mouth as he said, "I'm excited to do a full rework of all the palace workers and officials."

I wasn't quite sure what that meant, but something about it left me uneasy. Well, it wasn't like Stale ever smiled at anyone in the game either. In ORL, he reserved his smiles for scheming—or Tiara. He was a mysterious, cool kind of character. While the Stale I knew here certainly had his mysteries, he was far friendlier than in the game. He was already getting pretty popular with the rest of the castle.

I opened a history book, determined not to lose to Stale in wits even as I studied right there beside him. The Pride of ORL was a fast learner. Though evil, her wicked plans involved intricate, intelligent strategies. If I couldn't be as clever as Stale, the most intellectual love interest, perhaps I could at least be as clever as the Pride of the game. The memories from my past life were helping me with that, imparting knowledge I didn't have to relearn here. That was fine for the academic subjects, but what about things like empathy? I'd already failed at picking up on the feelings of the people around me to a frankly embarrassing extent. I'd need those kinds of skills too if I was going to succeed.

I spent day after day studying with Stale, trying to keep up with him, trying to improve myself to avert the disaster barreling toward me. But I had to admit it felt strange doing my lessons right next to the boy who might kill me in ten years, if things went the way they did in the game.

"Ugh…"

How depressing. I sighed to myself. These thoughts plagued me day and night, even when I wasn't sitting right next to Stale in the library. I just couldn't stop wondering how all this would play out now.

"Is something the matter, Your Highness? Are you feeling worried about today's birthday party?" Lotte asked while helping me dress.

I must have been sighing more than usual, but I tried to downplay it. "It's nothing like that. I'm excited to meet Mother and my sister. I guess I'm just a little nervous."

It wasn't a lie. I really *was* excited to see Tiara and Mother. However, burdened with my past life's memories and the knowledge of where this was all leading, it was hard to be very happy about this. Tiara was yet another victim of Pride's torment.

In the game, after Father died, Mother began to deteriorate. Pride played the role of a kind older sister around their mother, but turned harsh and cold the moment she was alone with Tiara. Day after day, she hurled insults at her younger sister, calling her a useless stain on the monarchy, and wore down Tiara's self-confidence. Once Pride inherited the throne, she forced Tiara to live in a faraway tower, but even there Tiara retained her compassionate nature and lived a noble life. She timidly addressed Pride as "Queen Pride" or "Your Majesty" due to all the bullying, but by the end of the game, after Pride died for her crimes, Tiara murmured "Elder Sister" in every single route. Even after so many years of torment, Tiara mourned Pride and the relationship they never had.

Knowing all that, I promised I'd try my very best not to let any of it happen. I didn't want to upset or hurt Tiara. But how much could I do when I was destined to become the villain, the monstrous final boss? In ten years, Tiara would stop my rampage and heal the land in the process.

My sister was the only ray of hope for the love interests, and for the entirety of the kingdom as well.

⚜

The whole kingdom came out to celebrate Tiara's birthday. From inns and taverns to large public squares, the Freesian people emerged in droves, abuzz with excitement over the new princess.

Naturally, the castle would host the most extravagant party of all. Visiting monarchs from neighboring lands, our own nobility, even some members of the middle class all filled the castle to bursting. Music drifted through every hall. Lavish food spreads awaited guests at every turn.

Yet the only members of the actual royal family present at that point were me and Mother, whom I hadn't seen yet thanks to having to adjust my makeup, accessories, and gown. When we actually went out to greet people, I would go first, followed by Stale. Tiara would arrive last, accompanied by Father.

I stood at the bottom of the staircase that led to the grand hall and gulped. I was used to these kinds of celebrations, between royal birthdays and national events, but this time my heart hammered against my ribs.

"Elder Sister."

I turned to find Stale standing behind me with a pleasant smile on his face. This was his first such event, yet he looked utterly cool and calm, unlike me.

"Don't worry. I'll be right here with you," he said.

"Thank you, Stale. That's good to hear," I told him.

I couldn't help but return his reassuring smile. My heart rate slowed just a touch, knowing he was by my side. But almost the moment I smiled back at him, Stale turned away.

"What's wrong?" I asked, but he waved away my question, still refusing to look at me. The red tinge to his ears made me think that perhaps he was just as nervous as me.

"Um, I...didn't say this earlier, but..." He turned back toward me with an effort, a strange flush heating his face. "Y-you look very...lovely."

"Oh!" I blinked. "Hee hee. Thank you, Stale. You look very handsome too."

I put my hand over my mouth like a proper lady, but I still couldn't hold in my laughter. Thanks to the memories of my past life, I'd mastered a dignified giggle in no time.

In his formal attire, black hair neatly styled and gallant features on full display, Stale really was handsome. He was only a child, but I knew that as one of the romanceable characters in the game, he'd grow into a dashing man. Plus, he had such a kind heart. He must have been nervous, yet he'd come here and tried to calm my nerves as well. As I admired his looks in silence, Stale stood there, flustered.

The maids and guards around us were smiling to themselves as they overheard our conversation.

"While it may be Princess Tiara's debut today, it's also the debut of Princess Pride as the new heir to the throne. You mustn't hesitate in holding your head up high today," one of them offered.

They were right. Tiara wasn't the only reason for this party— I had a leading role to play too. Stale cleared his throat and stood up straighter and I followed his lead, facing forward again and trying to get my racing heartbeat under control. Soon, the guards shouted a command and horns blared out a fanfare that rang through the hall.

With a gasp, I corrected my posture. The clamoring crowd fell to a hush as one loud, clear voice rose above the din to announce "Pride Royal Ivy." It was time.

Slowly but gracefully, I proceeded down the long carpet. Applause enveloped me on all sides, as the crowd parted so I could continue along my route.

They called Stale's name next. Even though he was the eldest prince, Stale was also my steward, so he followed behind me like my attendant. The guests around us let out cries of awe as they laid eyes on him for the very first time. I imagined they were struck by the beauty and aura he possessed, one so unlike any ordinary commoner. Besides, they'd seen me and Mother and Father before. Stale and Tiara would draw their attention today.

Slowly, I closed the distance between me and Mother.

"It's been a while, hasn't it, Pride? My dear daughter," she said.

Rosa Royal Ivy smiled down at me, framed by the soft waves of her blonde hair. She sat upon her throne with elegance, watching me with placid eyes. She was like a white rose perched upon a dais—regal, beautiful, and graceful, commanding the adoration of everyone around her.

"Yes, Mother. It's been a long time since we last met. I'm glad to see you looking well." I did my best to imitate her elegant smile.

"So this is the new member of our family, hmm?" she said, turning her gaze toward Stale.

"Yes, this is Stale Royal Ivy, my younger brother-in-law," I said. "We've entered into a subordination contract, so he'll be assisting me for the rest of my life."

Stale was already kneeling when I turned around, waiting for Mother's response just as he'd been taught. When Mother asked him to raise his head and introduce himself, Stale's responses were flawless. Everyone around us must have been just as impressed as me with how he handled himself before the queen.

We finished our official introductions and took our seats off to the side. The next round of fanfare echoed through the hall, announcing my father and Tiara. Tiara emerged with Father leading her by the hand as applause filled the hall.

With her fluffy blonde hair and pale skin, she looked so much like Mother. She regarded the large assembly with calm, gentle eyes.

"What a beautiful girl," someone said.

"Why, she looks just like Her Majesty," another onlooker added.

Uh-oh. I'm getting a little annoyed...

In my past life, I never thought twice about other children getting more attention than me. But something about being Pride sent a stab of jealousy right into my heart. Tiara was just so cute, so charming. Everyone kept remarking how much she looked like Mother. I wished they'd say the same about me, but no one ever compared me to my parents here, despite my sharp eyes and bright red hair.

No! I won't bully her. I definitely, definitely won't bully her! I focused all my attention on keeping a smile on my face and squashing down that petty voice inside me.

Meanwhile, Tiara stepped carefully down the carpet, struggling to walk in the kind of gown she'd never worn before. She and Father greeted Mother once they reached the throne, then turned toward Stale and me.

"Pride, Stale," Father said, "this girl is your younger sister, Tiara. Tiara, this is your big sister, Pride, and your big brother, Stale."

Tiara blinked her large, golden eyes at us in a rapid flutter. Stale and I rose, approaching Tiara to greet her. I went first, being her older sister and all.

"Tiara, I'm Pride Royal Ivy. Let's take good care of each other, my dear sister."

Perhaps her secluded life had made her shy, but when she responded, her voice hardly rose above a whisper, and she wore a timid smile. "I'm Tiara Royal Ivy. I'm so glad to meet you...Elder Sister."

Aaaah! So cute! No wonder everyone loved ORL's protagonist.

"She's the most likable heroine in the whole series," people used to say. "What an angel!" Despite being the protagonist of the very first game, Tiara's popularity persisted among fans.

That nasty voice in my head quieted when confronted with such a cute, shy girl. Stale, as the only love interest who got to see her this way, had to be luckiest of all the romanceable characters. Tiara looked like a tiny version of Mother, perfect and cute in every way.

Stale stepped forward to greet her next. At this point in the game's plotline, Stale was basically emotionless, having just killed his mother the night before. "My name is Stale Royal Ivy. It's an honor to meet you, Princess Tiara. I look forward to seeing more of you," was all he said in the game.

When Tiara saw him like that, she reached down to take the kneeling boy's hands, smiled at him, and addressed him as "my brother." To Stale, who'd lost all other relatives, it was the first warmth or familial kindness he'd received in some time. Tiara always referred to Stale as her brother after that day, and Stale looked after her more than anyone else. Even after Tiara was locked inside her isolated tower, Stale made regular trips to visit her, completely unbeknownst to Pride.

I hoped that, just like in the game, Tiara could provide such comfort and warmth to this Stale too. Nervously, I observed their first interaction. Stale knelt on the floor and took Tiara's hand.

"I'm Stale Royal Ivy, and I'm very honored to be your big brother, Tiara," he said.

Wait, what?

Stale had only ever called her "Princess Tiara" around me and the people of the castle. But now, all of a sudden, he addressed her without her title, and during their very first meeting at that. I'd expected him to be much more formal.

For a moment, I wondered if Mother, Father, or the palace nobility would be bothered by this, but no one reacted as far as I could tell. In fact, everyone looked impressed by Stale's refined manner and dignified introduction.

I was sure that Stale called her "Princess Tiara" in this scene in the game, though. I supposed things were different here, however. For one thing, in the game, Stale actually got to meet and confide in Tiara. For another, by this point in ORL, he'd already murdered his mother. This Stale, free of the burden of matricide, was able to greet his adorable younger sister with amicable charm.

"Pride, the firstborn princess and your older sister, is just as wonderful as Mother and Father," Stale was saying, still holding Tiara's hand. "Let's do everything we can to be of help to her, okay?"

Tiara's smile broadened and she squeezed Stale's hand in hers. "Yes, Big Brother."

All I could do was watch in utter shock.

Stale had certainly opened up to me more here than in the game, but I never imagined he'd say something like that in public. Though he spoke directly to Tiara, the entire assembly hung on his every word. Effectively, Stale had just declared to the people of the castle—no, to the people of the kingdom—that we were more than just siblings, and voiced his approval of me as the future queen in the process.

I bit the inside of my cheek as the implications hit me, holding back the tears that threatened to well up. Tiara turned her gaze to me. Stale was next, but soon Mother, Father, and everyone else watching the proceedings all focused on me. I gulped and took a shaky step forward to address Tiara.

"Thank you, Stale, and you too, Tiara," I said. "I'm so happy to have such reliable siblings." I set a hand on each of their heads.

This is it. This is where I have to say those words. But... I knew what I had to do, the right words to say, yet some nasty, ugly piece of myself, the part of me that was still Pride, fought against me. I dragged in a breath, gathering my courage.

"May the three of us, as siblings, protect this kingdom and its people forever."

Instantly, a chorus of cheers erupted in the room. Voices rose among the ruckus, shouting, "Long live Princess Pride!" and "Her Highness, the crown princess!"

I've never heard such cheers in all my life.

Stale wore a satisfied smile. Tiara reached up and squeezed my hand on her head, giving me a small nod. Father clapped right along with the audience. As for Mother, she smiled, glanced over at Father...then applauded with everyone else.

I could hardly breathe. My mouth hung open as I took in this roar of approval. The memories from my past life made it almost impossible to believe what I was seeing. I well knew all the gossip about Pride, having heard it from a young age. "She's so selfish."

"She's just a spoiled princess." "She's not fit to be royalty." No one ever showed such intense enthusiasm for me, not even at my own birthday parties or events.

Mother rose from her throne for the first time and stood before me. I gaped up at her, tall and beautiful and striking. Mother hardly showed her age at all. When she spoke, her voice rose above the crowd, though she did not shout.

"The people here are expecting great things from you," she told me. "I want you to make sure you never forget this moment."

Of course. There's no way I'd ever forget.

Mother faced the audience next. The moment she raised her hands, silence rushed to replace the ruckus. When she spoke, her voice boomed from her slender frame.

"One month ago," she said, "Pride, the firstborn princess, developed the precognition that serves as proof of her right to the throne. She will continue my legacy and serve as queen when her time comes. I hereby recognize Pride Royal Ivy as the crown princess of this kingdom!"

In that moment, I officially became Mother's successor and inherited the power that came with that title. Stale and Tiara, as members of the royal family, would serve as well and earn the love of the people. I could not hope for a similar fate. As Pride, I'd eventually fail in my mission of "protecting the land and its people." But I still had ten years before then and I swore I would use that time to do everything I could to help Freesia and its people.

Even if my dear siblings would despise me in the end.

⤙❋⤚

I endured a gamut of guests and introductions and polite conversations before the ceremony finally ended and I got a break.

I'd only just extracted myself from another conversation full of congratulations when Prime Minister Gilbert approached me. I let my shoulders relax. He was a shy man and my father's assistant as well; I didn't need to remain on my guard. Even Tiara seemed relaxed around him. She must have met him before.

I greeted him with a nod and thanked him for organizing the whole party.

"There's no need to thank me, Your Highness," he said. "It is I who am grateful to see each and every member of the royal family here in the same room today."

His easy smile still held the perfect poise expected of the prime minister. His constant flattery made me slightly suspicious, but how could I hate the man keeping the secret of those letters between Stale and his mom?

What's this? Father and even Stale look kind of scary all of a sudden... I couldn't figure out what their sudden shift meant.

"Princess Tiara, when I watched you today, I could hardly believe that this was your first public appearance," Prime Minister Gilbert went on. "But it's unfortunate, is it not? You would make as fine a queen as Princess Pride, if only you possessed her precognition for yourse—"

"I beg your pardon. What exactly do you mean by 'unfortunate,' Prime Minister Gilbert?" Stale cut in.

Stale?!

Before Father could even step in or correct him, Stale moved in front of Prime Minister Gilbert and met him with a glare.

"Ah, my sincerest apologies, Prince Stale," Gilbert said. "I only meant that Princess Tiara displayed the utmost elegance today, but it appears I was quite rude in my wording."

The Prime Minister offered a charming smile and changed the subject, ignoring Stale's obvious anger.

"Why, I hardly recognized you earlier, Prince Stale," he said. "In just the few days since I last saw you, you've become the very picture of royalty. I would love nothing more than to have a chance to converse with you sometime. I'd like to hear about your hometown and yes, even your previous family, or the kinds of special powers you've encountered among the townsfolk in your life."

"Thank you, Prime Minister Gilbert. I only made it this far with the support of the wonderful Princess Pride," Stale replied. "I'll do everything in my power to help her. I hope you'll support me as the *eldest prince* as well. Can I count on that, *Prime Minister Gilbert?*" Stale leaned into every title, making them heavy with authority and setting a challenge before Gilbert.

What's going on? He's being really, really scary!

Though Stale and Gilbert both smiled, something far darker lurked just beneath the surface of their pleasant expressions. Stale seemed to threaten the prime minister with every word, as though to say, "*My rank is higher than yours. Don't you dare look down on me.*" Could he already be this protective over his younger sister?

"Yes, of course, *Prince* Stale," Gilbert responded in a voice tight and tense with malice.

This wasn't going anywhere good. Tiara cocked her head in confusion, and I led her a few steps away, lest their conflict boil over right there and then.

"Ah, pardon me," Gilbert said. "Princess Pride, your conduct in particular stole the heart of everyone who laid eyes on you. By the way, I have a humble request of you, now that you're the heir to the throne. Might I hear your thoughts on the politics of this kingdom? For example, the topic of those who possess special pow—"

Thwack!

Prime Minister Gilbert reeled and rubbed his head, but it wasn't Stale who struck him. Father got there first and dragged the prime minister away by the collar.

"Are you all right, Elder Sister? I'm sorry, I said too much just now," Stale said to me.

"N-no, I appreciated what you said, Stale, thank you. I just..."

I hugged Tiara's shoulders, as if she were a stuffed animal I could squeeze for comfort during a storm.

"You just what?" Stale said.

"Stale...you've changed since you first came to the castle," I admitted. "You remind me of Prime Minister Gilbert now."

"What?!" he choked. His eyes flew wide, color draining out of his face. "Wh-what makes you say that?"

I'd never seen Stale so flustered before. His mouth hung open as though he couldn't summon the words to express his bewilderment.

"Well... Like...the way you...smile?"

"I-I've always been bad with...showing my emotions and such," Stale said. "Or rather...I can't do it properly..."

"What? Is that so? I'm sorry, I never noticed that," I said. I tried to encourage him to brush it off, but his shoulders slumped and he said, "No, I know that it's something I need to master."

With that, he turned away. I could hear him quietly mumbling things like, "Right... My face has to be...so that I can..." and "But why *Gilbert* of all people..."

I didn't really understand any of it. I hadn't realized that Stale struggled so much to express himself even before Pride gravely wounded his heart. Sure, he had trouble with that in the game and remained a stoic character even in his happiest ending with Tiara, but none of that trauma had occurred here. Perhaps I'd misread him, then, and he truly was just offering the prime minister a friendly smile.

My guilt weighing me down, I released Tiara and whispered, "Go cheer him up."

She walked up to him and tugged on his shirt. "Big brother," she said. With his shoulders still slumped, he patted her head. It was an adorable sight, unlike any scenes I ever saw in the game. How could I not root for them to eventually find happiness together?

"Princess Pride."

I turned when someone called my name, only to find...

"Oh, Commander."

A large man awaited me wearing armor and white knight's coat. I knew him from previous events. He was the commander of the royal order. Behind him stood two more knights, one of whom had to be the vice commander.

"I was incredibly moved by your earlier speech," he said. "I would like to congratulate you on your new title of crown princess and wish a happy birthday to Princess Tiara as well."

The commander bowed his head as he spoke. It was all a bit much to take in. He'd never offered more than a basic greeting before, and certainly never praise.

"Why, thank you," I replied. "I'm very glad to hear it."

His smile was as handsome as the rest of him. "The Unwounded Knight" had bright blue eyes and short-cropped silver hair. As his nickname implied, he didn't bear a single scar thanks to his exceptional prowess in battle. It was easy to see why as I took in his muscular frame. In my previous life, I might have even labeled him a "hunk."

"Truly, you've grown into a wonderful young lady since we last met," he said, ever the charmer.

My head swirled with déjà vu as I tried to figure out where I remembered this man from. It could have been the game itself, but there was no way a man his age was one of the love interests. He and Prime Minister Gilbert, both in their twenties or thirties... something just felt off about them.

"I hope that my son might one day have an audience with you as well, Your Highness," the commander added.

Yeah, I knew it. He might be too old to be a love interest in an otome game, but his son wasn't.

"Is your son a knight as well?" I asked.

"I...wish that were the case," he said with a laugh and scratched his head.

Uh-oh.

A bit taken aback, I smiled and replied, "I look forward to the day when you can introduce us."

Even as I offered the pleasantry, something in my gut told me things were more complicated than they appeared.

"Albert...I've been thinking."

I, Rosa, the queen of Freesia, was worn out from my day of official business at Tiara's birthday party. My husband, Albert Royal Ivy, joined me in my bedroom that evening.

"I just can't believe how much Pride has changed since I last saw her," I said.

Perhaps it'd simply been too long since I'd had time to see Pride. I knew my work had kept me away for quite a while now. But both Albert and I knew well that when Pride wasn't around us, she was an incredibly selfish and arrogant child. Her reputation around the castle had reached our ears long ago.

"I've been telling you, haven't I? Ever since her powers awakened, she's been different," Albert said.

"Pride would never have been able to become queen before. It was Tiara who was supposed to inherit the throne...until now."

"You've had a change of heart. Is it because of your precognition? Or is it..."

"My judgment as the queen, and as her mother, is what's changed my mind, of course. That's why I never visited Pride in person. I believed it was Tiara, the second-born princess, who was destined to become the true queen. But Pride is still my daughter, and I love her very much, which only made it harder to see her and know she wasn't fit to be queen. Especially after having Tiara. If Tiara ever developed precognition, I would have had to tell Pride that she wasn't the heir."

Albert insisted over and over that I should visit Pride more and show her a mother's love, but I couldn't bring myself to fill her with false hope about inheriting the crown. I sent him instead and he showered her with enough love for the both of us. Albert kept me up to date on what Pride was doing, but as soon as I gave birth to Tiara, I knew Pride would never become my successor.

"I was sixteen when I had my first premonition."

"That's just around the time we first met," Albert said. I hadn't noticed him move nearer, near enough to murmur into my ear and send a prickle of heat down my spine.

Precognition. I'd used that power to foresee many things. Long before I was even pregnant with Pride or Tiara, I saw both of them in my visions.

Of course, precognition was hardly a reliable power. I got visions at random. Sometimes, they were as momentous as the births of my daughters; other times, they were as trivial as tomorrow's weather. I could neither control nor predict it. The visions simply happened, and while they did occasionally influence the future of the kingdom, few queens actually relied on them.

For one thing, some of us got them constantly, whereas others experienced one maybe every ten years.

"I've foreseen many things since my first vision," I said. "However, one premonition that persisted was Pride, and a future beyond saving."

I never saw what happened after Pride took the throne. I couldn't bear to tell Albert all the horrible details of what I knew for sure, though—that Pride grew into a wicked queen who took pleasure from others' suffering. No amount of love or punishment would change that outcome.

"And yet, ever since you told me about Pride's precognition, I've stopped having visions about her future."

I didn't understand how or why, but ever since Pride awoke to her own powers, her future didn't appear for me, as though it had been diverted off course, erased, or changed in some way.

And then there was today's birthday party.

At first, I thought Pride was just playing the part of the perfect princess, putting on a show like she always did. But when she looked at Stale, I knew for certain that something was different. I'd seen the boy three months ago, but I didn't know who he was at the time. He simply appeared in my vision of Pride, a dead-eyed boy cradling Tiara's hand.

That very scene played out when Stale greeted Tiara at the birthday party...except this time, Stale had changed. The boy I saw in my vision only offered Tiara the most basic, formal introduction. But the real scene played out differently, with Stale speaking earnestly and familiarly.

Then there was his stalwart show of support for Pride in front of the entire assembly. That, too, was a significant change from my visions. I couldn't say for sure what kind of future it portended, but certainly a different one than what I'd seen before.

"Stale hasn't even lived in this castle for an entire month, and yet he did such a thing for Pride's sake," I mused. "The future...it changed. She's going to become a good queen. But how?"

At my sigh, Albert's smile twisted into a grimace. "This troubles you?"

"Yes, it does. I always thought that Tiara would take the throne, that Pride could never be queen. That's why I treated them both the way I did. Especially Pride... I couldn't..."

I held my head in my hands as the words hit me. *I couldn't be a mother to her.*

"Then it's just as I said, isn't it?" Albert said.

I peered up from between my hands to glare at him.

"Yes, sure, you were right," I said. Only my husband could get away with embarrassing me like this. "You were the one who always said that Pride was still young, that the future wasn't set in stone and she could still become the fine queen we always wanted her to be."

Albert just smiled, the same kind, soft smile I'd known and loved for so long. Just then, however, it twisted the guilt already knotted in my stomach.

"I'm not fit to be a mother...or a queen..." I said. I slouched over onto a table, and Albert set his hands on my shoulders.

"The way you treated Pride... Well, as her father, I can't say that it wasn't sometimes harsh," he said. "But as the prince con-sort, and as your husband, I just want to see you two repair your bond in the future. It isn't too late. She's still just a girl."

I heaved another sigh. "But I've always been playing the role of 'dignified queen' with Pride. It would be much too embarrass-ing to treat her like I treat Tiara all of a sudden."

When Pride was young, it was me, not Albert, who spoiled her. I wouldn't even rely on the wet nurse, insisting I would care for the newborn myself. So, really, this was all my fault. Pride was doted on as a young child. She was never told no, never scolded; she received only praise and pampering. Of course she grew up into a selfish girl willing to abuse her powers and station. Even so, when I finally realized that Pride could never become queen, I abandoned all my official business and wept for three days and nights straight.

"Things will work out this time," Albert said softly. "You've got me here with you, right? You don't need to go through this alone."

I trembled, drawing strength from those steady hands on my shoulders. "Albert..."

He knelt beside me and took my hand, pulling me into a tight embrace.

"I love you, Prince Albert," I said. "I'd be helpless without you. I couldn't do this without you by my side."

"I thought we agreed you wouldn't call me that anymore, back on that day when you officially inherited the throne," he said. "And besides...I love you even more."

Even after all these years together, heat flushed my face at his words. Albert helped me up. I could hardly breathe, chest clenching tight around my love for this man. Only he got to see me like this; only he knew about the queen's softer, private side. But it only seemed to make him love me all the more.

The Evil Princess and the Order of Knights

CLANG, CLANG! Metal clashed in the garden, interrupted by the occasional whoop or cheer.

"Please wait just a minute, Pride! There's no need to do this with me!"

Stale Royal Ivy, the eldest prince, was ten years old.

"Big Sister, please make sure you're being careful."

Tiara Royal Ivy, the second-born princess, was nine years old.

"Don't worry, you two. The instructor is right here with us."

And I, Pride Royal Ivy, was now eleven.

Three years had passed in peace since I first regained the memories of my past life. Stale didn't suffer more hardship; Tiara wasn't banished to a solitary castle tower. I even got to see Mother more often than before.

I spent a lot of that time studying. I'd recently finished every available history book in the castle and started to dive into books on Freesian law. Not only was it interesting in and of itself, but I could also pass the knowledge along to Stale and Tiara. I enjoyed teaching them. I even found a few truly interesting bits, such as a certain law enacted long, long ago.

"After this law was enacted, it wasn't uncommon for siblings-in-law to marry each other, even within the royal family," I'd told them. It made sense, thinking back on the royal family tree.

"What?!" Stale had blurted out. At first, his shock confused me; after all, I knew he married Tiara in some routes in ORL. But the Stale here knew none of that, of course.

Tiara had perked up as well. "Does that mean...you or I... could marry Big Brother Stale?" she said.

Before I could even nod in response, Stale had slammed his head down onto the table with impressive force. His face burned red, no matter how he tried to hide it. Did he already have feelings for Tiara, even earlier than in the game? In that case, my punishment at their hands might come sooner than I expected.

That thought chased me ever since that day. I no longer knew how much time I had left, but all I could do was continue on trying my best.

On this particular day, I wasn't reading, though. Stale and I were fencing. Stale had been studying the fundamentals for some time, but this was his first opportunity to experience the real deal.

My earlier attempt to reassure Stale that all was well and good earned me an angry "That's what you said when you joined my self-defense lesson this morning too!"

However, I was eager to get some combat training. Father insisted it wasn't something a queen needed to know, and in all honesty, I knew he was right, but I couldn't help wanting to learn.

Besides, there was something I needed to test.

Thus, I joined Stale in his training while Tiara watched us from a chair a few meters away. The instructor focused mostly on Stale, walking him through the basics, after which Stale got to take a break. I seized the opportunity and asked the instructor to practice with me in the meantime.

Shockingly enough, he agreed. I mentally ran through all the tips I'd heard him give Stale, then stepped forward with my blade at the ready. The instructor moved toward me and swung. I dodged his blade, then lunged to close the distance between us, parrying his sword along the way.

One meager step separated us. I set my feet and jumped with all my might, leaping right over the instructor to land behind him. He spun, thrusting his sword, but I rolled out of the way and used the opening to jab for his throat.

I knew it.

The instructor went wide-eyed with shock. Stale's mouth hung open. Tiara clapped her hands over her face as she yelped.

It happened again.

I'd never held a sword before. The most experience I had with fencing was watching Stale's lessons. Yet my body moved on pure instinct, and I even landed a hit on the instructor. It shouldn't have been possible.

The same thing happened this morning during self-defense combat. I'd never done more than watch others train, but when

I sparred with Stale's instructor, I dodged the man's every punch, shook away his grab, and jumped over his kicks, landing at his back and subduing a fully grown man.

I feared I knew what was behind this. The knowledge knotted in my stomach. I was using my "final boss cheats" to achieve these miraculous feats. More than anything else, this was proof that the memories of my past life weren't just delusions.

I knew from the game that Pride was strong. She even dueled the love interests, wielding swords and firing guns with uncanny skill and precision. There was a scene where Tiara tried to launch a sneak attack against her sister, only to get taken hostage instead.

"With my precognition, I see everything!" Pride would shout. But that strength didn't come simply from precognition. For example, if a boxer informed his opponent that he would punch them in three seconds, how likely would the other person be to dodge it successfully?

Now that I was Pride, I could feel her skill and tactical knowhow inside me. I needed no training to master combat. It was the ultimate cheat, but what else could I expect from a wicked otome villainess and the final boss of the game?

In some routes, Pride had to fight off the love interests themselves—including Stale. Sometimes, he tried to end his suffering by plunging a sword into his own gut. He didn't actually die, though he bled profusely while wearing a grim smile. But in other routes, he faced off against Pride with Tiara's help.

When I considered all this, it came as little surprise that I had a natural, perhaps even supernatural, knack for fencing and fighting. Although, frankly, I assumed the developers just made Pride OP without really thinking it through.

"It happened again..." Stale said. "Elder Sister's a woman and yet she has no need for me." Stale shook his head as though admonishing himself.

Tiara ran over to comfort him. "The instructor said you're doing great, Big Brother."

"No, our elder sister's the only impressive one here," he complained, clearly upset. "There's no point if I'm weaker than the person I'm supposed to protect."

"But my teacher said that you're the very best in the kingdom when it comes to studying, Big Brother." Tiara tried her best, but no matter what she said, Stale just collapsed in on himself yet further.

"Tiara's right," I said, hoping to help. "Plus, you're a boy, Stale. I'm sure you'll grow up to be stronger than me. Not to mention..."

I hesitated. Perhaps it'd be better just to keep my mouth shut, but Stale and Tiara were watching me, waiting for me to finish.

"If it was a simple battle of strength, then I certainly wouldn't prevail," I offered.

Stale would certainly overpower me someday. Already, he'd surpassed me in height and started filling out. I knew the Stale in the game became quite strong before his battle against Pride. He, along with many of the other love interests, ultimately prevailed against Pride by overpowering her.

"Strength..." Stale mused. He looked up to meet my gaze, finally coming out of his slump.

"Yes, that's right," I said. "For example, if a man pinned me down, I'd have trouble escaping something like that."

"Pinned down...by a man..." I was just trying to throw out a hypothetical, but Stale started muttering under his breath, and all the color drained from his face. "Not Pride," he mumbled to himself before hopping to his feet and taking up his sword.

"Let's continue," he said. "Teacher, please resume the lesson."

He faced his instructor stoically, his face set and hard. The poor instructor was still trying to steady himself after fighting me, but quickly readied to spar Stale, who awaited the bout eagerly.

That buzzing anticipation in him stirred suspicion in me. True, Stale was getting used to life in the castle, but he was also rapidly growing into the expressionless man I knew from the game. He still managed a smile in public, but outside of that, his face fell into that terrible, blank stillness.

Now here he was, suddenly leaping to attention and eager to spar. Was this all so he could slay me some day? His eyes shone with deadly intent, and I couldn't help but worry.

"Big Sister." Tiara tugged on my dress. "I'm not strong at all, and I'm not amazing like you are, Big Sister, but I-I'll always be with you!"

I blinked at her sudden determination. Tears shimmered in her eyes, but she set her jaw firmly. *Her too? What is going on here?*

"I'll be by your side so that nothing bad happens to you," she said.

Feeling a little pang of guilt at having suggested such a scary-sounding fate for myself as being overpowered by a man, I stroked her hair. "Thank you, Tiara. I didn't mean to scare you. But don't worry, we have Father and Stale and all our guards and knights to keep us safe."

It seemed Tiara truly wanted us to connect as sisters. My heart swelled at the very idea. Already, she'd grown more beautiful and ladylike. As in the game, the sickness that plagued her as a child ebbed as she aged, allowing her to grow into a normal teenage girl. Already she ran and played with me and Stale when we went out into the gardens. In fact, she spent most of her days with us, even if she couldn't participate in things like fencing. Seeing her love and determination, I longed to give her the sibling relationship she evidently craved.

After that day, Stale dove headfirst into daily fencing and self-defense lessons, honing his skills. I was invited to spar with the instructors, but I had no reason to keep practicing now that I'd proven I really did live in the otome game setting that I knew. I didn't want to get in Stale's way anymore either, so I politely rejected their offers. The last thing I wanted was some rumor about the crown princess being a savage tyrant. It was more important for me to study the etiquette and knowledge I would need in becoming queen, but before that, I wanted to teach Tiara everything I knew—she was the one who'd someday rule this kingdom.

Tiara also began to request physical training, perhaps wanting to follow in my footsteps after seeing me perform, and it took quite some time to convince her that such things weren't necessary for us. I was only allowed to participate just the one time myself, and that was with special permission. If the sickly heroine and second-born princess *actually* got hooked on hand-to-hand combat and fencing, well, that would be an ordeal all on its own.

"Elder Sister, your hand."

Stale reached out for me. I accepted his hand and let him help me out of our carriage.

We arrived at the training grounds for the order of the knights. With Stale so focused now on training, his instructor had invited him to observe the knights at their practice. I joined, making my first appearance as the crown princess. Even Tiara planned to join us once she finished her lessons for the day.

Though the practice grounds lay within the palace complex, we still needed a carriage to reach them. The castle sprawled out, so huge that it reminded me of the theme parks and large train stations from my previous life. I couldn't quite decide which world was stranger.

Mother lived and worked in one part of the royal palace, which connected via passageways to the buildings where Tiara, Stale, and I spent our days. A separate palace held rooms for guests, then there were the other buildings for visitors from faraway lands or for special use by royalty or nobility. That whole area where the royal family lived was called the "royal residence," but beyond it lay more manors and buildings for upper tier nobility. Thus, we'd needed a carriage just to get from the royal residence to the knights' training grounds—and it wasn't a short ride.

"Thank you very much for coming, Princess Pride and Prince Stale," someone said.

The knights stood lined up along a path. Two men waited at the end of the lane, one of whom was the man who'd greeted us.

"Oh, I don't see the commander here with you today," I said.

I'd assumed he'd be the one greeting us, but apparently he'd sent his vice commander in his stead. The second man was likely a squadron leader.

"My apologies, Your Highness," Stale's instructor, following behind us, said. "The commander had urgent business come up. He must attend a joint exercise with the new recruits of a neighboring country today." He sounded a bit flustered, and I realized I'd probably said it before he could inform me himself.

These "new recruits" were aspiring knights themselves. They served as reserve troops before they could join the main order. In this series, or, rather, in this world, the recruits were hand-selected for the order, which meant they had to show particular skill.

The knights here assembled appeared uniform in their white clothing and gleaming armor, but closer inspection revealed subtle differences. These slight embellishments differentiated between new recruits, main forces, vice captains, captains, vice commanders, and commanders. While subtle, the knights took these differences very seriously, especially because some troops remained "new recruits" for years before earning any mark of distinction.

According to Stale's instructor, a squadron from a neighboring kingdom had failed to show up for exercises with new recruits a few days ago. With no way to contact them, the commander set off for that kingdom with his own new recruits in tow. Mother and Father followed soon thereafter, taking a couple squadrons with them. One way or another, someone had to figure out what happened, report back, and decide what to do next.

"Mr. Carl, this is my elder sis—Princess Pride's very first observation," Stale whispered so that only his instructor and I could hear. "I'm sure that Mother already knew of this, but I believe that Her Highness should have been informed beforehand as well."

His instructor, Mr. Carl, bowed his head. "You're right. Please accept my apologies."

"It's all right," I said. "I knew about the joint exercises as well, so I should have confirmed the details for myself."

I was a bit disappointed to hear I wouldn't be meeting with the commander, but what was done was done.

"Princess Pride is always so understanding," Stale said with a smile, smoothing over the awkwardness.

"The commander told me that he trained you all to be the very best of knights," I said. "Even without his attendance, I'm certain my observation today will be just as valuable an experience."

Despite Stale's somewhat sharp rebuke, I hoped my words could set everyone back at ease. *Thank goodness. I didn't want them to think of me as some kind of overbearing princess.*

"You're always so clever," Stale whispered into my ear from behind as the vice commander led us inside a tower. I wasn't quite sure what he meant by that, and his customary blank expression certainly didn't help, but he seemed pleased, so hopefully it was a good thing.

Mr. Carl and the vice commander led us up to a tower bal-
cony from which we could look down and observe the training
grounds. Attendants had prepared a lavish chair for me to rest
in while I watched the knights go through their warm-ups. They
soon progressed to sparring, combat from horseback, and even
rifle practice.

That last took me a bit by surprise. In my past life, I always
wondered if knights actually used firearms. There was one scene
in the game where Pride used a handgun, so it didn't come as a
total shock for this world to have firearms. The vice commander
explained that while the troops primarily trained their swordsmanship, firearms experience was also required to become a
knight. Stale leaned forward in his chair as the vice commander
spoke, hanging on every word, his eyes glued to the scene.

As expected, the knights displayed perfect form during their
exercises, even without the commander present. They wielded
their blades with such passion and talent, yet the Pride of the
game used them only for waging war on other countries and op-
pressing her own citizens. What an absolute fool she was. The
vice commander indulged us when we peppered him with questions. His calm, mild manner contrasted sharply with the commander, but I found myself enjoying his patience and gentleness.
He almost reminded me of the type of man who worked in a
flower shop back in my old life. He kept the top layer of his blond
hair tied back, while the rest hung down to his shoulders. With
his placid voice and soothing demeanor, I wondered if he wasn't
more of a strategist than a soldier, in truth. However, I could see

scars peeking out from under his armor, proof of his experience on the battlefield. Through him, I got to learn about the chain of command, emergency preparedness, and anything else I wished to pester him about.

"While you're still only eleven years old, Princess Pride, it seems that the rumors of your wisdom are not unfounded," he said with a slight grin.

For a moment, I thought I must have misheard him. Surely he couldn't be praising me just for asking questions. "No, that's not—" I started to deny it when Stale jumped in.

"I see you're even well informed when it comes to castle rumors, Sir Clark," he said. "It just speaks to why you were made vice commander."

Huh? I thought he was completely focused on the knights. Was he actually paying attention to all this?

The vice commander, Sir Clark, smiled and said, "That one's quite well known by all."

It was certainly the first time I'd ever heard it. Me? Wise? How did a rumor like that get started? Thankfully, the conversation shifted, and we passed a pleasant hour just observing and chatting up in the tower. I was just about to stand up, thinking that Tiara would be finished with her lessons and want to join us soon, when a shout rang out below.

"Attention! Attention!"

As the cry sounded, Sir Clark leapt into motion. He hurried down the tower. We followed, but we couldn't keep up with his panicked strides. Eventually, we followed him into a separate building, the order's tactical strategy room. By the time we arrived, anxious knights filled the space, pacing back and forth. A few people gave Stale and me curious looks, but none of them had time to worry about us for long.

"Is Roderick safe?!" Sir Clark asked.

"Yes, sir! One of the troops is using his power to relay a transmission from Commander Roderick now."

The transmission contained a desperate request for backup. Apparently, while the commander led his new recruits on their journey to that neighboring kingdom, they got ambushed along the road. Multiple horses were dead or immobilized, and while none of the troops had yet perished, some had suffered grave injuries in the attack.

The vice commander froze for a beat, obviously trapped between his duty to his commander and his duty to the royal family. Technically, he had to protect Stale and me first and foremost. It would violate the rules of chivalry to abandon us or send us away, even if it *was* an emergency. Thus, we could make his job a little easier by simply staying with the knights, allowing the vice commander to look after us and his superior all at once.

Besides, I couldn't get the word "ambush" out of my head. The transmission came through as an image floating in the center of the room, like a hologram, but magical. In it, the commander pleaded for help and described the dire situation.

"The commander has forwarded us his coordinates!" one of the knights shouted. "I've determined his location, and we may now transmit back to him." The man's eyes glowed orange as he called on his power to produce the wavering image of the commander. The whole thing reminded me of a video conference call from my past life.

"Roderick, it's me! Can you hear me? Tell me what's going on!" Sir Clark said.

In the projection, the commander seemed to react to Sir Clark's voice. But he was still focused on something off screen, even as he replied.

"Yes, I hear you!" Commander Roderick said. "The situation hasn't changed since my last report. We still have no casualties, but we're seeing more and more injured."

"We're preparing to send backup. The vanguard of the special power forces is already on its way, and other squadrons will be out as soon as they're prepared."

"Get here as quickly as you can. Our new recruits are doing well, but there's only so much I can do as the only experienced soldier here." The commander turned his attention elsewhere for a moment and barked out orders.

"What about the enemy? Just who are you up against?" Sir Clark asked. All the cool calm he'd displayed up in the tower was gone now, replaced with urgency.

"I think they're an opposition group," Commander Roderick said. "They must be against our inter-kingdom alliance. First they dropped a boulder on our road from above so we couldn't pass. The attackers have been firing at us from the cliff tops ever since. We're sitting ducks out here! If we attempt to retreat, we'll have to do so with no cover. Right now, the squad's formed a shield to protect us, but it's only a matter of time. We're preparing all the horses we have left to carry the injured to safety."

"We can send horses from headquarters to your coordinates now," Sir Clark said. "They should arrive in about ninety minutes. The vanguard is already on their way, and though they're only a small group, they should arrive in thirty minutes. You'll have to find a way to hold out until then."

The vanguard. If they could just get there in time, there might be hope. Every one of them had special powers and had trained specifically for high mobility.

"I know," Commander Roderick said. "We can make it as long as we still have weapons and ammo... There!"

He turned suddenly as gunshots cracked and a distant scream rose. From the way he was pointing, the enemy must have come from above on the cliffs, meaning the knights could only fight with guns and not their swords. And that meant that their bullets—and time—were running out.

"What about Her Majesty? Do we have orders from her?" Commander Roderick pressed.

"We've been in communication, but she's currently outside the kingdom with His Royal Highness," Sir Clark replied. "The Queen has supposedly negotiated with their king to get you more backup, but..."

They won't make it in time. Sir Clark didn't need to continue. We all heard that horrible line hanging unspoken in the air.

Since the commander had left with new recruits, they'd probably traveled slowly. In all likelihood, they were pinned down closer to our kingdom than the next one over. Our allies' backup forces wouldn't arrive before ours did. I was sure Mother and Father were doing everything they could, but I wanted to help too.

"So backup will reach them in thirty minutes at the earliest. But what they need more than anything right now is supplies," I said.

Sir Clark and Commander Roderick both snapped their attention toward me.

"Princess Pride?" Commander Roderick said. "Why is she…?"

"Stale, I'll need your help with this. What do you say?" I asked.

"Whatever you wish, Princess Pride."

"Quickly, gather all the weapons and ammo they'll need and bring them here," I ordered. "Stale can use his special power to send them to the battlefield bit by bit."

It certainly wouldn't be quick, but Stale's teleportation afforded us an opportunity to shore up the commander's provisions a little faster. Unfortunately, Stale could only transport the equivalent of his own body weight at most and only to places he'd seen before. When he was first adopted into our family, he could only teleport things a short distance away, so he was already on the path of growth. I knew his power would get even stronger in the future—to the point of being able to carry three or four times his weight—but for now, he faced some stiff limitations.

Still, he was our best hope.

Sir Clark spoke up: "Please, the princess and prince needn't concern themselves with—"

"Right now, the only thing that matters is ensuring that as many knights survive as possible," I cut in.

Though reluctant, the commander and the other knights agreed. Sir Clark sent more than half his men out to gather supplies light enough for Stale to transport. I wished Stale could bring back some of those injured soldiers during his trips, but that simply wasn't possible for him yet. He had never left the country before, and even if he had, they'd simply be too heavy even if they removed their armor. At the very least, we could get them the supplies they so desperately needed.

It was time to strike back.

I couldn't believe my eyes.

In all my years as commander of the order, I'd never seen such chaos. My recruits writhed on the ground, clutching their injuries. The enemy blocked our escape route. Our supplies were depleting at an alarming rate. The vanguard would reach us soon, but their priority was speed, not supplies. We could send some of our troops to safety, but at that point, the tide of the battle would turn against those of us who remained. I wanted as many of my men to survive as possible, even if that meant I had to act as a decoy. But then...

"Commander Roderick, we've finished restocking the ammo stores!"

"We're continuing to treat the injured soldiers! May I send in a request for more bandages?"

"I managed to stop the bleeding. I'll join the others on the front lines."

"Some weapons just arrived over there. Someone go bring them in!"

Soldiers—my soldiers—shouted all around me, yet I wasn't sure how or if I could help them. I'd earned the moniker "the Unwounded Knight," yet here I was pinned down with my troops behind a hastily erected barricade, sheltering from gunfire, trying to tend to the wounded while only occasionally firing back at the enemy.

Then, by some miracle, shields, weapons, bandages, and ammunition started appearing out of nowhere. My fresh, green recruits gaped at the sight, but I soon realized what was happening—this power must've belonged to Prince Stale.

It had to be him. When I said as much to the troops around me, they let out a whoop, morale suddenly soaring.

I knew boys adopted into the royal family had to possess a special power. Some of them even posed a threat if wielded with malice. But it was quite another thing to witness that power all around me in the thick of battle. Plus, only the royal family knew the details of the prince's ability; I myself had just learned of it today. It wasn't a secret, but it also wasn't something the prince would publicly display. Some royalty took the secret of their powers to the grave with them.

And then there was Prince Stale.

He was famous within the castle for his wisdom and discretion. I'd heard that he busied himself forming friendly relationships with people throughout the castle, but not one of them knew of his power. There were even rumors that Princess Pride forbade him from divulging it to anyone. If you tried asking directly, he'd just smile and say, "I'm prepared to reveal it if that's what Her Highness desires."

I'd seen it myself at all the ceremonies I attended. Princess Pride always told him she didn't mind if he wanted to reveal his power, but he'd respond with, "I want to use it when that's what *you* want from me, Elder Sister."

Thus, in the three years since he joined the royal family, Prince Stale never once used his power in front of others, nor did he make it known to the public. What a powerful ace he had hiding up his sleeve.

I wasn't the only one impressed, most likely. The other recruits, Vice Commander Clark, and the knights on the other side of the projection all had to be shivering at the sight of what Princess Pride and her brother could do.

Why hadn't the crown princess made use of Stale's power before now, though? As princess, she essentially owned Stale's power. Even now, she could have kept his power a secret, yet she rushed to put it to use. The prince showed no reservations about following her suggestion, openly displaying his power even though he'd refused to reveal it before now.

He would only get stronger in time. Youth likely limited him, yet he could still send items to faraway locations, no matter how distant. Fear coiled through my awe as I watched item after item appear from nowhere, never more than three meters out of my reach.

But what if Prince Stale or Princess Pride... What if they misused those powers for something evil, like assassinations? A chill shot down my spine at the thought.

"Why don't we get Prince Stale to drop bombs on the enemy's position?" one of the recruits shouted.

"I'll agree to it, if that's what my sister wishes," Prince Stale said without a hint of fear in his face.

The princess responded quickly and firmly. "No, he can't do such a thing."

Even as the commander, I breathed a sigh of relief. What would have happened if she'd actually gone along with a plan like that?

She likely harbored the same fear I did. If we had Prince Stale start killing indiscriminately, he could become a threat more powerful than any army. I certainly didn't want him getting accustomed to murder with a power like his that was still developing. Already, I doubted he'd hesitate to take a person's life if the order came from Princess Pride.

Such unflinching devotion hinted at a fealty contract rather than a subordination contract, but I doubted that was the case. It was a feeling, a gut instinct. I had no proof, but I felt confident Prince Stale acted more from devotion than obligation.

Besides, Prince Stale clearly still had a will and purpose of his own. Those under fealty contracts rarely showed such voluntary devotion. Such arrangements left their actions completely under someone else's control, but that wasn't how Stale acted. Honestly, he showed more determination than even some of my own knights. Everything he did, he did for the princess.

For now, I focused on the supplies he delivered. They kept us from running out of ammo as we battled back the ambushers. Stale also delivered medical supplies for the wounded. With what he brought us, we could hold out until the vanguard, and perhaps even the main forces, arrived to support us.

"I'm truly grateful," I said, though I wasn't sure anyone heard me with the battle still raging on all sides.

I didn't just mean Stale. I also meant the person who ordered him to help us in the first place, Princess Pride.

"Prince Stale! Here's what we need next!"

"Prince Stale! We've brought the medical supplies you requested!"

"Prince Stale! Let us know how else we can help!"

I watched Stale send supply after supply to the battlefield, teleporting in and out. He always returned looking just as calm as when he left, but I planned to stop him if I noticed any kind of physical toll.

For now, he seemed entirely unaffected. I couldn't believe how easily he kept using his power. At the same time, I longed to be useful myself, but there was little I could do but stay out of the way. I didn't want the knights to think I was some good-for-nothing princess just being a nuisance, but everyone around me looked more frightened than annoyed.

"What's the matter?" I said, but the knights only shook their heads, apologized, and hurried away to some other task.

Wait...were they already scared of me?

With the rescue attempt smoothly underway, Sir Clark left his soldiers to their work and approached me instead. "Your Highness, I can't thank you enough for your help," he said with a humble bow of his head.

"It's too early for that," I told him. "Shameful as it is for me to say, I haven't done anything today. You should direct your gratitude toward Stale once he's finished here."

Sir Clark just kept his head bowed. "With all due respect, I believe everything that happened here was thanks to you, Your Highness. Once this is all over, I intend to express my gratitude again, and to His Highness as well, of course."

I shook my head, but as I did, I realized the vice commander wasn't the only one looking at me that way. His knights snuck glances at me as they hustled to and fro.

"Sir Clark," I said, "is it possible the knights...don't like me?"

Fewer people referred to me as the "selfish princess" behind my back now than three years ago, but nasty rumors still made their way around the castle. Some even suggested that I'd forced Stale into a fealty contract, but whenever I brought it up, Stale just laughed and said, "Don't worry about that." Easy for him to say; he didn't realize that a different Pride had done exactly that. The first time I'd heard it, my whole body had erupted in goosebumps.

"No, no, not at all," Sir Clark replied. "The knights are merely intimidated. Or rather, they are awed by your presence. I apologize if they've made you uncomfortable." He smiled, but it looked strained to me. "I also offer my apologies for that soldier's thoughtless remark earlier, and I thank you for your sensible decision."

By that, he had to mean the proposition that Stale drop bombs directly on the enemy. While plenty of nobles might have taken that opportunity—including the Pride from the game—I shuddered at the idea of ordering Stale to kill others. I didn't want him to have to do that ever, if I could help it. The weapons he teleported now were for self-defense. But to drop bombs on the enemy would mean taking their lives directly.

At this point in the game, Pride had already made Stale kill many people, including his own mother, but that only made me more dead set on never having Stale use his power to take someone's life. He wasn't evil and devious like me. He was a good person with a kind heart, and he deserved better than to become a murderer.

"I certainly was startled," I admitted. "Please reprimand that soldier once he makes it back. Well, I suppose the commander already did but..."

In fact, the commander had roared when that soldier suggested a bomb. Everyone in the room covered their ears and some went rather pale.

"My sincerest apologies, Princess Pride. I'll be sure to give him a good scolding as well."

"Yes, please do. Also, I'd like to ask that you keep the nature of Stale's power to yourselves as much as possible. I'd prefer for Stale to use his power for his own wishes and protection, rather than as a weapon for the sake of the kingdom."

The vice commander blinked before gathering himself and nodding, a kind smile gracing his countenance. "Of course, Your Highness."

"Vice Commander! The vanguard will arrive at the scene in ten minutes."

"Understood."

Thank goodness. This will change the tide of the battle, if only a little.

Stale continued sending weapons and ammo to the front lines. The knights, still amazed at the sight of the constant teleportation, placed more bundles of supplies before him.

"Send half of the forces to Commander Roderick's aid and the other half to the clifftops to capture the enemy," Sir Clark ordered. "We only need one alive to interrogate. Don't let a single one of them get away." The knights shouted their assent, and Sir Clark addressed the projection. "Just hold out a little longer, Commander. Don't let your guard down!"

The commander was still hunkering down on the ground from what we could see. He held his position, only turning to fire at the enemy.

"I won't," Commander Roderick replied. "Tell the vanguard that the ground here is loose. I'm sure the boulder they dropped on us was intentional, but unlike the lower level where we are, the cliffs will need to be scouted with extremely careful footing."

"Very well," Sir Clark said.

Wait.

"The ground?" I repeated quietly.

The ground is loose? Why does that sound so familiar?

"The ground there was always loose. And that's where my..."

Something from my past life—a line from ORL—suddenly rang in my head. It was one of the love interests describing his tragic past to Tiara. Assailed by the memory, I suppressed a scream.

I then shouted, "No! The vanguard mustn't go to the top of the cliffs! Those cliffs are going to collapse!"

All of the knights, Stale, and even the commander in the projection all gaped at me in pure shock. But now that it was out, there was no taking it back.

"I've just had a vision," I went on. "Those cliffs will collapse very soon, taking the attackers with it. Our knights are about to be crushed under all the rubble!"

I didn't have time for caution. Based on my recollection of the game, that cliff would collapse regardless of whether the vanguard arrived. But no one in the room was heeding my warning. They just stood there, stunned and wide-eyed, blinking at me in utter confusion. I had to snap them out of it, and quickly.

"I, Pride Royal Ivy, deemed heir to the throne for my precognition, give you my orders! Quickly! The vanguard must find an evacuation route and lead the troops to safety, as quickly as they can."

All at once, the spell broke, and the knights leapt into action. The projection shifted from the commander to the vanguard, so Sir Clark could issue new orders. All the knights hauling supplies to Stale changed course to help with the evacuation. The moment he finished with the vanguard, Sir Clark ordered his knights to connect him to the other backup squadrons on their way to the scene.

"Commander Roderick, did you hear that?" Sir Clark said. "Get out of there right away. Get as far from those cliffs as you can!"

"Right."

But the commander didn't move at all. He barked orders for the new recruits to flee from the front lines and put distance between themselves and the cliffs, but the commander himself stayed in place.

"I'm glad we placed the shields and defenses you sent us at our backs," he said. "We managed to form a wall just a few meters away that works as shelter from enemy fire. Anyone injured who can't move should go first."

"Commander Roderick! I told you to get out of there too!" the vice commander shouted.

Still, Roderick made no attempt to flee. "You're seeing me through one of the troop's powers, set from the perspective of the boulder that sits in front of me. Everyone else got away from the cliffs as much as they could."

"Then why won't you move?!" Sir Clark asked, frantic.

"I *can't* move." Commander Roderick's voice came through hushed and weak and I noticed for the first time how pale his face had gotten.

Why can't he move? Is he wounded?!

If that was the case, the troops should've carried him away to safety. The commander was a large man, but there was no reason uninjured recruits couldn't lift him.

"The boulder pinned one of my feet when they dropped it from above."

"What?! Is it broken?!" Vice Commander Clark's hands trembled. My stomach tied itself in knots as I imagined the commander's predicament.

"It's not broken, just completely pinned. There's nothing I can do to get it out. Even the new recruits couldn't get the boulder to budge. Blowing it up would only bury me under the rubble... If only my foot *were* crushed, then I'd be able to escape." The commander smiled far too casually as he added, "Before we began transmitting, I ordered the troops to leave me behind if they had to, and not to speak a word of it to any of you."

With that, he unsheathed the sword at his waist. Before I even had time to gasp, Commander Roderick sliced down, right onto his trapped foot.

I shrieked and covered my eyes, but when the blade came down, we did not hear rending flesh, but rather the screech of metal against metal. I peeked between my hands. The commander sat in the same spot, his blade utterly spotless—not a hint of blood anywhere.

"Anti-slash," he muttered through gritted teeth.

I didn't understand. I stood there in a daze until one of the grim-faced knights at my side offered an explanation.

"It's the commander's special power," he told me. "Nothing can cut him, no matter how sharp, and he has no control over that ability. In other words, he can't sever his foot to escape."

"The Unwounded Knight." That was how Father had introduced him, but I'd taken it as a nickname that resulted from his prowess on the battlefield. I never imagined something like this. The very power that had made him a celebrated commander now trapped him in a situation his troops couldn't save him from. At any moment, the cliffs could collapse, or the enemy could come to finish him off. Perhaps if the reinforcements completely wiped out the opposition, they could come help him, but there simply wasn't time.

The knights in the room murmured in disbelief as the reality of the dire scenario set in. Some collapsed to the floor. Sir Clark tried to suggest some sort of alternative, but the commander just shook his head.

"Sadly, it looks like my time is up," Commander Roderick said. "I'm counting on you to take care of things when I'm gone, Clark. Now that no one's firing back at them, the enemy will probably reach me any minute. As a knight, I'd like to die with—"

"Is this a joke?"

A new voice interrupted the commander. Everyone swiveled toward the sound to find an unfamiliar boy in the room.

The knights made to haul the boy out, but the commander shouted, "Stop!"

"He's Roderick's...the commander's son," Sir Clark said.

The knights froze. The vice commander stepped aside, allowing the boy to approach the projection of his father.

This kid is the commander's son?!

The boy looked nothing like the son of a commander. He had the same silver hair as his father, but long and unkempt, falling down to his back. His bangs covered most of his face. In his white tank top and worn-out pants, he looked more like a farmer than a soldier. He seemed a bit older than me, perhaps thirteen or so, but he was so small and lean, nothing like his stoutly built father.

"What are you doing there?!" Commander Roderick asked, eyes flying wide.

"A bunch of knights were passing by the fields, so I came to see what was happening," the boy said. "Tell me what the hell's going on!"

This wasn't the way the final conversation between a father and son should go, but the commander just stared at his son in silence.

"What kind of stupid dad are you?!" the boy asked. "What about Mom?! We have to worry about you all the damn time and now your time is just 'up,' huh?! Well, go to hell with that! You call yourself Unwounded?! You're supposed to be the commander! How are you gonna die from something like this?!" The harsh words didn't mask the boy's distress. "Stand the hell up. Go home and apologize to Mom a thousand times!"

"I'm sorry, I can't do that," Commander Roderick said. "I'll be dying a knight's death here. But I'd still like to teach you one last lesson of—"

"I don't want your stupid knight lessons! I already told you, I'm never becoming a knight!"

The commander's face fell a bit at this. Then he broke into a smile.

"I see. It's your life," he said. "I have no desire to force you into joining the order. I just wanted you to know what it means to be a knight. To put your life on the line for the sake of duty, just like my troops and comrades do. As your father, I wanted you to appreciate that." With that, the commander plunged his sword into the dirt and stood up, one foot still trapped under the boulder.

Distant footsteps sounded through the projection. They came from the cliffs where the enemy had hunkered down to fire at the knights.

"Finally out of bullets, are ya? Took long enough." Men dressed like bandits appeared at the edges of the projection as the pounding footsteps grew louder and louder.

"Cut off our transmission," Sir Clark said quietly.

The knight who'd been transmitting the signal regained his original eye color. The commander chuckled. "Good call," he said as our image closed in tight and narrow to focus only on the commander.

"Sir Clark! What are you doing?!" the commander's son cried.

"We need to get information from them without giving up any of our own."

Now completely on his own, the commander turned to face his attackers. They burst into laughter at the sight of his trapped foot, but the commander ignored their taunts.

"Those boys who made it out of here still have lives to live," Commander Roderick said. "I won't let you go after them. You'll have to deal with me until backup arrives."

"Tough talk for a guy who can't move, huh?! We'll let you live a little longer, if you promise to cooperate," one of the attackers jeered.

"Watch me, my son. Watch your father's final moments...my final triumph as a knight."

The commander lunged, slashing at the nearest attacker. He moved so quickly, the other enemies didn't even have time to react, then followed through with another swipe. He used his own arm as a shield, deflecting blows thanks to his special power, before driving his sword into one enemy's heart. Finally, the enemies gathered together to launch an attack all at once.

Oh, no...

My legs trembled as I watched the projection. Stale rushed to my side and held me by the shoulders. He tried to turn me away from the scene, but I refused to move. This was something I had to witness.

The commander's son let out a guttural scream.

"Go to hell, you thugs! Don't touch my dad! I'll kill you all! Let him go, let him go, let him go, let him go, let him go!" Fits of choking interrupted the boy's words, but he kept on screaming at enemies who could not hear him. Tears tracked down his cheeks, while insult after insult poured out of his mouth.

Sir Clark began relaying orders to the vanguard, who'd just arrived at the battlefield. He told them to get the young troops to shelter then evacuate to safety before the cliffs collapsed. He didn't order any of them to go help the commander, however.

There was nothing I could do. I'd pledged to use my remaining life to do whatever I could for this kingdom, for my people. But I was completely helpless in that moment.

The tragedy unfolded in slow motion. The commander cut

down his enemies, but they just kept coming. Each strike played out with agonizing slowness. I could see every movement of his sword, every terrified expression on the faces of his attackers. Then...

"That man!"

My eyes locked on to one of the attackers. He stood behind the rest of the enemies, a tan-skinned man calmly observing the struggle.

He was in the game. I remember him from one of the routes... He's part of a group of criminals in my kingdom!

I launched into action, scooping up a smaller sword from the pile of weapons once set aside for Stale to transport. Then I rushed closer to the projection. Commander Roderick's son did not so much as turn to acknowledge me, standing pale and shaking before the image of his beleaguered father.

Bang!

The boy jerked as a shot rang out. Commander Roderick fell to the ground, and the attackers around him whooped.

"Guns work on him! Everyone, stand back!"

"Nooooo!"

Howling, the boy reached out for the projection. His hand slipped right through it, and he sank to the ground as more screams rose. The boy slammed his fists against the ground and wailed in frustration. He twisted to glare up at me and the rest of the room.

"Somebody help my dad!" he roared. "Isn't he your commander?! Unlike me, he's supposed to be special, right?! So save him! Why isn't a single one of you knights doing anything?!"

The commander's pained screams cut in under the boy's shouting. "Why can't anyone save my dad?!" The rage broke, giving way to the grief waiting beneath the surface.

Vice Commander Clark and the other knights made no response. They merely glared at the attackers, watching their dear commander's final moment with awe. The boy hung his head again, and then...

"It'll be all right," I said, setting a hand on his shoulder.

He twisted to look up at me, jolting at the sight of the sword.

"I won't let a single person in my kingdom suffer," I told him.

Before anyone could react, I slashed the sword down, cutting my skirt into two equal halves so I could move more easily. My hair flew wild around me as I whirled and shouted, "Take me to that battlefield!"

The room fell silent.

The boy looked up at me in awe. The knights' mouths all hung open. And Stale...when I met his eyes, I knew he understood that I'd been speaking directly to him.

"You can't, Elder Sister!" Stale protested. "You're the one who saw the danger for yourself in that premonition, aren't you? You should know better than anyone how badly this can go."

"Don't worry. Just trust me," I said. I started to undo the metal fastener on my torn skirt.

Stale shook his head furiously. "No! You're the crown princess! You're the last person who should be going!"

"This is the only way to save the commander," I said.

Stale flinched. As much as I hated to frighten or worry him, however, I needed him to understand. I grabbed him by the shoulders, speaking close so he felt the weight of each word.

"I just had a premonition," I said. "I can still save him if I act now. I can save that boy's father."

Stale hesitated, and I knew he had to be thinking of his own father and the anguish his mother must have gone through when he died. Still, he said, "No, I can't let you go. I can't send the future queen to a place like that!"

I tightened my grip and looked him dead in the eyes. "I don't want to be a wicked queen who saves herself at the expense of others," I said.

Stale's throat bobbed as he swallowed. I'd chosen my words with care, hoping to remind him of that promise from three years ago, a promise I'd made as we hugged and sobbed. Stale held my gaze, even as more pained wails came from Commander Roderick through the projection. The taunting laughter of his attackers quickly followed.

Stale clenched his fists. "Are you sure you'll be all right?"

"I promise," I said.

Stale sighed, but then reached down to help me with my skirt, sending them away in a flash with teleportation. I gave his shoulders a final squeeze as I backed away and retrieved a sword.

But Stale didn't quite let me go. He wrapped his arms around me, pulling me into a strong hug.

At first, I flinched. Then I relaxed into his gentle, warm embrace. Stale squeezed tightly, breathing in deeply. The next instant, I blinked and he vanished.

Or, rather, I did.

One moment, I stood there in Stale's arms. The next, I was on the battlefield.

I lowered my arms after Pride vanished from within them. Her warmth and scent lingered, and I clung to it as long as I could. Around me, the knights murmured in disbelief. But I didn't care what they thought of what I'd just done. If Pride ordered me to send her to the battlefield, that was what I'd do.

"My princess," I murmured, "everything shall be as you desire." *As long as I can protect your beautiful heart.*

With that vow in mind, I placed myself near a box of explosives and coals. If things went downhill, I wouldn't hesitate to rain hell down on the enemy.

I guess this is it for me...

After all my years as commander of the order of knights, it had really come down to a foot stuck under a rock.

I dodged as many bullets as I could and fired back at the enemies, hoping to put up a fight during my last stand. But there was only so much I could do with the enemy keeping their distance. I wanted to stand to get a better angle, but the men on the cliffs would only get a clearer shot. Crouching wouldn't provide full cover either. On top of all this, my legs shook with exhaustion, and blood trickled from a gunshot wound. I didn't have much time left, no matter what I did.

Now assured in their victory, the men pointed their guns at me and sneered.

You won't be laughing for long, you demons. Her Highness has seen what happened here. You'll all join me under the rubble of the cliffs any minute now.

I smirked as they approached. One enemy screwed his face up in anger. He aimed right at my face and fired, but the bullet wasn't meant to hit—it merely grazed my cheek, sending a fresh stream of blood dripping down my chin. The other enemies reloaded, but I wasn't about to let them take down the commander of the order of knights that easily. I raised my sword to strike, but just then...

"Guh?!"

Someone screamed up on the cliffs.

Everyone whirled around, toward the sound. The two men who'd been preparing to fire down at me from the cliffs now shot in the opposite direction. Abruptly, their shots ceased, replaced by screams as they collapsed. Even the enemy paused, confounded by this turn of events. Soon, only one person remained atop the cliffs.

What the hell is going on? I braced for whatever new calamity awaited me, but nothing could have prepared me for what came next.

Bang! Bang! Gunshots rang out from the cliff, and the enemies around me howled as bullets struck them in the arms.

I had no idea what was happening, but I couldn't let the opportunity pass. I used my sword to drag one of their guns toward me, then fired it at my foes.

The enemy looked between me and the clifftop, trying to go back on the offensive. It was no use. Bullets rained on them from two angles now, and soon all of them were writhing on the ground.

The gunfire ceased, replaced only with the pained groans of the men on the ground. Then, a small figure leapt down from the clifftops. But how? Even the enemy had needed ropes and gear to get to me. Who in the world was I facing now? The enemy completely forgot about me, gaping at the figure who approached us now.

No, it can't be. I blinked and rubbed my eyes, but still couldn't believe what I was seeing.

"It looks like you were completely out of ammo too, weren't you? I'm afraid I used up the last of it just now," came the sweet voice of a young girl. She held a sword in one hand. Her skirt, torn in two, fluttered on the wind like a war banner.

"Prepare to meet your end, you demons," she said. She may have looked young, but that gleam in her eyes did not belong to a little girl. It was pure malice, and it struck fear into the enemies around us. "That man is one of my subjects," she said.

Subjects... But that meant...

No, Her Highness Pride Royal Ivy was the last person who should ever be on a battlefield. A crown princess had no place here.

My mouth fell open.

I could have taken on the attackers if I were free, but I was the commander of the knights. These were adult men with weapons they knew how to use. I couldn't fathom how a child was fearlessly facing them down. And not just any child—the crown princess. Perhaps I was hallucinating. Hadn't I just seen her back with the knights and Sir Clark in that projection? How did she get here?

I was still busy gaping while Pride launched into an attack, cutting down attackers. Even with her skirts split, her dress hampered her movements, yet she dodged enemy swords and immobilized man after man nonetheless. Even when they swarmed her, she slipped from their reach, knocking their feet out from under them. Her fine dress dragged through blood and her bright red hair flew loose, but she ignored it all as she crushed the enemy. Not even bullets reached her; she dodged each one effortlessly.

"That's it. I can just use this," she said to herself.

She exchanged her sword for a gun on the ground, shooting at arms and legs. Once she ran out of bullets, she snatched up the next gun and continued, wasting no time as she immobilized foe after foe.

The men were all sprawled out on the ground, and Pride still had some ammo left. Only moments ago, I'd hopelessly faced a whole swarm of attackers, but now, not a one of them still stood. Pride ignored my open-mouthed shock as she went about examining each foe.

"Wh-why?" I barely recognized my own hoarse voice. Princess Pride finally turned to acknowledge me. "Why did you come here? You should know the danger better than anyone." It came out harsher than I intended, but the princess didn't react.

"Stale said the same thing to me," she said, then went back to checking the faces of each of the vanquished men.

Why, why?! She'd saved my life, and yet...

"This whole place is about to collapse. You were the one who predic—"

The cliffs themselves trembled and groaned around us.

"There he is!" Princess Pride cried. At the same time, the flimsy rock around us started to flake off, then spill down in a cascade.

This is it. For the second time that day, I surrendered myself to my inevitable doom. At least the new recruits had hopefully gotten out safely.

I wished I had the chance to tell my wife and son how much I loved them one last time. I wished I could have died with honor as a knight. But all I could do was stand there with the princess and wait for the cliffs to come down.

She was the daughter of the queen to whom I swore my oath of loyalty. She was next in line to take the throne as queen herself. But now, my own mistake would cut both of our lives short. I could fathom no more shameful end for a knight.

Please... Please just spare Princess Pride somehow...

I dropped my sword and stretched my hand out to Pride, who truly looked like a helpless little girl now rather than the fearsome warrior who'd burst into this battle. I wanted to wrap her in my arms and protect her as long as I could. At least that way I could die a proper knight's death. My head swam from blood loss, but I clung to that one final thought as our end rushed toward us—

"Commander!"

Her shriek brought me back to my wits. Princess Pride held her sword against the throat of a tan-skinned enemy and forced him to stagger toward me. Somehow, amid all this carnage, he was completely unharmed.

"If you want me to live, then hold on to this man and don't let go!" Pride said. With that order, she turned and kicked the man in the back.

The attacker flew forward and collapsed at my feet. I had no choice but to obey the princess's words, even if I didn't understand them, so I grabbed the man and held him as tightly as my trembling arms allowed. He struggled, demanding I release him, but I held on with all my remaining strength. Princess Pride tossed her sword aside and grabbed the man as well.

"If you don't want to die here, then use your special power at once," she hissed. "You have to save all of us, or this will be your end too."

The man jerked at her demand. "How do you know about that?"

"Hurry! Do you *want* to be buried alive with us?!" Pride urged him.

The man growled, but he ceased his struggling. Already, rocks piled up around our ankles, and more were fast approaching.

"Damn it all!" the man cursed.

Then we disappeared.

"So this is where the commander was?"

An hour and a half after we were dispatched from the castle, we arrived not at a battlefield but a mountain of rubble.

The cliffs were gone, the roads completely blocked by large rocks. No one would be traveling between these kingdoms for some time to come. The rest of the vanguard and I used any special powers we had to get the most wounded recruits back to the castle. In all my years with the knights, I'd never seen anything quite like this. Scores of injured, an entire cliffside collapsed, frantic knights everywhere I turned. I helped up one of the less severely injured new recruits and tried to get somewhere safe.

"The commander was trapped under the boulder, so he stayed behind to buy time for us to escape," the recruit said. Tears shimmered in his eyes as he pointed a trembling finger at one particular area in the wreckage. "That's the spot. That's where the commander was."

I gulped. Not even the "Unwounded Knight" could survive something like this. I chewed on my bottom lip, trying to stay strong for the recruit beside me, but I couldn't help feeling like we in the vanguard had arrived too late.

The recruit and I knelt down in the rubble and started digging. Others had already taken up the task, all searching for some sort of keepsake we could bring back to the commander's family.

"Captain, I hear something over here!" one knight shouted. He waved frantically and we all rushed over to him. Sure enough, faint voices reached us through the rubble.

We dropped to the ground and dug with every bit of energy we had left, desperate to free whoever was beneath that rock. A wild hope rose in my chest, but when we reached the source of the sound, we found not a human, but a projection of the strategy room back at headquarters.

"Vice Commander!"

Several knights cried out in shock, but Sir Clark didn't seem to hear us.

"Get in contact with me as soon as you see this message," he repeated over and over again.

The knight in charge of transmissions quickly established a connection with the vice commander. Finally able to communicate, Vice Commander Clark rattled out our orders.

Sir Clark said the transmission we were seeing was being broadcast thanks to one of the troop's special powers. The transmission began an hour ago, with the commander's side of it anchored to the boulder pinning his foot. So if the transmission was still going, the commander could be somewhere nearby. We just had to dig until we found him.

Sir Clark tried his best to make it sound like a hopeful rescue mission, but we all heard the fear and anxiety in his voice, even through the shaky transmission. We also heard something along the lines of "You...also...ighness..." but the message was unclear.

Still, we immediately set to our task, gathering up anyone nearby who could help move the massive pile of debris. But as we dug, we found newly formed fissures in the earth, and the more rubble we moved, the deeper the holes went. We moved as much as we could, but eventually, we hit large rocks that formed a dome beneath all the other rock. The dome wasn't very wide, but it stretched downward for dozens of meters. Baffled, we gathered around it, tapping it with our feet or the pommels of our swords. It rang hollow, which only made us more confused.

"What is this thing?" someone murmured.

"Before the final transmission, we overheard that the man with Commander Roderick may possess a special power of some kind," Sir Clark said. "There's a chance Commander Roderick and that man are still down there."

The commander was alive? The suggestion filled us with fresh hope and renewed our strength for the monumental task ahead. But the vice commander tempered us, telling us to go about our search cautiously.

"Is anyone here?" a knight called.

"Commander?!" another shouted while we worked.

Finally, about two meters down... *Crack!* Something split, and just like that, the dome of rubble collapsed. We leapt away, startled as the dome fell apart. Except it wasn't really falling apart; it was cracking open like an egg.

"Look, the sky! The sky!" That voice was too high-pitched to be the commander. We rushed back to the dome, which was still crumbling away. What it revealed left us all stunned.

"Commander!"

Several knights cried out. The new recruit fell to his knees. From the other side of the projection, the vice commander went wide-eyed with shock while knights crowded around him, desperate to see the new development for themselves.

"Commander, please be sure not to let go of him yet," the high-pitched voice said.

As the dome fell away, we glimpsed the commander at last. He was hugging one of the attackers, who glared at all of us with indignation, clearly displeased about his circumstances.

"I can't believe we actually made it out," the commander said.

Cheers erupted around us as we saw our commander truly was alive and well.

"Commander, we're so relieved to see you safe."

"Thank god."

"It's truly a miracle."

"How could we go on without you?"

Sudden relief and joy suffused the former battlefield. It took us some time before we regained our composure enough to realize something wasn't right.

Who exactly was the owner of that high-pitched voice?

With the dome now completely gone, we beheld a fantastically unlikely sight—a young girl. She waited in total silence while we celebrated, staring straight up at the commander. Who was this child?

When she opened her mouth to speak, every eye went to her.

"Can someone from the order please tend to the commander's wounds?" she said. "Whoever else is available needs to quickly secure this man with handcuffs to negate his power. If you don't have any, then have Stale send you some right away." Covered in dust and wearing a torn-up dress, the girl was hardly more than a silhouette, yet she ordered the knights around with authority. "I'd also like to get in contact with the strategy room."

"Commander Roderick, just who is this girl?" I dared ask.

The commander gave a long, defeated sigh and said, "This is Her Highness Pride Royal Ivy, the crown princess of Freesia."

Every one of us erupted in shock. We dropped to our knees, terrified at having disrespected royalty so casually. Someone scrambled to get her connected to the vice commander as she'd requested.

CASE SUMMARY: Traveling knights were ambushed by a unity opposition party, then caught in a cliffside collapse.
INJURIES: All 30+ troops, Commander Roderick.
FATALITIES: Zero.

"Elder Sister..." I murmured.

Pride broke into a wide smile on the other side of the projection.

She was safe. Relief and exhaustion washed through me in tandem. I did my best to hide it from the knights, but I had to cover my face for a moment and drag in a few deep, calming breaths to manage it. My heart was still hammering in my chest, as it had from the moment I teleported Pride away.

She's alive. Thank god, Pride's alive. She's actually safe. She's going to come back to me. My throat tightened, eyes stinging. *No, I can't cry yet.* I wiped my closed eyes with my sleeve and managed to hold the rest in. I couldn't stand the idea of anyone seeing me like that, so I grit my teeth and forced myself not to cry. But I was so, so scared.

I really thought that Pride might die. And it would have been my fault for sending her to that battlefield. That fear was absolutely suffocating. When the cliff collapsed and we lost visual contact, my heart stopped, and I truly thought that I might die along with her. I froze inside and out, heart pounding in my ears.

"Roderick!"

I turned my head at the sound of a pained cry beside me. It was the vice commander, openly weeping as he watched the commander appear in the projection, somehow safe and whole. Sir Clark covered his eyes with one hand and sank down to the floor, tears streaking along his jaw. His shoulders trembled.

"Thank god," he said in pure relief.

So I wasn't the only one who was terrified. It wasn't just me and the vice commander either. Many of the other knights were rejoicing...and shedding tears as well.

"Thank god Commander Roderick's alive!" one knight yelled. He wiped his tears, raised his fists, and let out a shout of joy.

"She's incredible! Is the princess really only eleven years old?!" another knight said. He, too, was crying, but he smiled even as the tears fell.

"Where the hell did those rumors come from, anyway? She doesn't act anything like the spoiled princess I heard about," said yet another, laughing hoarsely.

Most knights just looked in disbelief between their crying vice commander and miraculously surviving commander. Some bit their lips and tried to hold back their tears, while others quivered from raw emotion. Back by the door, a knight stood with his hands on the shoulders of the commander's son.

"Everything's okay now," he said to the commander's son, his gaze warm.

On the projection, the knights surrounding the commander looked so excited that they didn't even seem to realize the crown princess stood in their midst. They, too, wept, even as they celebrated and cheered. One of the new recruits collapsed to his knees and dissolved into sobs. Another knight squeezed his shoulders and tried to smile at him, but couldn't get the expression out before he broke down as well. In both the strategy room and the projection, no one could contain their joy.

My gaze went right to Pride, however. She was covered in mud, all the way to the tips of her beautiful crimson hair. She wore her torn dress, tattered from battle, and a cold, determined expression. My heart clenched at the sight. I turned away, incapable of looking any longer. I couldn't protect her.

In my current state, all I could do was send her to the battlefield by herself.

That reality ate away at me, digging a hole in my chest. I'd sworn I'd stick to that vow from three years ago, yet right here today, I'd put her in harm's way. I clutched my shirt right over my aching heart and tried to hold down the revulsion and self-hatred crawling up my throat.

Thank goodness. I managed to save him.

A knight was using his special power to treat the dazed commander. Handcuffs doused the power of the enemy who'd protected us from the rock slide. By all appearances, we were safe. When I got a chance to talk to Sir Clark, I apologized for acting without his orders, but assured him we were all okay now. He looked like he was struggling to pick the right words. Eventually, he just shook his head and focused on issuing orders to the knights.

"Goddamn it! *That's* your princess?! How the hell do you have a monster for a princess?!" the enemy snarled. A knight led him away, barking at him to watch his mouth. "You bastards weren't there to see it. She's a monster!"

His cries fell on deaf ears. A knight shoved a gag in his mouth and forced him into a carriage bound for Freesia—the man's home country.

Val. He hadn't said it, but I knew that was his name. In ORL, he belonged to an enemy organization. Naturally, at the end of the game, when Tiara escaped her tower and fled to the nearest town with her love interest, Pride hired Val to drag her sister back to the castle. He was an extremely useful asset to Pride, especially because Val possessed the power of mud-sculpting.

In the game, Val and his gang destroyed the town Tiara fled to. Then Val used his power to block Tiara in with walls of mud. When Tiara and her love interest managed to defeat Val's cronies, Val shut himself inside a protective dome of rubble. Ultimately, Tiara and her love interest simply left him that way and made their escape. The player never had to see him again.

Despite his aggression against his own country, Val's special power gave him away as a true native of Freesia. He looked young, with even sharper eyes than mine and fang-like teeth that left a menacing impression. Truly the image of a villain, yet his power mostly served him as self-defense. He never really contributed to any battles.

That power was what I was counting on when I ordered the commander to hug Val close during the collapse. In order to protect himself, I knew Val would have to protect us as well, even if his power had some kind of size limit. I needn't have worried, however. The moment Val activated his power, it cleared out all the rock around us, even the boulder pinning the commander's foot.

We had to wait there a long, long time before we were sure the cliff wasn't going to collapse more. Even then, we feared another surge of debris would rain down on us. For a while, I thought we'd probably run out of oxygen, but I desperately hoped help would arrive before then. Only when we heard the knights' voices above us could we finally get out of that dome.

Val, meanwhile, was slinging all kinds of insults my way. In the game, Val was just a simple villain character and was probably executed for his crimes in the end. He'd been responsible for unforgivable horrors, after all.

Honestly, it was such a waste. Val could have picked any other path in life with a power as incredible as his. If only he'd gotten just one more chance...

"Princess Pride!" One of the knights hurried up to me. "I shall escort you to the castle. The vanguard is here for you, so please, come with me."

"But I'm not injured," I said. "The commander should be the first one sent home."

"Commander Roderick will be returning with the vanguard as soon as you're home safe. Please come with me for now."

"Well, in that case, the new recruits should go first."

The knights were probably on edge, having a member of the royal family out in a place like this. I understood why they wanted to prioritize my safety, but I was completely unharmed and wanted them to send the injured home first. I kept arguing with the knight, until shouts rose around us.

"Where are you going?!"

"Please don't hurt yourself."

"But, you're injured..."

Footsteps marched toward me. The knight before me was looking past me now, face draining of color. I whirled around.

"Commander," I said.

I thought they were still treating his wounds. He approached me shirtless, his uniform coat draped over his shoulders and bandages wrapped around his torso. Before I could even suggest that he go and rest, he reached down and scooped me off my feet.

"What?! Whoa!"

I shrieked as the commander lifted me into his arms, striding toward the vanguard. His silence was even scarier than the alternative.

"P-please let go of me, Commander. You're injured!" I struggled to wriggle out of his grasp.

"There are so many things I want to say to you," Commander Roderick said. "I don't even know where to begin. I truly don't. But for now, you must return to the castle."

Talk about scary! He's angry. I can totally tell! I started kicking my legs, desperate to get away, but it was no use.

"Ah! Noooooo!" I let out a scream, louder than any before it.

The knights, apparently as startled as me by this whole display, just stared as the commander carried me around.

"Don't all look at me," I said. "Look away!"

The knights obeyed my frantic order, but the commander still wouldn't let me down.

"All right, I understand, I understand!" I said. "I'll do as you say. Just put me d—Wait, no, my clothes." My voice withered to a whimper in my embarrassment.

Somebody... Please, bring me a change of clothes! My legs are laid bare!

I squeezed my legs together, but there was no helping it at this point. I was the one who'd cut my skirt for better mobility. The cuts acted like slits, which were fine on their own. But as

I battled enemies, rolled over the ground, and crawled out of a pile of rubble, all that frantic activity ripped my skirt to shreds, turning it into a miniskirt. No, more like a grass skirt. A princess in a grass skirt—could anything be more shameful than that?

The long layers of fabric covered me properly when I was standing, but now that I was on my back and kicking my legs, the skirt wasn't doing much to protect my modesty.

Having picked up on this, the commander finally set me back down. I smoothed the tatters of my skirt, but it did little to cool my embarrassment. I crouched down and quietly muttered for clothes again.

"Pfft!"

Did someone just laugh?! Who?! Who laughed at me?!

When I finally looked up, I didn't find rowdy soldiers, but Commander Roderick himself. He turned away to hide his face, and his shoulders trembled with laughter. The mirth even spread to the other knights when they noticed what was happening.

Ahhhhhh! How rude!

They obviously only saw me as a simple eleven-year-old child and nothing more, but I was still the crown princess. I knew how to behave like a proper lady. Besides, who wouldn't be mortified to have a bunch of people nearly look up their skirt? It didn't help that in my past life, I was pretty plain. No one had even seen my calves, and now a whole troop of knights had seen far more than that.

Maybe I should have them all arrested for blasphemy right here and now. The evil Pride inside me had several nasty solutions to this predicament, but then...

Swish.

Something fluttered down around me as the commander threw his jacket over my shoulders. It was so baggy and heavy, it actually dragged on the ground when I stood. Still, when I pulled it around me, it functioned like a shirt dress would. With this new "dress" to cover me, Roderick lifted me into his arms again.

He carried me a few meters more, toward a contraption that looked almost like a motorcycle. If I recalled correctly from the game, only the person who created the vehicle using their special power could operate it. It could pull carts that carried people or luggage, and ride-along passengers had to hang on to the driver's shoulders. Now, however, the wagon part was gone, replaced with a seat and handles.

I sat down and gripped the handles. From behind, the commander and the rest of the knights all knelt as they saw me off.

"I'll see you at the castle," I said.

The vehicle roared, then lurched into motion.

A large group awaited me back at the castle. Tiara and Stale were there, of course, as were Lotte, Mary, and the rest of my maids. Jack was there with my guards. Even Carl the instructor, the vice commander, and many of the knights welcomed me back. I also caught glimpses of the commander's son hidden among the knights.

When Tiara first laid eyes on my muddy, ragged clothes, she burst into tears and made a beeline toward me. My maids and guards paled and urged me to go to my room. But none of them compared to Stale, who looked a bit angry as he approached. I had probably scared him more than anyone else.

Just as I was about to apologize, he wrapped his arms around both me and Tiara and held us tight. He was tall enough now that I fit snugly in his arms. I felt bad getting the two of them all dirty, but they clung to me tenaciously with trembling hands and I couldn't bear to separate myself.

"You said... You said you'd be okay..." Stale managed, and I held him even tighter. I'd sworn that I would never cause him more pain.

"I'm sorry," I told him. "But I really am okay. I'm not injured at all. Can't you see that I'm fine? I just tripped and fell, and that's where all the mud came from."

I tried smiling and reassuring him, but he and Tiara only clutched me more desperately.

"How can you call *that* okay?!" Stale cried. "You were so reckless. If you messed up just once, who knows what would have happened?"

His voice shook. I pushed away to gaze up at his face and found tears shimmering in his eyes. I hadn't seen such softness in his face in years. He must have been watching that projection so anxiously, unable to tear his eyes away. Even Tiara, who hadn't witnessed any of it, burst into tears.

I wished I could ease their pain. They had grown up considerably since we first met, but they were still only nine and ten years old—younger than me. I'd put them through so much today, but at least I was back safe now.

Oh... I actually made it back alive.

Just as I was tempted to relax, a chill ran down my spine. Stale was right—I really could have ended up dead if I'd made a single wrong move. Feeling more fearful than I had during the cliff's collapse, I hugged Stale and Tiara again, trying to keep myself from shaking.

"I'm sorry," I repeated. "I'll be more careful next time."

But I couldn't promise that it would never happen again. For all I knew, I might end up doing terrible things in the future and hurting the two of them, even if all I ever wanted was to avoid that outcome at absolutely any cost.

Even if that meant my whole body needed to be torn to pieces.

"Princess Pride."

I extracted myself to face the vice commander and his knights. "Vice Commander, I sincerely apologize for all the disturbance I caused you." It was my second apology, but I owed him at least that many. Sir Clark just closed his eyes and nodded.

"It was your premonition about the cliff that saved the lives of so many knights," he said. "Each and every one of us is filled with gratitude for your help, as well as for your assistance in sending supplies to the battlefield. If you'll allow it, I'd like to find time to discuss today's events with Your Highness and Commander Roderick at a later date."

"Yes, of course."

We could try to talk about it here, but I'd have to order all these onlookers into silence, and that would only make me look like a villain. Instead, I suggested that we meet tomorrow. I probably needed to settle this before Mother and Father returned from their trip anyway.

I bid goodbye to the rest of the knights, and the maids escorted me away, with Jack and the guards at my side for protection.

At the end of breakfast the next morning, I received word from the order headquarters, requesting a meeting with me if I was available. Our superb royal order was as fast as ever. Apparently, the commander's son wanted to join us as well. I wasn't sure why, but he had been present at yesterday's chaotic events, so I didn't bother mentioning it when I sent a servant back to confirm my attendance.

We met in the castle throne room.

As the crown princess, I was only allowed to use this room once before: one year earlier, when Mother wasn't at the castle. It was the best possible location to speak privately with a large group of people, though, so I ordered everyone to clear the room and told the knights to meet me there.

By the time I arrived, the entire order, including the new recruits, waited for me. The commander's son even stood in the very back. I knew some of these men were still injured from the battle; I saw several bandages peeking out from beneath their uniforms, and I could smell the antiseptic as I walked past them. They stood ramrod straight and stepped aside to clear a path for me, and I made my way to the throne with Stale and Tiara at my back. Once I took my seat, with Stale and Tiara flanking me, the knights dropped to one knee.

"Raise your heads," I ordered, and the knights all looked up at me. "I've cleared the room, so it's only us now, along with my dear siblings." I'd hoped to leave Tiara out of this, but that was before the teary-eyed look on her face compelled me to include her.

"If there's something you wish to say to me, this is your chance to do so," I went on. "Don't worry. No one here will be punished for saying something improper, not for today."

The knights murmured and shifted, but they must've been wary because they still hesitated to speak up.

"Stale has told me that you've kept my presence at the battle-field a secret. I thank you for your cooperation."

The story of my orders to Stale to send supplies to the battle-field, my premonition about the cliff collapse, and my evacuation order to the troops had already made its way to Mother and Father through official reports. But the fact that I'd visited the battlefield moments before its destruction, fought the enemy, and spent thirty minutes trapped in a dome with only the commander and one of the attackers was still a secret, thankfully. Mother and Father would be furious if they knew I, a member of the royal family, did something so outrageous. They might even turn some of their ire on the knights for allowing me to get involved, result-ing in severe punishments.

Thus, Stale urged the vice commander to keep all of that secret. Naturally, he also ordered the silence of the guards, maids, and Mr. Carl, who'd all welcomed me back yesterday. Mr. Carl was es-pecially keen on keeping the secret, since he'd been my and Stale's escort to the knights' practice and failed to stop me from leaving.

The commander opened his mouth to speak. "No, it was a beneficial agreement for us as well... Now, let's get started. I beg your pardon, Your Highness, but where were you trained in fencing, firearms, and hand-to-hand combat?"

There was deep meaning to his question, and he spoke slowly, weighing each word. It figured a man such as he was curious about how I could fight the way I did. I had to give him an answer he could accept without revealing the truth.

"I only practiced fencing and self-defense combat a bit when Stale received lessons from his instructor," I said. "As for firearms, I watched the knights practice with them yesterday at the training grounds."

A flurry of murmurs passed through the knights.

I wasn't lying. I'd truly only practiced fencing and hand-to-hand combat once, and the rest of my experience came from watching Stale with his instructor. That was the best answer I could offer them. I couldn't exactly tell them that I was using my last boss cheats.

"Is she joking?" a knight muttered.

"That's all?" another said.

"Wait, so that was her first time firing a gun?"

"It can't be..."

I couldn't blame them for their reactions. My explanation left a lot to be desired, but it was the best I had in the moment. Sir Clark quirked an eyebrow, clearly surprised by my answer, but Commander Roderick simply said, "I see," and changed the subject.

"How did you know that man possessed a special power from Freesia?" Commander Roderick asked next.

"I saw it in a premonition," I told him. "He used his power to create mud walls and protect himself from the collapse."

Again, I couldn't tell the commander the truth—that I knew all about Val from an otome game. That probably wouldn't even mean anything to him.

"And why did you travel to the battlefield on your own?" It was frightening, how quickly his questions kept coming, but I did my best to meet him blow for blow.

"I was the only one at headquarters who could make it to you quickly enough. As you know, my brother, Stale, can only teleport items that are equal to or less than his own weight. So he couldn't send any of the knights—but he could send me."

"Then shouldn't you have instead made use of one of the transmission troops to convey all this information?" the commander countered.

"They'd already evacuated by the time I had my premonition. I had no way of knowing if they would arrive in time. I was also the only one who knew what the attacker looked like, s—"

"Still!" Commander Roderick interjected, his voice echoing around the room. "That would have been preferable to sending the crown princess to the battlefield!" His anger stung my ears; even some of the knights flinched away. "Even if no one else would have made it in time, you never should have gone there! You needed to tell the vanguard about that man's power and leave the rest to us!"

"Hey, calm down now," Sir Clark said, but Commander Roderick just barreled on.

"The vanguard—no, any knight at all would have put their lives on the line if it meant keeping you away from that battlefield!"

"But if things went wrong, you and that knight would have been swept away in the rubble. I was the only one who could ensure—"

"I would gladly accept such a fate! The lives of two knights for the safety of a princess is more than a fair trade!"

I couldn't muster a response. Two knights' lives for the safety of a princess. That was the natural order of things here, and every knight in the room likely agreed with their commander on that. But still, I couldn't.

"Do you understand how great a loss your death would be for everyone?!" Commander Roderick shouted. "Think about your position. Never mind me; your short-sightedness almost sent the entire kingdom into despair!"

I wanted to reel away from his tirade. I wanted to crouch down and hide. But I forced myself to keep meeting his eyes. He must've been holding all this in since yesterday. *I deserve to hear this. I have to just sit and listen.*

"We are knights," Commander Roderick continued. "We are the swords and shields that protect the queen, the prince consort, and Your Highness. But you almost cast terrible shame upon our entire way of life!"

The commander was right. He had simply wanted to die a knight's death. My slightest mistake wouldn't have just resulted in my own death, but sullied his as well. Even so, it didn't sit well with me.

While the commander scolded me, I noticed his son watching me from the corner of my eye. His wild hair covered his face, so I couldn't make out his expression, but it reminded me of how he'd looked inside the strategy room yesterday, when he thought he'd have to watch his father die. He'd screamed and pleaded with us to somehow save Commander Roderick.

"Your life holds more value than ours!" Commander Roderick said.

No, I have to hold back...

"We would gladly offer our lives for you or any of this kingdom's people!"

Don't say anything!

"We exist to serve the royal family and the people. You should never act out on our behalf like that!"

The Pride lurking inside me yearned to lash out at the commander's harsh words, but I kept a grip on my composure, struggling to stay in control while I absorbed the lecture.

"Just forget about us! Even if it means that I must die, you shouldn't hesitate to keep yourself safe first and foremost. You don't understand just how valuable your life is t—"

Snap.

Something broke inside me.

"That's enough," I said. My voice came out deeper and more powerful than I expected.

The commander stopped instantly. The entire hall fell silent as well, every eye on me alone now.

I'd had enough. They really wanted me to walk away and

leave them to die, even if it meant they'd see me as an arrogant and self-centered princess. Even if it meant the knights would lose their faith in me and judge me unfit to serve as queen. Even if it meant becoming the queen I saw in my past life, the Pride who would sacrifice anyone with a smile on her face. I'd do whatever it took to avoid that fate.

I rose and faced the hushed assembly.

"It is as you say, Commander," I said. "My short-sighted actions upset many people, and I rescued you in a way that was against your will. However…"

I set my feet and righted my posture, despite the ache in every muscle thanks to yesterday's adventure. I ignored the soreness and put everything I had into my next words, projecting my image as crown princess.

"You are not the only one I saved. I saved you and all the knights you'll train from this day on! Do you know how many citizens you might save throughout your life?!"

He gave no reply, so I took another deep breath, gazing down at the knights from my place before the throne.

"You're the one who doesn't understand the value of his own life, Commander! Do you have any idea how much the people in your life love, cherish, and rely on you?"

All of the commander's righteous fury dissipated, his eyes growing wide. Even Stale and Tiara were gaping at me by now.

"I belong to the royal family!" I shouted. "I am the firstborn princess, and I will inherit this throne! My role is to live for the sake of the people. You are knights, yes! You're our hope, the light that protects the citizens directly. When a single knight dies, he takes everyone he would have saved along with him!"

Once I let my emotions out, I couldn't stem the flow, and every word I wanted to say to the commander spilled out one after another.

"Even if you were a mere foot soldier instead of the commander, I would have rescued you. How could I let someone die when I knew I could save them? I will never allow any unnecessary deaths if I can help it. All of you are citizens of my kingdom, just as you are knights, and my people are my pride and joy. Our job as royalty is to protect each and every one of you. If you call yourselves knights, then concern yourselves not with dying an honorable death, but with those whom you'll save in the future."

I was panting by the time I finished. Still, I looked around at each and every knight in turn, meeting their wide eyes with steely resolve.

Perhaps I'd gone too far. Even after reassuring them that this room was a space without consequences, I'd lashed out at them. I couldn't tell if the men were disgusted or just in shock—every single one of them gawked at me. But either way, there was one last thing I needed to say.

"To conclude," I began, standing straight and tall. "By the name of Pride Royal Ivy, the crown princess of the kingdom of Freesia, I must apologize to you all. I carelessly set foot on your sacred battleground, left a mess on your hands with my selfish actions, and abused my powers as the crown princess for my own interests."

I bowed my head contritely. The knights, along with Stale

and Tiara, immediately responded this time. Members of the royal family didn't just go around bowing their heads like scolded maids. The gesture carried tremendous weight.

"Elder Sister, as the crown princess, you—" Stale started, but I held up a hand.

"We're the only ones here right now, Stale," I told him. "I couldn't do this in a public setting, but here I can give them my honest apology."

I kept my head down for a while longer, and when I finally lifted it back up, the knights' shock hadn't abated whatsoever. No one offered a response for so long that I was beginning to wonder if I had to dismiss them from the room.

"Your Highness, Princess Pride." It was the vice commander who finally broke the silence. It was his first time speaking out today, and he looked to be on his guard. "If we're not to consider this a public setting, and I can therefore speak freely to you, may I be the next to offer my thoughts?"

I nodded, and Sir Clark stood up, walked past the commander, and positioned himself directly before me.

"I thank you for the aid you offered the order, and I thank Prince Stale for his assistance as well." With that, he knelt before me once more.

The commander attempted to intervene. "C-Clark, you—"

"And also," Vice Commander Clark continued, voice rising so all could hear, "I give you my most profound gratitude for saving the life of my dear friend Commander Roderick. I cannot thank you enough."

Suddenly, he fell to the floor in a full bow, forehead against the tiles. I was too surprised to respond. But Commander Roderick looked even more shocked.

"As a knight, I can't approve of involving the royal family in an incident like yesterday's," Sir Clark said through gritted teeth. "There's no room for gratitude in something so reckless. But as for me personally, I do wish to thank you here and now. Without your actions, there's no doubt we would have lost our dear friend."

Another man stood and joined Sir Clark on the floor at my feet. Judging by his injuries, I assumed he was one of the new recruits.

"It brings me great shame to have had my life saved by Your Highness," he said, hardly taking a breath before adding, "Despite our own failings, we didn't have to lose our commander in the end. Thank you, Your Highness!"

Next came a knight who'd been in the strategy room, along with one from the vanguard, and then a new recruit after him. It was like a dam had burst. One by one, they came to bow before me and offer their gratitude. Before long, everyone in the room, aside from the commander's son in the very back, was bowing to me.

The commander froze, gawking at all the knights professing their thanks that he was still alive. To me, it just proved how loved he was.

Then, finally...his son stirred. He stood up slowly and approached the rest of the knights from behind. Though obviously inexperienced in these kinds of niceties, he lowered himself into the same silent bow as the troops. Commander Roderick's mouth fell open as his son joined the strange procession.

Upon seeing the commander's face, Sir Clark let out a chuckle. "I think it's time we take our leave," he said softly. He rose, signaling for the knights to follow him out of the room.

Each knight took a turn bidding me farewell before they left. Eventually, only Sir Clark remained, the last to reach Commander Roderick on his way out.

"Um..." the commander's son began. He was staring straight up at me now that most of the room stood empty. "May I...say something too?"

Unlike when he was in the strategy room demanding we save his father, the boy spoke demurely now, quiet and hesitant as he awaited permission.

"Hey," Commander Roderick began, but the vice commander stopped him.

"Yes, go ahead," I said.

The boy started slowly, one thought at a time. "Thank you for saving Dad...I mean, my father," he said, turning his face away shyly. His long hair fell over his shoulder, trailing all the way to the floor. "—we...and...for me?"

"What's that?"

He was too quiet to hear. He sat up, but kept his eyes glued on the floor.

"I...I've got a special power. But it's not...a power that can help me be a knight, like my father's. All it's good for is growin' the crops...Your Highness."

The boy studied his hands. I hadn't noticed the dirt smudges until now, but they stood out as the commander's son fidgeted. Behind him, Commander Roderick looked like he was doing his best in holding back his words, despite how he clearly wished to speak, and some of the knights who'd left were peeping back into the room.

"I'm nothing like Dad at all," the boy said. "I'm complete garbage..."

He banged his fist against the floor a few times, as though punching the ground in lieu of himself. Blood started to smear his hand alongside the dirt.

It sparked a memory of our first meeting. He'd screamed insult after insult at his father that time, but perhaps he'd been directing those insults at himself all along. Just how much hatred and pain had he inflicted on himself?

The commander was clenching his fists now, watching his son with a pained expression. But what came next changed his face completely.

"I'm gonna keep training," the boy said. "I'll learn from Dad's stupid lessons. I'll train, but..."

The boy raised his head for the first time. His hair flopped over his face, yet his eyes still bore into me.

"Can I... Can I become a fine knight like Dad someday?" Teardrops shimmered behind the curtain of his hair. His voice was hoarse as he added, "Even if I start now?"

I answered his cry. "Yes, you can." At that, he froze.

I did not offer that consolation lightly; becoming a knight

was no easy feat. There were probably thousands of people in this kingdom unable to achieve that dream. But none of that changed what I saw.

I was certain the boy would become a knight—a fine knight like his father. Despite his own self-hatred, he stood tall and held on to his dream firmly. Even living in the shadow of his father, he didn't back down.

"Even if everyone in this world rejects your dream, I will always support it," I said. "I believe you can become just as wonderful a knight as your father. From today forward, for as long as I live, I shall await the day you meet me again in this room as a knight."

I stepped toward the crying boy. Through his hair, his eyes never left me.

"Let me see your face," I said as I crouched in front of him. I reached out and gently parted his long, shiny silver hair.

A pair of deep blue eyes awaited me beneath, just like the commander's eyes. Though older than me, he came across as a small child when he cried, and I stroked his hair, hoping to comfort him.

"Promise me something. As long as I'm alive, I'll be waiting for you to become a knight like your father. No, I'll be waiting for you to become the kind of knight you dream of being. So when that time comes, please protect the people of this kingdom, whom I love so much, and my dearest family as well."

I placed my hands on his cheeks. His skin was warm and wet with tears. He trembled faintly, still burning with determination.

"I...I don't know if...someone like me...could do that..." His nose was running, but he never so much as blinked as he met my gaze.

"Yes, you can," I assured him. "I can see how kindhearted you are when you cry for your family. I've seen your hands weathered from hard work. And on top of all that..."

I took his hand in mine. Unlike my frail, tiny hands, his were large and strong, crisscrossed with scrapes and blisters that must have come from tilling the fields in his farm work. The boy gaped at the contact, but I just gave him a gentle squeeze. It was my turn to urge him on. The boy found so many faults in himself, yet he still aspired to knighthood. His ambition was palpable, his whole body radiating with this admirable wish.

"I can see just how badly you want to become strong," I said. "You'll succeed. I'm sure of it."

A fresh wave of tears spilled down his cheeks. "Ngh! Ahh!" He turned his face away, shook his head, and let out a wordless cry. But then, with a gulp, he fought through the tears to speak.

"I'll do it," he said. "No matter how many years it takes. I'll become a knight! And then..." He squeezed back, his hands warm, strong, and slightly trembling. "And then please allow me to protect you for the rest of my life!"

His eyes were red from crying, but he held firm as he waited for my response.

Me? Why me? What was the point of protecting the girl who would grow up to become an evil, heinous queen? Despite my doubts, I couldn't deny the boy's steadfast determination.

I smiled. "May I know your name?"

"Arthur... Arthur Beresford, Your Highness."

Arthur. I gasped when I heard that name.

Arthur Beresford.

Arthur? He's Commander Arthur, a love interest from the game!

Out of the blue, I recalled Arthur and how he'd spoken of the day the cliff collapsed in ORL. In the game, Arthur served as commander of the knights. Unrivaled in his physical prowess, he was the only love interest who managed to defeat Pride, the deadly final boss, in a contest of blades! His special power wasn't useless at all! He could...

So many details from the game flooded my mind. But now wasn't the time for that. I shoved it all aside and focused on the present.

"Princess Pride?" Arthur was blinking at me.

Arthur. I couldn't believe the commander's son was truly one of the game's love interests. But...

All of a sudden, my smile grew wider. *What a relief to know he really* will *become a knight.*

"Arthur," I said. "I don't think I'll have to wait very long for our promise to come true."

He tilted his head to one side in confusion. Perhaps it was wrong of me to go on, but I desperately wanted to offer the boy some comfort and motivation after all he'd been through.

"I've just had a premonition," I informed him, holding his hand even tighter. "You will become a fine knight in the near future. Everyone, including me, will recognize your strength. I believe you'll become a knight worthy of protecting me."

"What...?" he blurted out. The tears that arrived this time were much gentler, softer.

"I'll be waiting for you, Arthur. However..."

I was certain Arthur would become a wonderful knight, just like in the game. But that meant there was something else I had to tell him. I leaned forward and whispered into Arthur's ear.

"Should you ever look at me and see an enemy of the people, you mustn't hesitate to claim my head with your sword."

For the good of the kingdom, turn your blade against me.

Arthur was dumbstruck. I tried to let go of his hands and stand, but he pulled me back toward him. "What are you talking about?!" he cried.

Oh no, that came off like a threat again, didn't it?

"Don't worry, that last part wasn't a premonition," I replied, trying to smile as I let him clutch my hands in his. "You must become the kind of knight who uses his sword to protect those he loves. That is my wish for you."

Please protect Tiara. Please protect my family and yours and all the people of this land. Protect them from the threat I'll one day pose to them.

Arthur sat there mute for a time, but eventually nodded his agreement over and over again.

"I understand," he said. "I'll absolutely become a knight someday. I'll protect you and those you care for. I'll protect Mom, Dad, and all the people in the kingdom with everything in my power. That's the kind of knight I'll become!"

Vice Commander Clark had approached during our conversation, and he now set his hands on Arthur's shoulders.

"Shall we go?" he asked softly.

Behind him, the commander was crying. I didn't know when it started. He covered his eyes with those large hands of his, but the tears snuck between the gaps in his fingers.

I tried to go to him, but he said, "Your Highness..."

"Yes?"

The commander fell to the ground at my feet, pressing his forehead into the floor with a thud. "Thank you for saving my life. I'm so happy that I get to see my friends, my troops. My family..." Sobs interrupted his words, and I found his choking voice uncannily similar to Arthur's, but he pushed on. "But more than that... My son is to become a knight! I can hardly believe my ears."

Arthur gawked at his father, shocked all over again by this display. For a moment, the room fell silent aside from sobs. Then the commander forced out one more sentence: "I'm so glad to be alive!"

It made me happier than anything I'd heard all day. Tears stung my eyes. I bent to wrap my arms around the commander, who was curled up so small even I towered over him.

That body had saved and protected so many people. His troops, the upper ranks of the order, and his family all loved him so much for the sacrifices he'd made time after time for them.

And yet, despite all he did, the commander didn't survive in the game.

In ORL, the ambushers swarmed Commander Roderick. Then the cliff collapsed. He never got a chance to save his troops or reconcile with his son. I realized then what grief the Roderick of the game must have carried in his heart as he died that day.

But in this world, I'd been able to save him.

"Thank goodness!"

I hugged the commander close, letting my tears flow.

❧✳❧

"Your Majesty, may I ask you something?" a knight said.

He stood at the queen's side, at my side, except this time it wasn't me. This was the Pride of the game. I was watching a cutscene, helpless to change it the way I'd started changing things in the world now. The man looked straight ahead rather than at the queen as he voiced his query.

"When that cliff collapsed seven years ago... Do you suppose that was truly an accident?"

"What cliff would that be?" the queen responded, bored.

It took me a moment, but I finally recognized the knight. This was Arthur, his hair cut short so he resembled his father more. He'd finally succeeded in becoming the knights' commander, and this was the scene in which he sought the truth from Pride. Yes, I remembered it well...This horrific cutscene.

"Oh, of course it was an accident," Pride said, her voice devoid of emotion. "I saw it in a premonition before it even happened."

"A premonition? So you knew about it in advance. Then why did you send the vanguard to the cliffs instead of ordering them to evacuate?"

"Because those ambushers went after my knights, which is no different than going after me. Unforgivable. They all had to die. A quick death, really, once the cliffs came down. If I gave the order to evacuate, the attackers might've survived, you see." Pride revealed all this without shame. In fact, she smiled.

Arthur clenched his trembling fists, clearly forcing down rage and hatred. As the commander of the order, he was responsible for the safety of all of his knights. But he could not so much as raise his hand to the queen, and it seemed she knew that very well.

Even though she'd revealed all this in a flashback scene, I was painfully reminded of how she was...I was...an utter demon.

In the game, when Arthur watched those cliffs crumble over his father, Pride merely said, "My condolences." Like me, she knew the collapse was imminent. But she sent the vanguard to the cliffs anyway.

The scene suddenly changed.

"Ngh... Mngh... Ah..."

Once Stale returned, Arthur was free to leave Pride's side. He slipped away but did not get far, standing out in the pouring rain trying to cope with the queen's wicked words. She'd let his father and all those knights die, and Arthur was completely powerless to do anything about it.

Now Pride spoke of that horrific tragedy as if it was a means of entertainment.

He hated both her and himself, past and present. How could she do nothing? How could she stand by and let so many of her people die? Worse yet, how could he continue to serve a queen like that?

Somebody, please save him. He's done nothing wrong. Hurry. Hurry and save him.

He only had one chance for salvation, one chance to heal his broken heart, and that was the second-born princess. Tiara.

"Urgh…"

I groaned as I faced myself in the mirror, taking in my heavy eyelids. Well, that was to be expected after how much I'd cried yesterday. Though that nightmare hadn't exactly helped me recover either. When Lotte summoned me for breakfast, I groaned again, dreading facing everyone in such a state. I dreaded eating outside my room.

"You look much more beautiful than you did two days ago, all covered in dirt like that," Lotte said with a chuckle when I complained.

I called for Mary, the veteran maid, and tried explaining my dilemma again.

"Only Prince Stale and Princess Tiara will be there today, so don't you worry," Mary assured me. "The queen and prince consort won't be back until this afternoon."

Looked like I'd get no sympathy there either. With no other

choice, I let them usher me out of the room and found Tiara and Stale waiting in the hall.

"Good morning, Elder Sister."

"Good morning, Pride."

They smiled as they greeted me, and I smiled back.

"What're your plans for today, Pride?" Stale said. He took my hand as we walked down the hall. It was kind of him to offer me a steady hand like that, but I wished he'd prioritize Tiara instead.

"I have to go return the jacket Commander Roderick lent me."

I'd borrowed the jacket from him after the cliffs collapsed. Not only was it covered in mud, but it was also stained with blood from the commander and the attackers. Thankfully, Mary had been able to scrub it clean in just two days.

"Then I'll accompany you," Stale said.

"I'd like to go too," Tiara added.

We approached the next step and this time each of them grabbed a hand. They'd both gotten rather clingy after yesterday, which was a little embarrassing for me as the older sister. I'd made such a fool of myself, snapping at the commander, making that promise with Arthur, even breaking down and crying with Commander Roderick. Plus, there'd been all that business with the commander's son. During breakfast, I recalled the new memories I'd gained of him in my dreams.

Arthur Beresford was twenty years old in ORL, which made him four years older than Tiara. Just like his father, Arthur was a handsome and heroic commander sporting short silver hair and deep blue eyes.

Unlike here, in the game, Commander Roderick never got his foot out from under than boulder. Desperate to protect his troops until backup arrived, he fought alone against his tormentors without a single weapon while the young Arthur had to watch. Although the vanguard did eventually arrive, much to the child's relief, the cliffs came down right after and crushed his father in the landslide. Roderick and Arthur never got to reconcile in the game, and Arthur never got to prove that he could become a knight.

Pride, who was already queen by that time, forced her way into the strategy room the day of the ambush and issued her own cruel orders. She even demanded that the vanguard fight the attackers on the cliffs instead of aiding the commander, who fought back even as the cliffs began to fall.

And all Pride said in the face of Arthur's grief was those two cold words: "My condolences."

Later in the game, when Arthur asked her about the truth of what happened that day, she laughed and told him she sent the vanguard to the cliffs even knowing thanks to her precognition that they would collapse. Her desire to wipe out anyone who defied her far outweighed any sliver of compassion for her own knights.

"The ground there was always loose," Arthur said, his words thick with despair and hatred. "And that's where my father lost his life. But to die like that, left behind for no reason, it never should have happened…"

Arthur's grief in the game was so great that he even rejected Tiara at first, saying, "Please don't touch me. I don't want anyone who shares that woman's blood to lay their hands on me."

In the horrible cutscene I dreamed about, Arthur stood out in the rain and cried alone until Tiara rushed to his side, coaxing him to talk about his pain while still respecting his wish that she refrain from touching him. In that moment, she was like a goddess sent from heaven.

I wished I could have remembered this sooner, but this all happened in the very first game. And Arthur as a child didn't look much like the love interest character. He looked much more like his father in the game and spoke more formally, like the gentleman knight he was. Whenever Tiara praised Arthur's conduct, he would write it off as "a simple imitation of his father."

In fact, it was the commander's passing that motivated him to pursue knighthood in the game. That day lit a fire in him, a burning desire to feel closer to his late father and uncover the full truth of what Pride had done. He was a man caught in continuous torment, yearning to imitate his father and become the perfect knight, the perfect commander.

He achieved that goal on Tiara's sixteenth birthday. From the moment they met, she began healing his heart. From what I could recall, he spoke very harshly whenever Tiara was in trouble and when he defeated Pride at the very end. The contrast between his gruff and tender sides earned him a lot of fans among ORL players.

"My dad...was my dad, and even though I've pretended to be him, I'm still me," he said later in the game.

Remembering all of this also meant I remembered more about his special power, which was far from "useless," as he claimed.

He didn't understand the power well in the game either. Perhaps I would need to tell him, but only later. He'd learn the truth by the time he reached twenty either way.

"Pride, why aren't you moving?"

Stale's voice snapped me back to reality. I blinked and realized I was sitting frozen at the table, my fork partially raised. Tiara and Stale cast me nervous looks.

"Big Sister, is something on your mind?" Tiara asked me.

"Y-yes, you see, I was just wondering if Arthur is doing well."

I couldn't tell them the full truth—that I was remembering his backstory from the game. But I truly was worried about Arthur. My siblings glanced at each other and then smiled in unison.

"I'm sure Mr. Arthur will be all right," Tiara said.

"Tiara's right. You did so much for him, Pride," Stale added.

They must have meant my premonition about him becoming a knight. Sure, that wasn't the kind of thing royalty usually bestowed on commoners, but still...

"It was nothing. If something so simple served as motivation for him, that makes me very happy." I forced another smile, but it didn't seem like I was fooling either of them.

"What on earth do you mean?" Stale said.

"You showed so much compassion to a boy who was a total stranger," Tiara noted.

Something about their remarks carried further implications.

"You're a wonderful person, Elder Sister."

"You should take more pride in your actions."

Their praise came laden with gentle chiding. My siblings were such kind souls.

Stale offered one more comment on the matter. "Besides, I'd like to become closer with Mr. Ar—with Arthur too." A hint of a smile ghosted across his lips.

Stale and Arthur never developed any real relationship outside of their work in the game. In fact, Stale once coldly called Arthur "hard to make use of." Their interactions were hardly pleasant.

"I see a darkness of incredible depth in that man," Arthur told Tiara in the game, urging her not to trust Stale. Yet here Stale was, professing his desire to become friends with Arthur. I couldn't help feeling a twinge of concern, knowing how their relationship played out in the game, but hopefully they wouldn't just start fighting right from the start. Stale's smile seemed genuine, but also...thoughtful.

After breakfast, we completed the day's lessons with our tutors. By the end of the day, my eyes weren't quite so puffy anymore.

After all our duties, the three of us, along with Jack and a few other guards, boarded a carriage bound for the knights' training grounds. The men went through their paces as usual, even just two days after the ambush. Minus the injured recruits, of course.

Stepping out of the carriage, we made our way toward the grounds. Vice Commander Clark, who'd been overseeing the exercises, rushed up to meet us.

"Princess Pride! Along with Prince Stale and Princess Tiara as well," he said.

"Good day, Vice Commander," I said. "I'm sorry to stop by so suddenly. I'd like to return something I borrowed from the commander. Is he around today?"

Injured or not, Commander Roderick didn't seem like the type to lie around and rest. If anything, he was sure to be right here at the training grounds.

"Just a moment, if you would. Someone go call Commander Roderick!" Sir Clark ordered. "Princess Pride has come for a visit."

Several knights responded all at once, all trying to get closer to verify the claim themselves.

"Princess Pride's here?!"

"The princess is visiting us?"

"Hey, don't push me, idiot! I was here first!"

The men crowded behind the vice commander, trying to get a look at me. Feeling utterly tiny, I struggled not to shrink away from their eyes.

The knights went to one knee, but kept watching me avidly. They'd seen me the past three days in a row, but looked just as stricken as they had the first time. If they wanted to stare at someone, why not take in Tiara's beauty instead?

"Princess Pride, what brings you to our training grounds today?"

"Princess Pride, allow me to introduce myself. My name is Alan."

"Don't act so familiar with the princess!"

"Your Highness, might you do me the honor of sparring with me?"

"We're not supposed to talk about that, idiot!"

Their requests and offers and praise overlapped in a cacophony. I turned to Stale for help.

"It's no surprise that you're so popular, Elder Sister," Stale said with a smile.

That's not the problem here! Please help me out a little!

I was still flailing around searching for the right words for all the knights' requests when I spotted the commander sprinting toward us.

Indeed, here was Roderick Beresford, father of Arthur, a love interest in the game.

"My apologies for the delay, Your Highness!" he called. He joined the other knights, going to one knee while he tried to catch his breath. A red spot marred his forehead.

I shouldn't ask about the forehead, but I really want to!

"I'm sorry that the commander must present himself in such a state, Your Highness," Sir Clark said. "He's been resting up on account of his injuries, but he apparently still wants to train with the rest of us, and, well..." The vice commander trailed off and chuckled. "He had a bit too much to drink last night, and on top of that, he started training his son at the crack of dawn this morning, then showed up at the training grounds like this. He's been resting inside until now."

"Clark!" Commander Roderick said, face flushing red.

Sir Clark seemed wholly unperturbed. "Doting parents can be so troublesome."

It was nice to see the commander so lively, and to hear that he was on good terms with Arthur now.

"I wasn't drinking until dawn on my own, now was I?" Commander Roderick retorted. Once again, he failed to upset Sir Clark's cool.

"So Arthur is already receiving training?" I said.

"Yes, Your Highness," Commander Roderick said. "He was up at dawn just to train. My wife was as surprised as me to see that."

The commander smiled to himself as he recounted the story. The knights behind him wore similar grins. I imagined they were thrilled to hear their commanding officer doting on his precious son.

"He's so skilled with a sword, you would never imagine it's been years since he last held a blade," Commander Roderick gushed. The knights behind him snickered. "Don't you laugh! Oh, but that reminds me. Well, I suppose I can tell my knights about this too... Even this morning, my son was still talking about Your Highness and how—"

"Shut up, stupid Dad! What the hell're you tellin' them that for?!"

A yell cut the commander off mid-sentence. I whirled toward the sound, only to find a red-faced Arthur.

"What? What are you doing here?" Commander Roderick said.

"You went and left this at home after we finished training, and I had to come bring it to you," Arthur said. "You're the worst, stupid Dad! You better start apologizin' to me!"

Arthur tossed a sword toward his father like it was a sack of potatoes and not a sharp blade.

"I see," Commander Roderick said. "I'm sorry for forgetting my sword, but, son—"

"Seriously, I can't believe you!" Arthur cut in. Done berating the commander, he snapped his eyes toward me instead. "Princess Pride, about yesterday..." All the heat had gone out of his words. In an instant, he'd turned from a raging child to a contrite subject of the crown princess.

"Good afternoon, Arthur," I said with a smile. I tried to put him at ease, but his face flushed the moment I addressed him. "I'm glad to see you looking well."

"Thank you."

It was hard to believe this was the same boy I met in the throne room yesterday. Perhaps he couldn't do anything about feeling nervous around someone of higher social status, but I wished he wouldn't treat me differently just because of that.

Also unlike yesterday, I could see his whole face today. He wore his long silver hair pulled back into a ponytail this time. *Now that I see him like this, I can definitely tell he's the same Commander Arthur from the game.*

"I'll be taking my leave now," Arthur said, averting his eyes.

"Oh my, Arthur. Are you sure about that? Don't you want to stay and talk to Her Highness a little longer?" Sir Clark said, a teasing edge in his voice.

"Shut it, Clark! I'll kick your ass if you say that again!" Arthur yelled, going right back to his rowdy screaming. He turned to me instead. "We can talk once I officially join the order." With that, he offered me a short bow and made as though to leave.

Arthur wouldn't be able to participate in the training exercises until he joined the order, of course. He was visiting today as a relative of the commander, but usually, anyone allowed inside the headquarters had to have a history of intense training under their belt. That must have been why he and the commander were practicing together at home. I wished there was something I could do for them...

"Please wait a moment." Stale suddenly spoke up, stopping Arthur in his tracks as he attempted to leave. Arthur turned, blinking at the smile Stale greeted him with. "If you have the time, would you care to join me in my own training?"

It was such a casual question, but I could hardly believe my ears.

Sure, he said he wanted to become closer with Arthur, but what if they become enemies like in the game?!

Commander Roderick seemed just as surprised as me. "Prince Stale, whatever do you mean?"

"I've been looking for a partner to practice with," Stale explained. "Mr. Carl is a busy man, so I've been unable to spar with him outside of my actual lessons, which is very unfortunate. What would you say to giving it a go later today? If it suits you, we could even make it a regular arrangement. It might feel strange to practice methods that aren't used by the royal order, but I think studying a wide range of fighting techniques will help the both of us become stronger." Stale offered his hand to Arthur.

"Stronger..." Arthur mused, then reached out and squeezed Stale's hand.

Knowing what I did about the otome game, this was a shocking development.

"Very well then, Mr. Arthur. Once my elder sister is done with her errand, please join us in the carriage. That's all right, isn't it, Commander?"

Commander Roderick needed a moment to recover before he said, "Of course."

"Oh!" Tiara gasped. "That's right. Here you go, Big Sister." She handed me a package, and I remembered what we'd come here for in the first place.

I thanked her, then presented the package to the commander. "This is the jacket I borrowed the other day. Thank you again for lending it to me."

The dazed commander took the package and unwrapped it to find his jacket inside. "Pfft!" He spluttered a laugh before turning his face away, but his shoulders shook with mirth. Surely he was remembering that embarrassing incident when he picked me up in front of all of his knights.

The troops around us covered their mouths and averted their eyes, but it was clear the commander's laughter had rekindled the recollection in them as well. Heat crawled up my neck, and I balled my hands into fists.

"P-please stop laughing!" I cried. I stomped my foot, but the knights were too far gone now. Stale and Tiara had their heads cocked in puzzlement.

"Dad is laughing?" Arthur murmured.

The little chuckles erupted into full-blown laughter, and there was nothing I could do to stop it anymore. I bundled Stale and Tiara back into our carriage with a hasty, "We'll be on our way now."

The knights saw us off properly, of course, but they still wore smiles and chewed their lips. I glared back at them.

"Don't you breathe a word of that incident to anyone!" I said. The men nodded their agreement...while snickering.

I was all too relieved to climb back into the carriage with Stale, Tiara, and Arthur. After a moment, the driver flicked the reins and sent us back toward the castle and away from the giggling knights.

What a humiliating situation that was... Maybe I should have some new clothes made just in case I ever need more mobility again sometime.

At least one good thing came of that visit, though. My embarrassment aside, Stale gained a valuable training partner in Arthur from that day forward. That put me even further off course compared to the events of the game. At this point, I had no idea where this would all lead.

"Go to hell, you thugs! Don't touch my Dad!"

My throat ached.

Where am I?

In the projection before me, a group of threatening men surrounded my dad. They leveled their guns on him as Dad shouted to keep them from chasing down the new recruits.

Right. I was in the strategy room of the order headquarters.

How long had I been screaming? The minutes passed with no hope of backup to sweep in and save Dad. The vanguard was late. After an hour of this, Dad was running low on ammo, barely hanging on. Red stained his white uniform, the uniform he always wore so proudly, the uniform I so admired.

"Just a little more," Sir Clark said. "Hold out just a little more, and the vanguard will—"

But then, a girl spoke over the vice commander. "Here are your orders. Station every member of the vanguard at the top of the cliffs." I tried to figure out who she was, but her face was too blurry in the projection.

"But Roderick and the troops won't be able to—"

"The vanguard can kill the enemies on the cliffs first, don't you see? Or do you plan on defying an order from the queen, Vice Commander?"

You've gotta be joking! Dad's already half-dead, though. Can't you see that, or are you blind? Dad can hardly even scream anymore!

I was just about to refute the queen when Sir Clark grabbed hold of me.

"Very well," he said with shaking hands.

I could hardly believe what I was hearing. The queen planned to let Dad die. But then the vanguard arrived at the clifftops, offering a fresh wave of hope as they engaged the enemy. I cried for them to wipe out the attackers as quickly as they could and save Dad.

"The cliffs!" Dad shouted.

The image on the projection went fuzzy as the sides of the cliffs themselves began to tremble.

"Wha...? Dad... Dad, run for it!" I yelled.

I screamed so loud, I could taste blood in my mouth. But the collapse cut the transmission short. Dad would never hear me. And he didn't even attempt to run.

Rubble began to rain down, but Dad just ordered the troops behind him to retreat. He was too late. The rumble of crushing rocks drowned out their cries of fear and pain as the cliff consumed them.

"Run!" Dad shouted again and again with the very last bit of energy he could muster. And then...

"Roderick!"

It was Sir Clark yelling this time. A shadow occluded the transmission as something loomed over Dad. He looked up at the cliffs in grim realization. Then he reached a hand out toward us.

"Clark, tell Arthur—"

CRUNCH.

Before the screen went black, I caught sight of something beyond horrific. Dad collapsed and a spray of red splashed up where he'd been standing only a moment ago.

Aaaahhhhhh!

I screamed before I even processed what I'd just witnessed. I didn't even recognize my voice.

"Roderick! Commander!" the knights cried. But their calls did no more good than my own.

Dad was gone.

Crushed right before my eyes.

"That was your 'Unwounded Knight,' was it? It sure didn't take much to kill him, huh? What a pathetic showing from the man who's supposed to be the commander."

The girl in the projection sounded almost amused. I could barely process her words. I wanted to run. I wanted to berate her. I wanted to tear out my own hair. But all I did was stand there and scream and scream and scream.

"Commander Roderick fought until the very end so that our new recruits could make it out!" Sir Clark hollered, his voice heavy with grief. He stepped forward to glare into the projection, crying and gritting his teeth.

"Hmm," the girl mused. "But a death like that's nothing to be proud of, and all the other troops died anyway."

My world turned red. If I could have reached through the projection and strangled the queen right then and there, I would have.

"Well, I suppose it's a good thing that most of the dead were just newbies," she said. "You can always recruit new knights. And now that the commander's dead, you can step up and take his place, right? Seems simple enough." She offered all of this as though it were just another trivial little detail for someone else to work out.

My dad and all those knights... Are they really that disposable to you?

"That dunce of a commander was responsible for everything that happened today, anyway," the queen went on. "Let's just leave it at that. Stale, end the transmission now." A moment later, the projection flickered out, and the girl disappeared.

"My condolences." Those two words, the first words she'd said when she saw me through the projection, still rang in my mind.

She knew all along. She knew in advance just how my dad was gonna die, and she didn't care at all.

I couldn't take it.

He's dead! Dad is dead! He was your knight! Why didn't you do anything about it?! He fought so hard for his troops, so why, why did he have to die like that?! And why are you saying those things about him?

All my life, my dad had told me I could become a knight someday, just like him. But what good was any of that now?

No. Someone like me could never be a knight.

Around me, knights cried, still whimpering my father's name or the names of the new recruits. Some outright wailed. Others balled their hands into fists like they wanted to hit something. A few covered their faces in their hands. There was nothing I could do for them.

As for Sir Clark... He was perhaps the most distraught of all, standing off by himself and weeping openly. Sir Clark shouted for rescue teams to go to the site of the landslide and search for survivors, desperate to not let my father's death be in vain.

It all seemed so pointless to me. I'd never see Dad again. I'd disappointed him my whole life and I'd never even get the chance to rectify that.

Is this really how you want things to end? Your dad just died and that girl doesn't even care!

But I wasn't a knight. What was I supposed to do about the queen?

Goddamn it!

What could I do for Dad? What could I do for anyone? I was trash, even more useless now than when Dad was still alive. At least then there'd been some hope I would become a knight like my father.

No, I'll do it. I'll become a knight. And then I'll get revenge for Dad's death.

I'll become like my father.

I'll destroy myself. I'll destroy who I am. Every trace of me will be gone, until there's nothing left but Dad.

If I could just live like Dad did, perhaps I could become a knight like he did. I would never reach his level, I was sure, but at the very least I could imitate the man I'd spent my life watching and emulating.

I would rise from my own shortcomings and become a knight!

It didn't matter if I was a shoddy impostor. I was going to train and act just like Dad, until I was strong enough to reach...

Her.

The girl who dishonored my dad's death as a knight. She would receive her punishment by my hands.

I'd do anything to make sure of that.

"Arthur! You're awake already? You're such an early bird," Mom said as I left my room. She'd already prepared food for the day.

Arthur Beresford was the name my mom and dad had given me.

"Ah, I think I had a weird dream or something, but I don't remember what it was," I muttered. "Ugh, what a way to wake up."

I rubbed my eyes. I'd fallen out of bed this morning and woken with tears on my cheeks, the vague tendrils of a nightmare drifting out of my mind as I roused. I still couldn't recall the dream, but uneasiness lurked within me.

Mom shook her head at me, trying to hide a smile. She was already hurrying around the restaurant Gramps had passed down to her. We didn't need the money, thanks to Dad's work as a commander, but she enjoyed the job and didn't want to give up the restaurant her father had entrusted her with.

"Besides, I can never relax until your father comes home safe, anyway," she always said.

I didn't share her worry. Dad was strong, so strong I'd never reach his level. Once, I dreamed of being just like him, of becoming a knight and riding horses and using a sword to defend the kingdom. He made me prouder than anything or anyone else in the world, after all. His lessons were tough, and probably not suited for a kid like me, but I worked hard and glowed when I received his praise. I never even doubted myself, not when I was young. But one day I realized that all the training in the world, even from him, wasn't going to help me overcome my biggest weakness.

My special power was simply useless. I could use it to make crops grow nice and healthy, but that was about it. One day, I'd found a field of shriveled, rotten plants, but as soon as I touched them, it was like I breathed new life into them. I was really young at the time, so all I felt was excitement when I learned that I had a special power of my own, just like Dad. My parents were both so excited when I told them.

But for some reason they were the only ones who reacted that way.

"That's too bad, huh?" others said.

Soon, I grew old enough to understand the truth: While Dad's power made him an invincible knight, mine just made me...a farmer. Compared to the Unwounded Knight and his anti-slash, I was practically powerless. My ability certainly wasn't helpful in battle. I couldn't even control how the plants grew or how fast they grew. My power just ensured they were healthy. How pathetic.

Some said the powers only the people of Freesia possessed came from God himself, divine gifts granted only to those who were worthy. That was why we made sure our queen and royal family and everyone of high rank had some kind of power.

But if all I could do was grow crops, did I even count?

"There are many knights who don't even have powers. It's nothing to worry about," Dad said.

That wasn't enough to satisfy me. I didn't want to merely become some rank-and-file knight. I wanted to be as strong as Dad, or even stronger. Yet no matter how much I trained, no matter how much practice I put in, my weak, useless power would always hold me back.

It was the insurmountable gulf between Dad and me.

At first, I was too upset to keep up with my practice anymore. I quit the training exercises I used to do whenever Dad wasn't around.

If I became close to my dad in strength, then I could still become a knight, and that was good enough. That's what all the customers at Mom's restaurant always said, anyway. But my dad's name would follow me around like that forever, always reminding everyone that I just wasn't as strong as him.

The more I grew, the more I feared that gap between us. No amount of hard work would ever help me catch up to him. When I finally told Dad I didn't want to be a knight anymore, he was aghast and kept on demanding to know why. I made up a random excuse, but he didn't buy it for a second.

"You're giving up just because you don't think you can be stronger than I am?" he said. "That's the only thing that drove you to be a knight? To surpass your father?"

"Screw you," I said. "You don't know anything about me. You don't know what it's like."

Dad was right, of course, but that only pissed me off more. He threw my petty ambition right back in my face, forcing me to confront it, but I wasn't ready then.

The truth was, I wanted to protect Mom and Dad.

I was jealous of Dad, and of his vice commander, Sir Clark, who stood shoulder to shoulder with him.

I wanted to grow up and fight alongside my dad. I wanted to be like the man I so looked up to. The fact that that was impossible because of something completely out of my control crushed my motivation.

Fighting for the kingdom like Dad did, saving so many people like Dad did, protecting those I cared about like Dad did, growing stronger like Dad... I wanted to be a knight that could hold his head high, worthy of the name Beresford.

Mom and Dad both scolded me that day. I just ran off, fleeing to the fields to be alone. Beneath it all, I really did want to be a knight still, and that realization brought me to tears.

But it was too late. I let years pass without training. New recruits had to apply when they were fourteen, and only a few made it through the rigorous trials. Then they had to pass an exam as well. And even after all that, the order might not choose them. That was why Dad spent so much time training me as a kid. Many new recruits spent a full decade preparing before they turned fourteen, and even then, most didn't make it.

I was too far behind to even begin. Meanwhile, my father had become the youngest commander in the history of the order. Even if I tried to start my ten years of training right now, I'd just be a stain on his reputation. How old would I be by the time I finally did make it, assuming I did? The youngest knights were still old enough to have families of their own. Maybe, just maybe, I could become a newbie by then, but my father had been the youngest commander in the history of our kingdom. We didn't even compare.

Once, I'd resembled my father pretty closely, but after I abandoned the idea of becoming a knight, I couldn't stand to look in the mirror and find a pale imitation of him. Instead, I grew my hair out long, so I could hide my face. I forgot about swordsmanship and focused on being a farmer. I tended to the hidden fields behind our house as a means of escape. At least I'd never struggle to put food on the table.

Soon, there was no turning back. My hands were stained with dirt, my body too slender to don an armor and shield and protect the people. It was too late for me, yet the frustration only grew every day. To everyone else, it looked like I'd given up. But that latent desire to follow in Dad's footsteps gnawed at me persistently.

I want to be stronger. I want to be a knight, I thought every day, no matter how hard I tried not to.

And every day, Dad would twist the knife by asking if I was really serious about giving up.

"It's not too late, you know," he'd say. "You can begin your training again."

Rage boiled inside me each time he asked. It wasn't his fault, yet I still had to grit my teeth and dig my nails into my palms to keep from lashing out.

I'd been working in the fields for a full year by the time I turned thirteen. I was even settling into the idea of being a farmer. Dad still bothered me about it sometimes, but he was beginning to change his tune.

"If this is really the path you want in life, I won't stop you," he said.

"Knights are pointless," I spat. "It's embarrassing as hell to put your life on the line to protect a spoiled little princess like her. What a waste of taxes. You just die in the end anyway, like a common soldier." I flung all kinds of insults at Dad, but he never raised his hand to silence me.

And, eventually, he gave up. I gave up too. It was all too pain-ful a reminder—I was the worst heir he could have hoped for.

I want to be a knight. I want to be a knight, some voice in the back of my mind kept screaming. I shoved it down every time, sticking to my farm work instead of training, knowing I was just a worthless embarrassment to my dad. Maybe I was better off dead, in that case. These thoughts plagued me day in and day out.

If I'm going to die, I want to at least die as a knight, that voice said, fighting back against my despair. I thrust my hoe into the dirt to distract myself from that sentiment.

"Hurry! The commander needs our help!"

"There's no time! We have to save the commander and all the new recruits!"

All of a sudden, hooves thundered past the fields and men shouted in panic. Knights rushed past in a flurry, too numerous to count, and my heart leapt into my throat.

"Save the commander!"

"We have to save them!"

Their words finally sank in.

"Dad?"

I'd been to the strategy room at order headquarters many times, but today felt different. The gatekeeper let me in when I told him I was Commander Roderick's son, but he never met my eyes. The whole place just felt wrong. I'd come here enough as a kid—to learn from Dad and Sir Clark—that the shift in atmosphere immediately put me on my guard.

This takes me back.

Dad used to tell me I'd be a regular here one day, his voice loud and proud. I never thought I'd come back here after giving up on becoming a knight. But when those knights rode past earlier, shouting in alarm, it sparked a worry in me that I just couldn't snuff. I lied to Mom and raced out of the house.

The moment I opened the door to the strategy room, chaos poured out. I reeled back for a moment, but no one even noticed me. Everyone was focused intently on a projection, and as I followed their eyes, I saw Dad wavering in the image.

"Sadly, it looks like my time is up. I'm counting on you to take care of things when I'm gone, Clark. Now that no one's firing back at them, the enemy will probably reach me any minute. As a knight, I'd like to die with—"

"Is this a joke?"

The words slipped out before I could stop them. Was this real? Was that really Dad saying his farewells, telling everyone he was about to die?

The knights tried to grab me, but Sir Clark stopped them. I stumbled up to the projection, desperate to see it for myself. Dad looked startled, terrified. He was sitting on the ground, totally defeated. The scene was so surreal, I could hardly trust my senses.

"Stand the hell up," I said. "Go home and apologize to Mom a thousand times!"

"I'm sorry, I can't do that," Dad replied. "I'll be dying a knight's death here. But I'd still like to teach you one last lesson of—"

"I don't want your stupid knight lessons!" I shouted. "I already told you, I'm never becoming a knight!"

I won't be a knight! I won't take your lessons! As long as... As long as you're alive, nothing else matters!

I looked down at my feet, at anything aside from the desperate, doomed man on the projection.

No. I don't want Dad to die.

"I see. It's your life," Dad said. "I have no desire to force you to join the order. I just wanted you to know what it means to be a knight. To put your life on the line for the sake of duty, just like my troops and comrades do. As your father, I wanted you to appreciate that." Pain and sorrow strained his voice.

I couldn't face him like that, so I studied the floor instead.

"Finally out of bullets, are ya? Took long enough," a new voice cackled.

When I dared look up again, a group of men surrounded Dad. The thugs formed a circle around him, closing in slowly—until Sir Clark cut off the transmission.

"We need to get information from them without giving up any of our own," Sir Clark said firmly.

You're kidding me, right? Clark's been Dad's friend for ages, so how is he staying so calm through this?! I glared, at least until I noticed the blood dripping from his clenched, shaking fists. *Why...?*

The thugs were laughing at Dad, mocking him for being foolish enough to get his foot trapped under a boulder. But Dad didn't seem to care—he kept his back to us and addressed his enemies.

"Those boys who made it out of here still have lives to live. I won't let you go after them. You'll have to deal with me until backup arrives."

Why are you even thinking about that right now?! You can't run, you can't even move! Why are you acting so calm?!

"Watch me, my son. Watch your father's final moments...my final triumph as a knight."

Dad lunged, slashing at his attackers. Though I'd practiced fighting with him many times, I'd never seen him like this—going full force at a real enemy. He radiated brilliance and power, without even a beat of hesitation—the exact man I'd always seen in my dreams, ever since I was a kid. How I'd wished to fight alongside this man. But what was I doing to help him now?

Nothing. I was useless. I could only stand and watch him fight.

He was completely outnumbered. The attackers swarmed him as a group, pressuring him to fall back. One pointed their blade at him, and another leveled their gun at his face with murderous intent.

Dad was about to die.

"This isn't funny! I never said you could die, Dad!" I screamed. "Go to hell, you thugs! Don't touch my dad! I'll kill you all! Let him go, let him go, let him go, let him go, let him go!"

I started yelling before I even realized it. It felt like the only thing I could do, useless though it was. Still, I kept shouting at the projection, trying to prevent the inevitable tragedy playing out before me, all the while nearly succumbing to despair.

I hadn't even mustered up the courage to open up to Dad yet, to tell him my true feelings about becoming a knight. I disappointed him and he lost his patience, gave up on me, and abandoned me...but for some reason, he wanted me to watch him in his last moments.

No. I can't just want to watch. I wanted us to battle together as knights. This isn't how it's supposed to end!

But there was no way for me to say any of that to him now. I was trapped in the strategy room watching Dad die, like getting stuck in some horrible nightmare I couldn't wake up from. *Maybe this is what I dreamed about this morning.* I felt my mind attempting to distance itself from reality.

Watching Dad's demise, my hatred of my own worthlessness only increased, gnawing at my guts. *I should be the one to die, not Dad. I'm the one who's worthless.*

Bang!

A dull crack dragged me out of my thoughts. Someone had shot Dad in the foot. He fell to the ground and his cackling enemies closed in around him, making some snide remark about how guns worked on him. I reached out for him, pointless though that was, and kept screaming and screaming, trying to reach him any way I could. My legs gave out under me and I fell to the floor, my hand passing through thin air. I couldn't reach him. No matter what I did, I couldn't reach him, I couldn't reach, *I couldn't reach!*

"Ahhhhhh!"

I slammed my fists against the floor and howled.

When I turned, all I saw was a bunch of people dressed as knights, wearing that same uniform I always hoped to wear someday, but doing just as little as me in my pathetic state.

"Somebody help my dad!" I cried. "Isn't he your commander?! Unlike me, he's supposed to be special, right?!"

Dad *was* special. He wasn't scum like me—he had the strongest power possible for a knight and the physical skills to match. He was one of the chosen ones. So how could everyone just let him die like this at the hands of these bastards?

"So save him! Why isn't a single one of you knights doing anything?! Why can't anyone save my dad?!"

Someone... Someone help him! I'll take his place if I have to. I haven't been able to say anything to him yet, or pay him back for anything he's done for me. But I swear I'll do anything if someone just saves him. Please, I love him so much! You have to save him!

Not a single one of the knights moved. They watched the projection as helplessly as me. All these knights with their uniforms and their training and their weapons, all these knights I'd once dreamed of joining, and yet they were no better than me in that moment.

The world closed in around me, darkening my vision around the edges. I slumped forward again, sitting there frozen and mute. It was too late... There was nothing anyone could do...

"It'll be all right."

Someone set a hand on my shoulder. I gazed up, hardly

believing my eyes. The girl looked totally out of place among all the knights. She was young, for one thing, even younger than me, and had bright red hair.

"I won't let a single person in my kingdom suffer," she said.

She unsheathed a sword, the weapon unnatural in her small hand, and slashed her fancy dress. I blinked, still not quite believing my eyes or ears. Did this girl really think she could do what the knights couldn't?

"Take me to that battlefield!" she said, raising her sword.

In that moment, she looked more like a knight than anyone else here. She looked like Dad.

Everyone in the room gawked at the girl. I clung to her words, to her promise that she wouldn't let anyone suffer, including my father. Oh, how I prayed she meant that.

"You can't, Elder Sister!" a boy—her little brother—said. "You're the one who saw the danger for yourself in that premonition, aren't you? You should know better than anyone how badly this can go."

Premonition? What in the world was this boy talking about? His older sister stood her ground, refusing to back down. I could barely keep up. The crown princess...was going to save my dad? Or had I gone completely nuts, sinking into some impossible fantasy of salvation?

"I just had a premonition," the girl declared. "I can still save him if I act now. I can save that boy's father."

There was that word again. "Premonition." The little brother looked at me, but I couldn't read his impassive face. He shook his head again, muttering something about refusing to send the future queen onto a battlefield.

"I don't want to be a wicked queen who saves herself at the expense of others," the girl said.

My thoughts were in total disarray.

Queen? How could this girl be a queen? The boy's eyes went wide when he heard that. The pair stared at each other in silence for a while, with Dad's screams still coming through the projection behind me.

Hurry! Hurry! Hurry! Get on a horse if you're gonna save Dad!

Even with a horse, I couldn't fathom how she'd get to the battlefield in time. Dad seemed completely out of strength already. Would she even make it if she left right this minute? Was there any chance at all that she could save my dad? The questions raced through my mind as the siblings came to some sort of agreement beside me. He wrapped her in his arms...and the girl vanished into thin air.

"Wait, Sir Clark?! What was that?! Where'd she go?! Why'd she just..." I stuttered.

Still on the ground, I turned toward Sir Clark, but I never managed to get the rest of my questions out. The knights all around us stood stunned as well.

"Don't tell me..." Sir Clark said to the boy.

"Sir Clark, what happened to that girl?!" I asked.

Unable to rise, I crawled toward Sir Clark on the floor.

"Prince Stale," Sir Clark said, mouth agape. "He used his teleportation to send her away."

He looked down at me.

"P-Prince Stale?" I parroted. That boy couldn't be...

"This is the firstborn prince, Prince Stale," Sir Clark said. "The girl who just disappeared is Her Highness, Pride Royal Ivy, the crown princess."

"What?!"

I choked out a single shocked sound before falling silent.

The crown princess? That little kid?! Why are the prince and princess here?! Does that mean everything she said about premonitions and becoming queen was actually true?

Everything finally fell into place. Sir Clark ordered a backup squadron to rush to the battlefield, but Prince Stale stopped him. The two argued back and forth until suddenly a scream rose from the projection.

"Guh?!"

The scream wasn't Dad's this time. Some other man was shouting now.

Sir Clark, Prince Stale, and all the knights focused on the transmission. Dad and all the attackers surrounding him stared up at the cliffs, but we couldn't see what they were so intent on through the projection. After all, we had only a sliver of a visual to go by.

Gunshots rang out, followed by screams up on the clifftops.

What the hell's happening?

Even Dad was frozen in place. The knights broke into confused chatter.

"Could they be battling in close quarters on the clifftops?"

"No, the vanguard wasn't supposed to go up there."

"Then who's firing?"

"My elder sister."

Clark and I whipped our heads around when Prince Stale spoke. He stared fixedly at the projection, clutching a box of explosive powder.

No way. That girl is Princess Pride? Princess Pride's shooting at those enemies up on the cliffs right now? What the hell is she thinking?! She's tiny. There's no way she can beat men with guns. They'll kill her like it's nothing. I've heard the princess is spoiled, but I guess she has rocks for brains too. I can't believe I was desperate enough to ask her for help. I was such an idiot!

Even as I cycled through these thoughts, the gunshots fell silent. She was dead. She was dead, and it was my fault for begging her to save Dad. The princess was...

Bang! Bang!

Two more gunshots cracked. The men aiming their guns at Dad suddenly howled in pain, clutching arms and legs as they fell. Dad plunged his sword into the men who'd fallen.

What the hell's going on?

Lost for words, I focused on the projection. Silence suffused the battlefield until soft footsteps approached. It couldn't be possible. Miracles like that didn't exist in this world.

Dad slowly rose to his feet. Past him, I caught a glimpse of a familiar dress. She was so small and fragile-looking. She wasn't even a boy, much less a knight.

But my eyes weren't deceiving me—the tiny little princess stood before Dad.

There was no way... She couldn't be the person who'd just swooped in like some hero out of a picture book. Yet the image didn't change, and as the reality sank in, tears blurred my vision.

"It looks like you were completely out of ammo too, weren't you? I'm afraid I used up the last of it just now."

It was that same voice, that same voice that had reassured me here in this room.

"It'll be all right."

"Prepare to meet your end, you demons," she said.

Goosebumps broke out all over my body. I shivered from her words and the force of her presence. The crown princess had actually stepped in and saved my father, even though she was the one all of these knights, including him, were supposed to protect.

"That man is one of my subjects."

I couldn't see through my tears. I couldn't follow her words. All I could do was weep with relief.

She'd made it in time.

It was going to be all right. She was really there, and it wasn't just hypothetical anymore.

Her Highness, Pride Royal Ivy.

The young lady we were all supposed to protect.

A man who'd been lurking at the back of the band of thugs faced the princess. He made some snide remark before lashing out, but she twisted around his sword and leapt at his undefended chest. The princess swung, and with a loud, wet slash, the man collapsed, clutching his legs.

No one could believe what they were seeing, least of all me. An eleven-year-old girl was cutting down fully grown men without the slightest hesitation.

Princess Pride continued her rampage while we watched. She dodged any attack thrown her way before slicing down her foes. Every time her sword flashed, another man fell, taking a deadly hit to the arm or leg.

How is this possible?

My mind went fuzzy. I couldn't even remember how long I'd been watching her fight to defend Dad. She never slowed, never reeled back in surprise or fear. She bested every enemy who dared challenge her, the very picture of a knight.

Still, I gulped when the thugs rushed her together. I lost sight of her tiny body within the cluster of enemies. Then, Princess Pride reemerged, swiping at the men's feet, sending them backward, and taking out their legs with one swish of her sword.

"Whoooooooa."

All the knights in the room cheered when she popped back up out of the huddle of attackers.

"Incredible..."

I was so amazed, the word just slipped from my lips. The way she fought was actually *beautiful*. Even guns didn't stop her. The immobilized men grabbed weapons off the ground and fired straight at Princess Pride. But quick as lightning, she vanished, and the bullets struck the man behind her instead.

"What just happened?!" multiple people said. We got our answer when the princess reappeared, falling from above. She had actually jumped over the bullets and now plummeted back down.

"That's it. I can just use this," she said to herself, picking up one of the guns with a grin.

She dropped to the ground. Had someone struck her, or had she lost her footing? I was still trying to figure out why when more gunshots whizzed past, followed by cries of pain.

"What skill!" a knight said. "Was Her Highness really the one doing all that shooting we heard earlier?"

Seeing her roll across the ground, popping up to fire with deadly accuracy, I had to believe she *was* the person who'd wiped out the enemies up on the cliff. She was mesmerizing as she tore through the group of thugs with unnatural ease.

I suddenly realized I wasn't trembling anymore.

"Is that her special power?" someone asked.

"No, the princess has precognition," another person replied. "There's no way she could have any kind of power related to combat as well."

"But, her aim... I don't think even *we* could pull that off!"

Even the knights—Dad's proud, chosen knights—couldn't figure out how a little girl was taking out so many enemies on her own. While they pondered it, the projection filled with fallen foes, until only Princess Pride and Dad remained standing.

"Wh-why..." Dad said. "Why did you come here? You should know the danger better than anyone!"

I couldn't believe he was actually scolding the girl who'd just saved his life, but my relief that he could stand and speak overwhelmed that feeling.

"Stale said the same thing to me," the princess told him. Unperturbed, she paced through the carnage she'd caused.

Wait. Dad's safe now, so why is everyone still upset? It's all over n—

"This whole place is about to collapse," Dad said. "You were the one who predic—"

What?

I latched on to those words, churning over them, refusing to process them.

Then a terrible rumble rose, like the earth was splitting open. The cliffs started to flake, flecks of rock pattering down behind Dad.

"Vice Commander! The cliffs are beginning to collapse," a knight said.

"The vanguard has just finished evacuating our troops," another reported.

"Reinforcements on their way to the scene can see the collapse from a distance."

"Vice Commander! The vanguard has just confirmed that they can't make it to the commander's position due to the landslide."

The knights' reports overlapped, coming one after another to deliver the dire news.

What's going on? Even though she defeated all of Dad's attackers, he's still not safe?! But she said everything would be all right...

The noise in the room made it impossible for me to demand an explanation from Sir Clark or anyone else. Suddenly, the cries turned to shouts of "Princess Pride!" In the projection, the princess kicked one of the attackers toward Dad, then cast aside her sword and embraced both of them at once in some strange hug.

"What's going on?" someone said.

The rumbling cliffs made it tough to hear the princess, but I picked out the phrase "your special power" and an outraged shout from the attacker hugged between her and Dad. Then rubble spilled down, tumbling into view until it filled the projection. Both Dad and Princess Pride disappeared among the debris.

"Wha...? Ah... Aahh..."

It all happened in the blink of an eye, and at first, I could hardly react, too dazed from the whole experience.

"Ahhhhhh!"

When I recovered enough to respond at all, all I could do was scream.

How many years must've passed after that? In reality, it was probably just a few minutes. But I stood there in a total daze for so long I couldn't tell anymore, screaming and screaming until my throat went raw and I started to cough. I was still on the ground, slumped over and too weak to stand. How did it come to this?

My thoughts grew sluggish. The projection was empty now. It'd been connected to a boulder that rolled off somewhere in the landslide, yet I kept staring at that empty image, hoping against hope.

Sir Clark issued orders to the knights, demanding they start their search once the rubble settled. He also added the reinforcements to the search effort, once all the new recruits were safe.

It took me a moment to process what Sir Clark said. It wasn't a rescue mission. It was a search party. They were looking for Dad's body—and Princess Pride's.

Everyone died someday. I wasn't so naive I didn't realize that. But how could this happen? I shook my head, refusing to accept it.

"I have to go save my elder sister," Prince Stale said.

"You mustn't! Pull yourself together, Your Highness," Sir Clark said.

I managed to turn my head just enough to look at the prince, who was pale and quivering. "Elder Sister... Elder Sister..." he repeated under his breath.

He lost a family member too.

The death of Princess Pride would be a huge stain on the order. Part of me wanted to take the blame for this. After all, she'd only gone to that ill-fated battlefield because of my pleading and begging. I was even willing to face execution for the fate to which I'd doomed the amazing princess.

And then there was Dad. As my thoughts turned to him, my despair washed over me anew. He'd died so easily. I never even got to tell him anything. I never even...

"Get in contact with me as soon as you see this message," Sir Clark said. He was stomping around the strategy room, shouting the same orders over and over in an endless refrain.

Eventually, the knights did manage to make contact with someone. The projection changed. The knights in the image provided an update on the situation—they'd just arrived at the scene and assessed the pile of rubble while searching for the commander and Princess Pride.

"Why don't we go outside and get some air?"

I jumped when a knight addressed me. The man lent me his shoulder, which I had to lean on to stand up and shuffle out of the room. When we made it outside, he propped me up against a wall.

"I'll come get you if anything happens," he said before returning to the strategy room.

He took me here so I wouldn't see Dad's body, I realized, still reeling. *They can't show a kid like me a mangled corpse.*

But as soon as that thought crossed my mind, a vivid image of Dad and the princess crushed beneath a mass of stone flashed before me, and I vomited on the ground.

Pathetic.

Empty inside, I leaned against the wall and looked up at the sky. The murmur of voices within the strategy room still managed to reach me, but I couldn't make out the words anymore.

What am I gonna tell Mom?

She'd cry when she heard the news. She lit up every time he came home from a long mission, and now I had to tell her he was never coming back again. Even though Dad and I were always fighting, I was happy to see them together. Not only would I never see Dad again, but I'd probably never see Mom smile.

Why couldn't I do anything?

Why was I so powerless?

I hugged my legs and pressed my face against my knees while the image of Dad standing tall and proud flooded into my mind.

"Watch me, my son. Watch your father's final moments...my final triumph as a knight."

I was watching, Dad. You were so amazing. I watched you fight to protect your troops, refusing to retreat. You were the hero I always knew you were.

A hero...

"Take me to that battlefield!"

The princess wielded her blade with such majesty. She radiated beauty as she fought.

Princess Pride took on all those grown men, but she was younger than me. It was unbelievable. But she was dead now too. Both of my heroes were gone.

I'm sorry. I'm so sorry.

I'm sorry I'm so weak. I'm sorry all I can do is cry. I'm sorry I couldn't protect you. I'm sorry I'm worse than scum, weak, pathetic. I'm sorry all I can ever be is the victim. I hate myself so much.

But, what if...

Just then, a commotion rose in the strategy room.

"It can't be!"

"The commander!"

Voices overlapped. It sounded like they'd found Dad's mangled body, but I didn't want to know. I didn't want to hear their cries of disgust. I pushed my face harder against my knees and hugged my legs closer. Then the door flew open.

"Beresford!" The knight who'd walked me out stood over me, out of breath despite the short distance.

No, please, I don't want to hear it.

He grabbed my shoulders, forcing me to meet his eyes. "It's your father!" he yelled, clearly a bundle of nerves.

But what if I could do it all over again?

He dragged me back into the strategy room. Chaos ruled the space. Knights raised their hands in the air. Some screamed; some wept. And then I heard it...

"I can't believe we actually made it out."

Dad's voice.

I blinked, not believing what I saw on the projection. Dad, standing there right next to Princess Pride. She was covered in mud, but she smiled as knights rushed up to her and Dad.

They're alive. Dad and Princess Pride are alive.

My body went limp with overwhelming relief. I crumbled to the floor and burst into tears. All around me, the room filled with cheers of pure joy.

But what if I could do it all over again?

This time, I'd protect them with my own two hands—Dad and the princess and everyone else I cared about.

I'd be just like them.

The strategy room never quieted back down once they confirmed that Dad and Princess Pride were safe. Sir Clark inquired about my dad's injuries, figured out how to get the princess home safe, and debated whether to inform the queen and prince consort. Prince Stale stood at his side, quietly conferring from time to time.

Eventually, Sir Clark told me that the vanguard was escorting Her Highness and Dad home, specifically a knight who specialized in transportation thanks to his special power. I thought that might mean more teleportation, but Sir Clark said the journey would take thirty minutes. All this time, the battlefield had felt so close because of the projection, but that made me realize just how far away this all unfolded.

The moment we knew Princess Pride was returning, Prince Stale disappeared, just like the princess had before. I asked Sir Clark about it and he explained the prince's power. I had a lot of questions, but Sir Clark stopped me, warning me to keep my silence on the topic.

Just then, I was happy to oblige, much more concerned with seeing Dad healthy and whole. I followed the knights when they headed toward the castle, as eager as anyone to see the princess.

Prince Stale and a young girl waited for us outside the castle, along with a row of maids and guards. The girl was probably Princess Tiara, the second-born princess. Her face was so pale and she clung to Prince Stale's shirt like she needed to hang on to him to stay standing. He stroked her back and murmured reassurances, though he looked plenty pale himself.

We waited there a long time. Finally, a strange vehicle raced toward us. It skidded to a stop before the assembly, and a knight climbed off, offering Princess Pride his hand to help her off the contraption. Princess Tiara gulped. The maids and guards drew deep breaths. Mud covered Princess Pride from head to toe, except where she wore a knight's jacket, far too baggy for her slight frame. The beautiful dress beneath was nothing but tatters, and Princess Pride's wavy red hair drooped like dried-up vines of ivy. It was no fit state for a princess.

It's my fault, I thought and realized I had no idea how to face her. I cowered behind the rest of the knights and hid.

Prince Stale and Princess Tiara rushed to Princess Pride and burst into tears when she embraced them. Even after all she'd just gone through, Princess Pride was the one comforting people now that she'd returned.

How can she be so calm about everything? I looked closer and realized the princess was trembling as she hugged her siblings.

She wasn't fearless, and she wasn't invincible, yet she stood up and faced the enemy with unwavering strength. She even had the courage to accept the weaknesses of others. Her radiance in that moment could have blinded me.

People led Princess Pride and her siblings to the castle. The moment they disappeared inside, Sir Clark approached to tell me that Dad and the vanguard were about to arrive at the infirmary and join the rest of the injured recruits.

There were already dozens of injured soldiers at the infirmary by the time we got there. Among them, in a wagon carrying the injured, was my dad. But I didn't feel ready to meet him face-to-face yet, so I hid myself away behind the knights.

The men roared with joy the moment Dad arrived. The new recruits disembarked first. Then, the moment Dad stepped down, the knights swarmed him. He greeted each and every one, still dazed from the battle. Sir Clark shouldered to the front of the pack and wrapped his arms around Dad, shouting, "Roderick!" Soon, all the rest of the knights were following suit, trying to get closer as they called out the name of the commander they couldn't believe had survived.

I stood by the wayside, casting nervous glances at the group. *I wish I had a bond with him like the order does. It's like they know Dad better than I do. What do I even say to him?*

"Commander Roderick?!" someone cried, and not with elation this time.

Dad's legs gave out under him. He collapsed against Sir Clark's shoulder, completely drained. The rest of the men rushed to carry him to the infirmary.

Finally, my worry overwhelmed my shyness; I ran up to be next to Dad. He still slumped against Sir Clark, relying on the other man's shoulder all the way to the infirmary. The doctor hurried out to greet us and got Dad into a bed right away. We waited anxiously for the news, but the doctor returned quickly, saying Dad had been treated back at the cliffs and wasn't in mortal danger.

"He probably collapsed from exhaustion. I'm sure he'll be well soon," Sir Clark said.

Yet Dad still had to get more treatment before they took him to a different room in the infirmary to rest and recover. Perhaps his injuries were so bad that they wanted to monitor him. I hoped he just got a special room because he was the commander.

Two knights guarded his room at all times, but they gave us privacy when I finally went to visit him. Sir Clark was too busy to hang around the infirmary once things settled down a bit, so I was on my own.

I leaned against the wall by Dad's bedside the moment I arrived. For a while, I just listened to his breath and watched his shoulders rise and fall.

Dad's alive. He's here, and he's alive. My vision blurred with tears. I slouched down to the ground, hiding my face against my knees.

I really thought I'd never see him again. I thought it was goodbye. I thought I'd regret it for the rest of my life. And once I accepted that, the guilt nearly broke me. I prayed for a second chance, a way to undo it and try again. As a knight, Dad had put himself in danger well before now. I thought I'd accepted that. Knights fought and died—that was just a reality of the procession. But today, I'd had to see it up close. And surely, this wouldn't be the last time. Surely, he'd end up in mortal danger again someday. How could I repair things before then so I wouldn't face this guilt all over again?

"...thur... Arthur... Arthur."

Someone touched my shoulder. I raised my head, bleary with tears and exhaustion. Sir Clark was looking down at me, concern in his eyes. Had I fallen asleep? How long had I sat here moping?

"Sir Clark," I said.

"Are you well?" he said. "If you're tired, how about heading home for now? I'm sure Clarissa is worried about you."

Oh, right.

My mom—Clarissa—had to be worried half to death. I'd told her I'd be back soon when I left, but now most of the day had passed. Still half-asleep, I clambered to my feet, asked Clark for the time, and went cold when I heard the answer. I dashed for the door, but turned around at the exit.

Dad was still sound asleep. I watched him, watched one last breath rise in his chest just to reassure myself.

"I'm going to wake him and give him a status report," Sir Clark told me, having noticed the gesture. "Would you like to speak to him before you leave?"

I bristled at Sir Clark's presumption. "No, there's no need. I'll go see Mom and come right back here." I turned to leave, and he snuck in a final word.

"All right. Good to hear you'll be returning."

"Shut it," I growled.

I'd known Sir Clark since I was a little kid, but I still hated the way he acted like he knew everything about me. I didn't bother elaborating after the quip; I just turned on my heel and left before he could get under my skin further.

By the time I got home, Mom was pacing. Apparently, she'd heard all the knights passing by our fields and that only made her worry more.

"What happened? Did you visit the order? Is your father safe?" she asked.

I assured her that everything was all right; it was a bit of an oversimplification, but it eased her worries. Anxiety tightened her face all over again when I told her I had to leave again and might not return for a while.

"Why do you need to go?"

"I'm gonna see Dad," I told her.

Her face flickered through emotions—surprise, doubt, joy. I told her Dad was at headquarters if she needed anything, but she didn't ask any further questions this time.

When she agreed to let me go, I staggered back down the road and returned to the infirmary. Dad was awake and sitting up in bed, talking softly with Sir Clark. Bandages covered most of his body. He was still looking pretty beaten up, but he waved me over when he noticed me, his eyes widening in surprise. I crept closer while Sir Clark continued delivering his report. It sounded like they had a formal meeting with Princess Pride tomorrow.

"You're right, I think we should move quickly. I plan to inform her that I'll be taking responsibility for her actions," Dad said. Determination burned in Dad's eyes. I wasn't exactly sure why, and Sir Clark ignored it as well.

"Very well," Sir Clark said with a nod. "If Her Highness is available tomorrow, we'll tell her then." Then, Sir Clark turned to address me at last. "Hey there, Arthur. Where were you off to?"

Damn him for seeing through me so easily. He knew I wanted to keep it a secret that I'd stayed by Dad's bedside while he slept, and he was actually covering for me. Somehow that was more frustrating than him just outing me.

"I went to see Mom," I answered.

"You what?!" Dad said, raising his voice. "Don't tell me you told Clarissa—you told your mother about everything that happened?"

Sir Clark looked like he was biting back a smile.

"What the hell?! Of course I didn't tell her, moron!" I said. "Then I'd have to sit there and calm her down for the rest of the day."

"I see." Dad sighed. "That's good to hear."

"But I'm telling her next time I see her." Shock renewed on his face, but I just kept going. "I swear, I'll tell her. I'll tell her you went and got your foot stuck under a rock, and you got crushed by a landslide, and you got yourself all shot up, and you collapsed when you made it back to the castle. Oh, and I'll let her know you were babblin' about how you were about to die, and during that whole embarrassing final spiel, you never once mentioned her name."

"B-but I think about Clarissa every day!" Dad stammered, looking deflated.

I ignored his excuse. "She'd cry, y'know that? And I'm not helpin' you out when she gets upset. You better get ready for Mom to scold the hell out of you when you go home. It's gonna hurt, but you deserve it, stupid Dad."

Dad didn't even try to retort this time, mouth hanging open.

"Looks like you're not getting out of it this time, huh, Roderick?" Sir Clark laughed.

Just like that, Sir Clark confirmed that Dad had certainly brushed up against death before now. Dad froze, clearly trying to think of a way to wave this all away.

"I won't mention this to Mom," I said, "on one condition."

Dad tried to get out of bed at this, but he whimpered when he attempted to move.

"Condition... What do you mean, Arthur?" Sir Clark asked.

Dad was still wincing from pain, but he focused on me.

"I want to see Princess Pride again," I said. Dad and Sir Clark shared a glance at this. "You're gonna see her tomorrow, right? So let me come too. If I can't join the meeting, at least let me see her again. I'm not goin' home until I get to see her, no way. I told Mom I wouldn't be back for a while, anyway."

Dad and Sir Clark held a silent conference, heads cradled in their hands, sharing a look of mingled horror and resignation. They knew I wouldn't give up when I was being stubborn.

"Clark..." Dad muttered.

"Very well," Sir Clark said. "I suppose it can't hurt. I'll put in a request with Her Highness."

Victory was mine.

"'Kay. I'm gonna go lie down out there, then." Assured they'd meet my condition, I headed for the door.

"Wait a moment, Arthur! You don't have to leave," Dad called.

"Even as your son, I don't deserve some fancy room in the castle," I said. "I'll be fine outside."

I brushed past Sir Clark, who grabbed my arm to stop me.

"Why are you like Roderick in all the worst ways, Arthur?!" Sir Clark yelled, his voice bouncing off the walls. "You share the strangest sense of honor!"

I tried to fight them both on it, but I was outnumbered and

eventually gave in. I ended up spending the night in Dad's infirmary room, since he needed more bedrest anyway.

"You're sure you don't want a blanket?" Dad said.

"What right do I have to borrow something like that?" I snapped.

I'd have been lying if I said I wasn't cold, but it wasn't unbearable, and more than anything else, I hated the idea of borrowing castle supplies when I was already on their property completely uninvited. I had some folded-up bedsheets on the floor. That would have to be good enough.

"What do you intend to say to Her Highness when you see her?" Dad asked me.

"I dunno. I'm goin' to bed, so don't talk to me anymore, stupid Dad," I replied, turning away and curling up into a ball.

In truth, I really didn't know what I wanted to say to her. I just knew that I had to see her again.

Dad didn't pester me further, and I soon drifted off to sleep.

The next time I opened my eyes, someone had laid a blanket over me. I quickly pretended to still be asleep, but I could hear Dad letting out a grunt of pain as he clambered back into his bed.

Stupid Dad.

The next morning, Sir Clark arrived after his morning duties to inform me that I'd be allowed to join the meeting with Her Highness.

I trailed the rest of the order through the halls of the royal palace. Chandeliers glittered overhead. The floors were polished to a shine. Everything shone and sparkled and I shrank down in the dingy clothes I'd been wearing since yesterday. Dad and Sir Clark had changed into their armor, but I'd rejected all their offers of fresh clothes. I wasn't some helpless little kid. They even tried to get me to tie back my hair, but I resisted, too terrified by the idea of the whole order getting to see just how much I looked like Dad.

The procession paced through the palace until we encountered tall double doors that opened into the throne room.

Princess Pride arrived right on time. She wore an immaculate dress, unlike yesterday, and had Prince Stale and Princess Tiara flanking her as she walked through a path created by the knights.

It was the first time it really hit me that this girl was an actual princess. She practically glided to the throne, taking one careful step after the next, otherworldly in her elegant beauty. It was dizzying, trying to equate her with the girl on the battlefield yesterday.

As she passed, Dad, Sir Clark, and then the rest of the knights went to their knees. I followed suit, waiting with the others as Princess Pride took her place.

"Raise your heads," she said. Everyone gazed up at the crown princess. "Stale has told me that you've kept my presence at the battlefield a secret. I thank you for your cooperation."

Sir Clark had issued a strict gag order. Even I was ordered not to speak a single word, not even to Mom or my friends. I was happy to oblige if it meant helping the order and the princess.

"No, it was a beneficial agreement for us as well," Dad replied.

He launched into a stream of questions, asking if she had previous combat experience, how she knew about one attacker's special power, why she went to the battlefield alone. The longer it went on, the more aggressive his questioning became.

It might have been shocking to see Dad address a princess so, but it was even more shocking when Princess Pride said she had almost zero combat experience. How had she slain so many foes then? If this was a lie, it was a terrible one, but nothing about this made sense. My head swirled with confusion, but Dad pushed on, and the conversation shifted to the princess's precognition, the limits of Stale's teleportation, and details like that.

"Still! That would have been preferable to sending the crown princess to the battlefield!" Dad's angry shout echoed in the throne room, slapping against the high ceiling. "Even if no one else would have made it in time, you never should have come there. You needed to tell the vanguard about that man's power and leave the rest to us!"

Sir Clark tried to get him to calm down, but it was no use. Dad had clearly already made up his mind, and he was going to keep on yelling, even at the very person who'd saved him.

In a way, he was right. A member of the royal family had no business being at that battlefield, and Dad knew that better than anyone. The people of this kingdom obeyed the royal family and paid them taxes out of more than mere tradition. Every knight knew they were training to protect the royalty, with their life if it came to that. To have that reversed—to have a princess trying to trade her life for a knight's—it was downright absurd, even if she was trying to save a commander.

Princess Pride bit her lip like she was holding back some retort, but Dad just kept going, talking about how knights put their lives on the line for royalty, how the death of any royal could rock the whole kingdom. Dad even said Princess Pride's actions would have dishonored his death, as though he was *meant* to die out there on that battlefield.

What a joke. The despair and the loss I felt yesterday is still just as suffocating as it was then. Do you have a goddamn clue how happy the knights are that you're alive? Do you have any idea what I...

"Just forget about us!" Dad said. "Even if it means that I must die, you shouldn't hesitate to keep yourself safe first and foremost. You don't understand just how valuable your life is t—"

I clenched my fist as hard as I could, quivering with the urge to punch him and make him stop.

"That's enough," Princess Pride cut in.

Her voice echoed through the room, silencing everyone, even Dad. Unlike Dad, her authority wasn't raw rage. The power of her words rippled through the knights as she rose off her throne.

"It is as you say, Commander," she went on. "My short-sighted actions upset many people, and I rescued you in a way that was against your will. However..." She spoke low, her anger palpable, each word sharp and cold as an icicle waiting to fall. "You are not the only one I saved. I saved you and all the knights you'll train from this day on. Do you know how many citizens you might save throughout your life?!"

Goosebumps spread down my arms. She was right. She hadn't merely saved Dad; she'd saved everyone he and his knights would help in the future.

"You're the one who doesn't understand the value of his own life, Commander!" she said. "Do you have any idea how much the people in your life love, cherish, and rely on you?"

She understands. She understands how I feel. She understands how all of us feel, and she put it into words.

I trembled, but for the first time in days, it wasn't from dread or sadness.

"I belong to the royal family!" Princess Pride declared. "I am the firstborn princess, and I will inherit this throne! My role is to live for the sake of the people. And you are knights. You're our hope, the light that protects the citizens directly. When a single knight dies, he takes everyone he would have saved along with him."

I shuddered down to my bones. "Living for the sake of the people..." What an act of selflessness that was. She'd even called the knights her "hope" and "light." Knights were the first line of defense for the people. Even a single knight's death should be avoided at all costs.

She was right about all of it.

How did she see through us all so easily? She understood the ideals of knighthood on a level few outside the order ever did. It was those ideals that first inspired me, those ideals that I still admired in Dad and yearned to achieve.

"Even if you were a mere foot soldier instead of the commander, I would have rescued you," she continued. "How could I let someone die when I knew I could save them? I will never allow any unnecessary deaths if I can help it."

I couldn't imagine how much her words meant to the knights.

It struck me then that Princess Pride hadn't gone to that battlefield for my sake; I'd just happened to be in the strategy room that day. She would have gone either way. It wasn't pity. No, she went because she *could*, because it was possible to save Dad and she knew it. Simple though it sounded, it required a strength and bravery I could hardly fathom.

"All of you are citizens of my kingdom, just as you are knights, and my people are my pride and joy," she said. "Our job as royalty is to protect each and every one of you. If you call yourselves knights, then concern yourselves not with dying an honorable death, but with those whom you'll still save in the future."

As her words sank in, they echoed in my mind, replaying over and over as I quivered before her.

"Concern yourselves not with dying an honorable death, but with those whom you'll still save in the future."

I wanted to protect everyone—Mom, Dad, all the people of this land. That was why I despaired when I realized I'd never be stronger than Dad. How could I protect him when I'd never measure up to him? I longed to be like him, but I could only cause him shame in my current state, and I'd therefore abandoned my dream of knighthood.

When I thought Dad was going to die, what was I most concerned with? What was the thing in my life that filled me with constant, constant, constant regret?

"I wanted to be a knight. I wanted to protect people. I wanted to become strong."

Who was it? Who looked down on me, telling me I'd bring shame to my dad, who shoved all the blame on him and said it was too late for me to become a knight? Was it Dad? No, he always said there was still time, that I could still become a knight if I started training now. The person who constantly poisoned me with negativity—with the idea that I'd be a disgrace, that it was too late to become a knight, that I didn't have any talent, that I'd never be like Dad...was me.

Ah... There I go again.

I couldn't stop shaking. I sank to the ground and tried to focus on Princess Pride's voice, although I was enduring the aftereffects of my epiphany. She was apologizing to the knights for her rash actions. Sir Clark thanked the princess for saving Dad, to my delight. At least someone had finally said it. Yet while all this went on, Princess Pride's voice kept on echoing in my head.

"Concern yourselves not with dying an honorable death, but with those whom you'll still save in the future."

The knights bowed on the ground before the princess, thanking her for what she'd done. My heart swelled with pride. Meanwhile, Dad stood frozen amid all this. I stood too and walked right up to the princess. I'd been watching from the very back, so I wasn't sure if I'd be able to do it right, but I clumsily lowered myself down to the ground, pressing my forehead to the floor.

I was terrified. Terrified that I wouldn't be strong enough to protect anything or anyone I cared about in the future. But I had to at least thank the princess for all she'd done.

"I think it's time we take our leave," Sir Clark said softly somewhere above me. The knights filed out one by one at his command.

I kept my head down and tried to hold on to my composure. What if I gave up again, right here and now, and lost my one chance to save the people I cared about? What if I failed all over again?

"Um..."

I forced the words out. Princess Pride watched me. I wasn't even sure she remembered me. The last time she saw me, I was bawling my eyes out in the strategy room just before she went to save Dad.

"May I say something too?" I said.

I wasn't ready to give up, yet I was almost too nervous to speak. Princess Pride, the crown princess, the future queen, waited for me to continue. I didn't deserve to speak to someone like her, and I knew that better than anyone, but I had to keep going now that I had her attention.

"Hey," Dad started, but Sir Clark stopped him.

Dad had to be terrified for me right then. I could get thrown out of the castle if I made some misstep now, but for all I knew, this was my last chance to speak to the princess for the rest of my life.

"Yes, go ahead," Princess Pride said.

I actually get to talk to her.

"Thank you for saving Dad...I mean, my father," I said. At least I'd managed to say the most important bit.

Unfortunately, Dad and Sir Clark were standing right next to me. I kept my head down, cheeks burning with embarrassment. But I'd been dying to thank her since yesterday. If it weren't for her, I probably would have spent my life burdened by regret. I certainly wouldn't have realized my true feelings on the matter.

"—we...and...for me?" I muttered.

"What's that?" she said.

This was it. I had to confess my true thoughts before my nerves got the best of me, but my throat closed up before I could speak. When Princess Pride asked me to repeat myself, I sat up a bit straighter, though I still couldn't muster the courage to look at her. With my head hanging, I let the words spill out at last.

"I...I've got a special power," I said. "But it's not...a power that can help me be a knight, like my father's. All it's good for is growin' the crops...Your Highness."

I studied my hands on the floor. No matter how hard I washed, the dirt and mud never quite scrubbed off. They weren't the hands of a knight—they were the hands of a pathetic loser who hadn't even held a sword in ages. That stinging reminder of my shortcomings dug into my chest like rending claws tearing me open, leaving me raw before the princess.

"I'm nothing like Dad at all," I said. "I'm complete garbage..."

I slammed my fists down so hard, blood smeared my skin alongside the dirt. Such feeble hands to bruise so easily. And every word only left me feeling weaker, more pathetic. I wanted to crawl away and hide.

I know better than anyone that I'm total scum. I know I'm just bothering her by asking her this question. She's just gonna shoot me down anyway. But still, I want to hear it from her, even if I'm weak and useless as I am right now.

"I'm gonna keep training," I said. "I'll learn from Dad's stupid lessons. I'll train, but..."

Please. I need an answer.

Even if it wasn't the answer I wanted to hear, I could live with it. But she was a hero in my eyes, just like Dad. She'd saved the both of us with her actions. I had to hear this from her and no one else.

"Can I... Can I become a fine knight like Dad someday?" I asked. My vision went fuzzy with unshed tears, Dad and the princess blurring along with it. "Even if I start now?"

How pathetic and miserable I must have looked. I was back to wailing and moaning just like in the strategy room.

Please... Please... I was practically praying, hoping against hope that Princess Pride wouldn't dash my dreams right there and then. *Please tell me... I need the motivation to carry on, a reason to get up off my knees and fight again.*

Scum like me can't even stand up on his own. But you're the one who helped me figure it all out. You saved me from this crappy life I've been living. Now that I wanna be a knight again, you're the one who can make or break me with your—

"Yes, you can."

I froze.

She didn't hesitate. She didn't flinch. She stared straight at me, and no matter how I tried to make sense of it, I could tell she wasn't just being polite.

Was I dreaming?

When I blinked, the tears finally fell. For a moment, my vision cleared and I could see Her Highness clearly.

"Even if everyone in this world rejects your dream, I will always support it," she told me. "I believe you can become just as wonderful a knight as your father. From today forward, for as long as I live, I shall await the day you meet me again in this room as a knight."

I hardly dared to breathe. I couldn't have heard her right. She not only said yes, but she also believed I could even measure up to Dad. And she'd be waiting for me. How was this real? She was our crown princess. We lived in separate worlds. Why would she wait for someone as insignificant as me?

Regardless, I couldn't look away now, afraid if I blinked this would all disappear. Yet no matter how long I knelt there, the girl who'd given me back my life in so many ways remained right there before me, smiling down.

"Let me see your face."

She elegantly came and crouched down close to me. I hadn't seen her so close since she'd patted my shoulder and assured me that things would be all right in the strategy room.

I went even more still, unable to do more than blink as she parted my bangs with her delicate fingers and peered at my face—the face that so closely resembled my dad's, but tainted by dirt and shame. I'd come here with my long hair down in order to hide, to shrink away from probing eyes looking to compare, and here she was, looking me right in the eyes and stroking my hair.

"Promise me something," she said. "As long as I'm alive, I'll be waiting for you to become a knight like your father. No, I'll be waiting for you to become the kind of knight you dream of being. So when that time comes, please protect the people of this kingdom, whom I love so much, and my dearest family as well."

There it was again—that declaration that she'd wait for me. She really meant it. And she was waiting for *me*, not Dad. Me. Though she looked into a face that appeared so similar to Dad's, she acknowledged me for my own abilities, she asked *me* to protect her subjects and family, the things she cherished most. She chose *me*, Arthur.

I was to become the kind of knight *I* wanted to be.

Joy and fear consumed me all at once.

She slid her hands down to my cheeks. With smooth, gentle fingers, she stroked the face I'd been desperate to hide for so long.

"I...I don't know if...someone like me...could do that..." I stammered.

Despite her conviction, I didn't want her to meet with disappointment later. I desperately wanted to live up to her hopes, but was that actually possible for someone like me? How could I possibly protect all that she held dear? In spite of her words, the doubt seeped back in.

"Yes, you can," she assured me. "I can see how kindhearted you are when you cry for your family. I've seen your hands weathered from hard work. And on top of all that..."

Princess Pride gripped my hands, covered in scrapes and blisters, blood and dirt—the result of my work in the fields. She didn't even flinch, her gaze unwavering.

"I can see just how badly you want to become strong."

I crumbled.

How I'd wished for strength hundreds, no, thousands of times. How I'd agonized over being weak, useless, broken. How I'd prayed for someone to notice and tell me I was capable, I was strong.

"*I want to be strong. I want to protect people. I want to be a knight.*" I'd buried those feelings deep inside, hiding them all this time, while desperately, desperately wishing for my dream to come true.

And here was a princess, actual royalty, seeing right through all of that, putting my feelings into words.

What would I call this, if not salvation? The princess had given me my life back in more ways than one these past couple days, but I had nothing to give her in return. Still, perhaps I could request just one more thing from her.

With a sniffle and a suppressed wail, I declared, "I'll do it. No matter how many years it takes. I'll become a knight! And then..."

I was the least suitable person in the whole kingdom to ask such a thing of the princess. But I squeezed her hands and faced her nonetheless.

"And then please allow me to protect you for the rest of my life," I said.

You've given me everything. That's why I can ask this. I want to return that kindness however I can. It's not much, but it's all for you. I want to protect you and everything you hold dear without rest. If you'll wait for me to become a knight, I'll fight for you as long as I live. I'll die a knight's death for you.

Princess Pride froze, taken aback by my declaration. Perhaps she was struggling to come up with an answer, but I'd already made up my mind. Maybe I was out of line, but that wouldn't deter me. I would spend my life protecting this person. I knew it with every iota of my being. I would serve this girl who showed such strength and nobility, whose name so perfectly suited her regal personality. But for the moment all I could do was wait for her decision. After an interminable moment, she smiled again.

"May I know your name?" she asked.

With a sliver of hope burning in my heart, I answered, "Arthur... Arthur Beresford, Your Highness."

It was the name my mom and dad had given me, the name of the man who was here offering his very life to her.

Princess Pride froze again, and her eyes grew hazy and distant, as though she was remembering something she'd nearly forgotten. *Is it possible we've met before?*

"Princess Pride?"

Princess Pride snapped out of it, shaking herself. When she noticed me again, some new joy lit her face. "Arthur, I don't think I'll have to wait very long for our promise to come true."

Not very long? I had no idea what she meant, but she spoke as though it was a certainty, as though she was glimpsing some inevitable future.

"I've just had a premonition," she announced. "You will become a fine knight in the near future. Everyone, including me, will recognize your strength." She squeezed my hand. "I believe you'll become a knight worthy of protecting me."

"Premonition," she'd called it. It really had come on so suddenly. Princess Pride possessed the power of precognition and through that power she declared with confidence that someday I would be her knight—that I would be a fine knight, whose strength was recognized by the people.

This can't possibly be real. She just told me what I'll be capable of in the future. With a smile on her face, she told me I'll be worthy of protecting her. She saw that I have value!

My eyes went wide with disbelief. The joy that rose in me overwhelmed every sense until tears streamed down my cheeks.

Someone like me... Someone like me gets to protect Princess Pride...

"I'll be waiting for you, Arthur. However..." She leaned forward to whisper in my ear. "Should you ever look at me and see an enemy of the people, you mustn't hesitate to claim my head with your sword."

Her voice was clear and strong, but I couldn't believe the words I'd just heard. She couldn't possibly foresee a future where she died on my sword. I rejected the very notion.

No way... Never, never, never, never! I could never hurt her!

Princess Pride tried to stand back up, but I reached out and stopped her. "What are you talking about?!"

"Don't worry," she said, "that last part wasn't a premonition." I could have sighed with relief. At least that last bit wasn't part of her premonition. "You must become the kind of knight who uses his sword to protect those he loves. That is my wish for you."

"Those I love?" Then why did you ask me to kill you?! You're the one I mean to protect. I'd already told her as much, and she'd said I was worthy.

"Should you ever look at me and see an enemy of the people, you mustn't hesitate to claim my head with your sword."

Are you absolutely sure that wasn't a premonition?

I trembled at the idea that that was part of her vision, a fate neither of us could escape. But I'd already made up my mind to pledge my life to her, so I would accept any order she issued, even that.

"I understand. I'll absolutely become a knight someday. I'll protect you and those you care for. I'll protect Mom, Dad, and all the people in the kingdom with everything in my power. That's the kind of knight I'll become!"

Even if the whole world turns against you, I still want to be the one to protect you. If your wish is to die at my hands when you become an enemy of the people, then I'll continue to protect you and your loved ones, even then.

I would be there to keep her on the right path, to keep her heart noble and pure. Nothing would get in the way of her strength. I'd walk that path beside her, protecting her and the things I cared about without fail. I would never, ever let her go astray.

I would cut down anyone who tried to corrupt her or stand in her way. And if the princess, the strong, dignified princess before me, ever came to the verge of collapse...

"How could I let someone die when I knew I could save them?"

I will be there to save you, without fail, just like you saved me today. No matter what hardship befalls you, I'll reach my hand out to you and rescue you as you've rescued me.

Arthur Beresford.

I vowed on that name, vowed right then and there. No matter the cost, I would protect the princess until the very end.

With everything I had.

"Arthur."

Sir Clark's voice pulled me out of my thoughts. I turned to him, lighter than when I'd entered this room. Princess Pride slipped her hands out of mine, but the phantom of her fingers lingered against my skin long after she was gone.

Sir Clark set his hands on my shoulders. "Shall we go?" he said.

It pissed me off, the way he always knew exactly what I was feeling. Sir Clark was almost the same age as Dad, but he acted like my older brother, and sometimes...sometimes it was exactly what I needed.

I nodded and finally shambled onto my feet.

I really did it. I'd told her everything I needed to say. A massive weight lifted off my shoulders. My head swam with dizziness.

Sir Clark had to help me to the door, but along the way I realized I had no idea where Dad was.

"Your Highness..."

I whipped around at the sound of Dad's voice, but the sudden motion made the whole world spin.

A thud rang through the room as Dad fell to the floor and thumped his head against the tiles, bowing to Princess Pride.

"Thank you for saving my life," Dad said through tears.

Even after my vision steadied, it took me a moment to process what I was witnessing. I'd seen Dad get angry so many times, but this was the first time in my entire life I'd ever seen him cry.

"I'm so happy that I get to see my friends, my troops. My family again."

So many moments in Dad's life were worthy of tears—when I said horrible things to him, when he thought he'd die on that wretched cliff, when he miraculously returned to the castle healthy and whole. But he never cried at any of those times. Now, he wept right before my eyes.

"But more than that..." he said. "My son is to become a knight! I can hardly believe my ears."

Me?

My eyes were so fixated on Dad, I forgot to blink. Until only a few minutes ago, I always believed I was a disappointment to him.

Whenever I heard "Don't give up," and "Are you sure about this?" from Dad, I assumed he'd given up hope for me already, and would only think of me as a burden if I changed my mind and decided to become a knight. I was so sure I'd be an embarrassment to him.

But that changed when I heard Princess Pride's words, and realized Dad never once gave up on me. In fact, right now...

"I'm so glad to be alive!"

Dad was crying for me.

As elated as I was by Princess Pride's assertion that I would become a knight, Dad seemed equally overjoyed. It was everything he'd ever wanted to hear from his son; how had I ever imagined I was an embarrassment to him? Even after so much crying, my vision blurred once more. After a life spent thinking I was cursed with a useless power and dead-end future, I suddenly felt like the luckiest person in the room. I had a dad who'd waited all this time for me, a mom who let me see the world, even the support of an older brother in Sir Clark. I hadn't been able to see all those blessings until I met Princess Pride, though. I covered my eyes, but the tears slipped past my hands.

After all this time, it still wasn't too late for me to realize how fortunate I was. Yet I'd nearly let it all slip away. I'd nearly lost all the good things in my life out of sheer stubbornness.

I wiped at my eyes with my fists and saw that Prince Stale and Princess Tiara were staring at my Dad, who was curled up on the floor, even smaller than me. Princess Pride smiled and wrapped her arms around my dad, tears shimmering in her eyes as she held him. It was the first time I ever saw her cry.

Even with all the excitement and drama yesterday, Princess Pride hadn't yelled or cried. But today, I saw her get angry. I saw her chastise Dad for giving up hope and assuming his death was an acceptable outcome.

Now she was crying too—crying not for her own sake, but because she was so happy to hear Dad say he was glad to be alive.

"Thank goodness!" she said, voice strained and quiet. I knew I heard her correctly, though. She was like a goddess then, tears glinting, the sun haloed around her as she comforted Dad. I clung to that image, burning it into my heart for the rest of my life.

I never wanted to forget that sight, not for as long as I lived.

"Stupid Dad."

"Don't call me that inside the castle."

Dad and I followed Sir Clark and the other knights down the hall after leaving the throne room. I assumed Dad was heading to the training grounds with the others.

"Fine. But what are you planning to do about that, *Commander*?"

I pointed at the knights ahead of us still rubbing their swollen eyes. They murmured quietly to themselves.

"I can't stop crying."

"Thank god. Our commander is safe."

"Princess Pride is truly wonderful." When we were leaving the throne room, I noticed the door stood ajar. Meaning all these knights had watched everything that happened in there. I could have dropped dead from embarrassment.

Now, Sir Clark led the chattering knights while Dad hung back with me. I couldn't bear to look at him, but I felt him smiling over at me.

"So, what are you going to do now?" Dad asked, rubbing his red eyes with a furrowed brow.

"I'm going home. Mom's waiting for me."

"Don't speak a word of this to your mother."

"Ugh. I know, obviously."

I tried to turn away, but his eyes prickled at me. I had to beat him to the punch.

"I don't care when we do it," I said before he could speak. "Whenever you've got the time...um..." My voice fell to a whisper. "Please start helping me train again."

I refused to look at him, bracing for his response, but it never came. When I finally glanced his way, he had a hand over his mouth, and his shoulders were trembling.

"Dad!" I yelled, assuming he hadn't been listening. He replied by smacking me in the head. My whole life, he'd never once hit me. I was more stunned than angry.

"Of course I'll help," he said, smiling gently for the first time in ages. "I'll be home first thing in the morning. Be sure you're ready as soon as I get there."

"Yeah," I said, numb and shocked.

We continued in silence. When we reached the front doors, palace servants opened them for us. Feeling a little annoyed by the realization that he still saw me as a little kid, I decided to ruffle his feathers a little.

"I bet you've almost gotten yourself killed a bunch of other times too, and you kept it from me and Mom."

"What?! N-no, I..." His reaction was answer enough.

"I knew it. What, are you scared of Mom scolding you? You're such a baby."

Dad mumbled some kind of excuse. We passed through the door, exited the castle, and made our way toward the front gates on the other side of the garden.

"Just so you know, you won't be able to hide it from me anymore," I said. I knew he simply didn't want to worry Mom and me, but that wasn't going to work anymore. "Because I'll be there with you on the battlefield next time."

Dad halted, eyes going wide. It was such an odd look on him that I grinned like a little kid. I didn't even know I still had it in me to smile like that.

Flush with victory, I took off running before he could fit in any kind of retort. I dashed past the knights, slapping Sir Clark on the back as I ran by.

"Don't get that close to death again, not till I'm there with you! Stupid Dad! And you too, Sir Clark!" I yelled over my shoulder.

Then I kept on running, sprinting with my eyes fixed only on what lay ahead.

"Ha ha! Are you still with us, Roderick?"

I laughed, watching Arthur dash off into the distance, before calling out to Roderick. My old friend looked completely stunned from the day's events, and the knights were beginning to take notice.

"Don't any of you turn around, got it?" I ordered before the troops could get any ideas.

How many years has it been since Roderick or I saw Arthur smile like that?

I could only imagine that Roderick felt as proud as I did in that moment.

⁕

"There," I murmured to myself as I faced the mirror.

I'd pulled my long hair away from my face, tying it back into a ponytail. I couldn't remember the last time I'd seen this much of my own face. The hair spilled over my shoulder now, but that didn't make my reflection look any less like Dad. When I furrowed my brow, the resemblance only grew stronger. Once, that might have sent me into a panic, but now I very nearly felt proud of the face I saw staring back at me. I gently smoothed out the crease.

If I cut my hair off, I'd look even more like Dad, but I couldn't bear to do it. *She* had touched this hair, and I swore my scalp still tingled from the brush of her fingers. I pinched the ends, approving of the length.

The world outside my window lay pitch black, but I stayed up cleaning my sword. Dad said he'd be home first thing in the morning, but I hardly slept that night and woke up early the next day. After finishing up with my hair, I cleaned my sword once again and did a bit of training on my own, the first time I'd done something like this in so many years.

"Arthur! Your...your hair!"

"Took you long enough, stupid Dad."

The sun hadn't yet risen when Dad returned on horseback. He gaped at my pulled-back hair. He hadn't seen my face much these past several years either.

"It's easier to move around like this," I said.

"I see." A smile seeped across his lips. Ugh, he reminded me so much of Sir Clark in that moment. "Did you get any sleep?" he asked.

"Yeah, but I woke up early for some reason, so I decided to warm up while I waited."

I wanted to train with you as soon as possible. I swallowed those words, terrified to utter them aloud.

"Anyway, are you even ready to teach?"

"What do you mean?" Dad said. He had dismounted, but he still held his horse's reins. As we talked, I picked up the distinct scent of booze on his breath.

"You were drinking with Sir Clark again, weren't you?"

"It was just one glass."

Yeah, right. It wouldn't smell this strong if you'd poured that whole glass over your head.

"If you're already warmed up, then that's perfect. Let's begin," he said.

With that, Dad and I began our first training session in years. We started with how to hold and wield a sword. The very, very basics. But by the end, he let me spar with him.

Between exercises, Dad told me all about Princess Pride. I couldn't get enough. He told me about her life in the castle, the rumors that swirled around her, all the good and the bad. He started with Princess Tiara's sixth birthday, however, then moved on to the troubling rumors that arose when Princess Pride was very young. I'd heard these sorts of things about her around town, including the whispering about her forcing Prince Stale to sign a fealty contract. But all of it sounded completely incongruous with the girl I'd just met. I vowed to find whoever had started the vicious rumors.

I couldn't remember the last time I'd had such a long conversation with my dad. And the training was even better. He didn't go easy on me for a second, forcing me to work hard during every bout. I couldn't possibly be happier. Although I never even came close to beating him, by the time we stopped, he wore a look of surprise.

"Arthur, you really haven't been practicing with your sword all this time?" he said.

What's that supposed to mean?

Of course I hadn't practiced. I barely remembered how to hold a sword before he reminded me. In fact, I was still using the same sword I'd used as a little kid, though it had taken me forever just to clean the darn thing enough to use.

"I can't believe it," Dad said. "You really *are* more talented than me."

I was still mulling over his words when Mom came to see what we were up to. She blinked in disbelief when I said I was training to become a knight. Her gaze flickered between me and Dad, but Dad slinked away, saying he had to return to the castle. While she clearly hungered for an explanation, he'd foiled her attempt to pry any further.

Stupid Dad.

He even left his precious sword behind. I had to go drop it off for him after I had breakfast and tilled the fields. During breakfast, Mom asked what had changed my mind about picking up my training again, but I didn't know how to explain myself without telling her everything about the ambush. I didn't know what to say that wouldn't break my promise to keep the events a secret, so I just hurried to do my chores for the day so I could rush off to the knights' training grounds instead.

"Don't you laugh!" Dad was yelling when I arrived.

I peeked around the corner of a building and nearly gasped. Princess Pride, Prince Stale, and Princess Tiara stood among the knights.

Crap. Should I come back later? After everything that happened yesterday, I didn't really have a clue how to approach the princess anymore.

"Oh, but that reminds me," Dad started.

His conversation kept everyone distracted while I slipped away and did a lap around the castle. Hopefully, the princess would be gone by the time I returned. Yet the moment I turned to leave, I overheard Dad again.

"Even this morning, my son was still talking about Your Highness and how—"

What?!

"Shut up, stupid Dad! What the hell're you tellin' them that for?!" I was shouting before I could stop myself, stomping out into plain view of everyone—Dad, the knights, even the prince and princesses.

"What? Why are you here?" Dad asked me.

"Because you went and left this at home after we finished training, and I had to come bring it to you. You're the worst, stupid Dad! You better start apologizin'!"

I tossed the sword at him.

"Ah, I see. I guess I left my sword at home. Sorry about that." The way he shrugged like this was all no big deal only ratcheted my anger higher.

Stupid Dad. Why'd you have to go and say that to everyone, not to mention Princess Pride?! I've gotta tell him to keep his mouth shut next time we're alone.

Busy with those thoughts, it took me a minute to realize I was still standing right in front of Princess Pride. The moment I noticed, we locked eyes, and all the blood drained out of my face.

"Princess Pride..." I stammered. "About yesterday..."

Oh no, I've gotta say something, I urged myself, but the embarrassing memory of yesterday left me at a total loss. *Stupid Dad, if only you didn't say anything, I'd... Wait, am I blushing? Crap, I didn't think I'd run into her again before I became a knight. What do I even say?*

However, she was the first to break the silence. "Good after-noon, Arthur. I'm glad to see you looking well."

I muttered a "thank you" as my face grew even hotter. I glanced at the knights, but that provided little relief. I met sev-eral smirks, including Sir Clark's. *Damn it!*

"I'll be taking my leave now," I said, assuming that was that. I bowed my head, face burning, and turned to leave.

"Oh my, Arthur. Are you sure about that? Don't you want to stay and talk to Her Highness a little longer?" Sir Clark said.

"Shut it, Clark! I'll kick your ass if you say that again!"

Bastard! He's teasing me! I'm gonna punch him next time I see him. But the damage was done. I was facing the princess again. And the truth was, I *did* want to talk to her more. Little would make me happier.

I wasn't worthy of that yet. I couldn't protect her. "We can talk once I officially join the order," I said.

I bowed once more and tried to leave.

"Please wait a moment."

Foiled again, but at least this time it wasn't Sir Clark. Rather, Prince Stale addressed me.

"If you have the time, would you care to join me in my own training?" he said.

What the hell? Prince Stale wants to train with me?! What's going on?

Dad asked what His Highness meant by that, and the boy responded immediately and without a drop of hesitation, like I was actually worthy to train with a *prince*. He even offered me a handshake. I just stared at his hand for a moment. I couldn't possibly be a good enough training partner for him, yet his words kept ringing in my mind.

"I think studying a wide range of fighting techniques will help the both of us become stronger."

"Stronger." That was it. I wanted to be strong. Dad spent most of his days with the order, and practicing by myself during that time wouldn't be enough. But maybe there was a different way I could train. Maybe I could use all that wasted time and put it toward becoming stronger.

I shook Prince Stale's hand at last and he smiled. *Is it just me, or does this kid's smile look kinda suspicious? It's creepin' me out.*

Still, he was Princess Pride's little brother, and from what I heard, he'd played a big part in saving Dad and the rest of the knights. Perhaps he was hiding or holding back something, but the terror he'd felt when Princess Pride disappeared in that landslide was definitely real. That was enough for me to trust him for now.

"Very well then, Mr. Arthur," Prince Stale said. "Once my elder sister is done with her errand, please join us in the carriage."

"So, um, is this it?" I said.

"Indeed," Prince Stale replied. "I keep a few spare swords over here, so please take whichever you like."

Prince Stale had taken me to a special practice room the royal family used. Yet when I surveyed the room, I sighed. It was smaller than the practice spaces the order used, though it would be more than enough for a private session. It only had two changing rooms, one for each participant. Among the practice swords sat some real weapons, as well, all polished to a shine. The room was so lavish, it hardly looked like it ever got used for actual sparring.

"Is something wrong, Mr. Arthur?" Prince Stale asked, surely having picked up on my gawking.

"Ah, no..."

I wasn't sure how I was supposed to reply, now that I was alone in a room with a member of the royal family. Prince Stale didn't seem to care, but I retreated a step, too overcome by awkwardness.

He held out a practice sword toward me. "You needn't be so nervous. It's only the two of us in here right now."

"Um, you don't have to be so polite," I told him sheepishly. "I'm not the kind of guy a prince needs to be on his best behavior around and I don't think you should be callin' me 'Mr.,' Your Highness..."

Having him address me so formally only made the whole thing worse. He should have just treated me like any other subject.

"All right, then you don't need to speak formally with me either," Prince Stale said. "You're older than me anyway, Mr. Arthur, so what say we both speak to each other as equals?"

Hang on, that's not right either!

It wasn't a matter of age. Dad and the rest of the knights all spoke to Prince Stale properly, even though they were much older than me. I couldn't go around talking to a prince like we were buddies.

"Okay, I'll start, then," Prince Stale said when I hesitated. "When you feel like you're ready to see me as a friend, go ahead and talk to me like one. Right now, I'm just going to be myself with you...Arthur."

The creepy smile finally faded from the prince's face. His expression went completely blank as he raised his sword.

Wait a second! I just picked up a sword for the first time in years. Don't tell me you wanna fight already!

The prince definitely wanted to fight already.

He lunged at me, leaving me no choice but to jump aside and block his sword. I had no armor or shield to protect myself with, so I just had to bat him aside and keep moving. Prince Stale stumbled, but he kept his weight on his right foot to steady himself.

"I was going to stop before I hit you," he muttered. "Arthur, you really haven't been practicing fencing at all?"

There it was again, the same question Dad had asked earlier.

"This morning was the first time in years I'd touched a sword, Your Highness," I said.

It still felt too strange to ignore his status when I spoke. Prince Stale blinked, then lowered his weapon.

"I knew it. I definitely want to keep you as my training partner." I had no idea what that was supposed to mean. But Prince Stale watched me with keen, blunt interest now. "Also, I'd like you to take the order's entrance exam as early as next year," he said.

"Wh-what?" I croaked.

What the hell is he on about?!

"N-no way. I can't do that. I don't know any of the basics, and I can hardly use a sword. My plan is to start with the basics now, then take the exam in three years at the earliest."

"It's not like you're only allowed to take it once," Prince Stale said. "If you don't make it through next year, there's always the years after that."

"No, but even if I take it early, I won't..."

"I'll support you to the fullest. I want to see you as a knight in the near future."

Why? Why is he saying all this? It made my head hurt trying to contemplate it. We were essentially strangers, yet here he was, the firstborn prince, vowing to support me in becoming a knight as soon as possible.

"Can I ask you something?" I said, desperately trying to make sense of all this.

"Sure."

"Why do you care if a guy like me becomes a knight? And does the firstborn prince really need someone like me to train with at all? When your instructor's done teaching you, shouldn't you spend your free time studying laws and whatever else a member of the royal family's gotta know?"

Princes were busy people. I knew that much, at least. Prince Stale was originally a commoner too, so I imagined there were all sorts of things he still needed to learn about being royalty. Even if he did choose to train, any knight would be honored to join him, and they'd all make better partners than me.

"To protect my elder sister," Prince Stale said.

My whirling thoughts stopped short. The answer came to him so simply, so immediately—and it explained everything.

"My elder sister is very strong," he went on. "But what you saw her accomplish was actually her very first day on any real battlefield."

What she "accomplished" that very first day was the complete destruction of an enemy army, along with rescuing Dad.

"I have no doubt she'll do something reckless like that again someday," he added. "As long as she feels she can make a difference, she'll try.

"But my elder sister isn't invincible. She has said so herself. 'If it was a simple battle of strength, then I certainly wouldn't prevail.'"

The battle flashed through my mind all over again. I saw the princess dodging and sidestepping attacks—but never once trying to overpower the enemy head-on. Suddenly, that made perfect sense.

"In the end, she is but a lady, one who simply can't rely on raw physical strength to win," Prince Stale said, as if he'd read my mind. "When the royal family adopted me, my elder sister was only eight years old. But even then she was already afraid of something, and she's remained fearful all this time."

Afraid?

That jogged a memory loose, the princess speaking close to my ear, strange words that made no sense at the time. "*Should you ever look at me and see an enemy of the people...*" A chill ran down my spine.

"I don't know what she fears," Prince Stale said. "But all I can say for sure is that something in her life is lurking silently, threatening to crush her. That's why I study whatever will help me protect her and spend so much time practicing with a sword. But..." Prince Stale leveled his blade at my chest. "It's still not enough."

His dark eyes were burning with ambition, too keen and focused for a mere kid. Even so, his voice grew quieter, and even his sword slumped low, representing his emotions. Shadows crossed his gaze, and I recalled the more frightening rumors regarding Princess Pride that, even today, coiled around the castle like snakes.

"I want to become stronger. Strong enough to protect my elder sister, but I'm still too weak. Even if I grow strong enough to be her equal, I still have to get stronger. I want to protect her with my life. But even that's not enough. If I die without saving her, then it'd all be for nothing."

Prince Stale stepped back and charged at me, bringing his sword down from above. I blocked on reflex, and metal clanged through the room.

"It won't be enough," he said as we struggled. He glared, but not at me. That look was for himself. "Adults may have authority and disputes and ways to work around problems, but even if I used those to protect her, it still wouldn't be enough. If someone stronger than her decided to resort to violence..."

Leather groaned as Prince Stale tightened his grip. He leaned his weight into his sword, pressing the blade closer to my face.

"I wouldn't be able to protect her."

The tip trembled before my eyes. I jerked back, knocking his blade aside, and Prince Stale stumbled back.

"Arthur," he said. "I know you'll grow to be strong. Stronger than me, or my elder sister. Stronger than anyone."

I couldn't fathom why he believed such a thing. Maybe it had something to do with his sister's precognition. Sure, I was the commander's son, but I hadn't even held a sword in years.

If, as he said, strength was within my reach, then I wanted it. No, I *needed* it.

To protect Princess Pride, I needed to be stronger than anyone.

I'd never planned to have the prince as my practice partner, let alone to receive such high praise from him. And yet...

"Can I ask two more questions?" I said.

"As many as you like."

"Why are you doing so much for someone like me? I know you're Her Highness's assistant, but why're you so desperate to protect her?"

Rude though the question was, I couldn't help but wonder. The prince was just her assistant, a former commoner adopted into the royal family. Yet at such a young age, he threw himself into her service. That, combined with his mysterious smile, nurtured a budding suspicion about his true motives. I waited patiently for him to continue.

"I thought you were like me," the prince murmured.

I paused, confused by his response.

"My elder sister is the crown princess, and I owe everything I have to that fact. I can't tell you the specifics, but I'll never forget what she did for me, not for the rest of my life. I took a vow, not to anyone else, but to myself, that I would protect her, that my existence would always be for her sake."

He bore into me, eyes bright with determination. I gulped and didn't dare break his gaze. Yet something more lingered there, the ghost of a memory, the weight of an unseen burden.

"I can't trust very many people."

He was only a ten-year-old kid, yet he spoke like he'd seen the face of evil.

"I can't trust very many people."

As I spoke with Arthur, I saw again that scene from three years ago, when Gilbert met with his subordinates to conspire against the crown princess.

Reputation meant nothing if a man held in such high esteem could turn out to be a traitor. For these past three years, I'd wondered what traps Gilbert was planning, what schemes he was devising. It meant I couldn't trust anyone in the castle, except Pride, Tiara, Mother, and Father. Now, I counted the commander and vice commander among my potential allies. But I had to view everyone else with suspicion, including Uncle Vest, Lotte, Mary, Jack, Mr. Carl, and the rest of the castle staff. And Prime Minister Gilbert, of course.

Despite my wariness, I'd forged as many useful connections as I could during my foray into high society. But I didn't trust a single one of them. I had no way of knowing who would one day betray Pride, or who already had.

That left me with few allies. I'd hoped becoming strong on my own would be good enough. But it wasn't. Pride had too many potential enemies. Then, just yesterday, I witnessed that moment between Arthur and my elder sister, and I realized something.

This boy will protect her.

Running into him again felt like destiny. On top of that, and much to my surprise, he truly was strong. Arthur dodged my lunge on his very first attempt and forced me to retreat. I'd only just begun to study the fundamentals of fencing myself, but my basic training started years ago. Mr. Carl said I was doing well. He told me I had natural talent with a sword, that I was performing wonderfully, that he wasn't just being polite. Thus, when I struck at Arthur, I gave it everything I had, hoping to find a dent in his defenses.

But I didn't.

Despite not touching a sword in years, Arthur met me blow for blow. He seemed oblivious to his potential, but I wasn't. I saw how powerful he could become, more powerful than me, more powerful than Pride. More powerful than...

"Please allow me to protect you for the rest of my life." The moment he made that honest declaration...

"I knew I could trust you," I said. Arthur received that news with wide eyes. "When you said you'd protect her, you meant it from the bottom of your heart. It felt like a vow to me."

He was someone I could believe in. Even Pride said she

foresaw a future in which Arthur was a fine knight worthy of standing at her back.

I needed him. *Pride* needed him.

"I will be my elder sister's shield that protects her from political influences and threats unseen. Arthur, I want you to be her sword and cut down anyone who tries to hurt her by force."

Arthur didn't respond. He just stood there, lips softly parted. Did he doubt me still?

"Do you think I'm lying?" I said. "Trying to entice you to join me? Do you think I would make all this up to control you or my elder sister?"

"Hell no, I don't think that," Arthur replied, the words bursting out of him. Finally, he addressed me as an equal.

"Okay, I'll start, then. When you feel like you're ready to see me as a friend, go ahead and talk to me like one."

"I don't know why you feel like you owe Princess Pride or just what the hell you see in someone like me..." Arthur said. He drew in on himself as he spoke, becoming smaller right before my eyes. At the same time, he held up his sword. "But I believe you when you say you wanna protect Her Highness. I can tell that's what's really in your heart. I want to protect Princess Pride, and so do you. That's why you wanna become strong with me, right? So let's practice together every single day." His eyes bore into me, as if judging me.

Rather than interrupt him, I nodded my agreement right away. He'd said every word I wanted to hear.

"Ha ha! Callin' us a 'sword' and 'shield' and stuff like that is really embarrassing," Arthur said. "Kids can be so annoying, I swear. But..." An easy smile broke across his face. At last, he seemed relaxed around me. "I guess I don't hate being called a sword."

I couldn't resist his boyish smirk and found myself grinning right back. His smile shone right through me, lighting me up from the depths of my heart.

"Just so you know, I wasn't lyin' about how long it's been since I held a sword," Arthur went on, scratching his head. "I don't wanna hear any complaints if I can't become a knight as fast as you want. Got it, Stale?"

"Stale," he'd called me. The moment the name dropped from his lips, I realized it was the first time I'd been called by name alone since the royal family adopted me. Well, except by people like Pride.

"Of course," I replied. "You'll get stronger, and I'll be your support."

"Will you stop acting like the future's set in stone?! Plus, you're gonna get stronger *with* me."

He pointed his sword at me, and I had no choice but to respond by raising my own.

"You're gonna get stronger too, right? For Princess Pride."

It was clear he still had some wariness about me, but at least now we knew we shared a common cause.

"I'll teach you everything I learn from Dad—and the order, once I make it in. So, teach me what you know too. There's gotta be stuff I can learn, right? Like the royal family's fencing style or self-defense combat or something like that."

Even if we weren't the sort of people who should be teaching each other, as long as it was to achieve our own goals and protect the princess, it would be all right.

"Yes. Thank you, Arthur."

"No problem."

Thus we forged our unusual alliance. I could see some joy in his eyes, even as his expression was stoic. I did my best to smile, but Arthur turned away and scratched at his head again, grumbling to himself.

"Oh. One more thing," Arthur said.

He glared up at me, gaze suddenly sharp. His shyness of a moment ago evaporated in an instant and I found myself taking a step back.

"I don't wanna see that creepy smile anymore. The one you made last time I saw you. Just make the same face you did when we were talking about Princess Pride."

I gulped. No one had ever seen through that fake smile I affected, not until now.

"It was...weird? I thought I was smiling pretty we—"

"Hell no you weren't," Arthur said. "You made me think I'd have to keep an eye on you, but I guess you're not that scary after all."

Scary? No one had called that smile scary before now. If I wanted to frighten them, I certainly could, but the bland smile I wore most of the time was supposed to appear genuine and inoffensive. Not even Princess Pride or Princess Tiara remarked on it.

"You've seen how unfriendly my Dad looks all the time, but Mom's actually got a really expressive face," Arthur said by way of explanation. "Then there's all the people who come to her restaurant. Basically, I've seen all kinds of expressions my entire life."

A restaurant. I didn't know much about Arthur's background, but if his mother owned a restaurant, it made sense that he learned how to read people. He seemed almost painfully sensitive, now that I understood. He must've helped her out a great deal, interacting with customers on a regular basis, and eventually enduring all sorts of superficiality once his rumored power was discovered. Perhaps that was why he hid his face with that long hair, as though he could shut out some of the information around him behind the curtain of his hair before running off to the fields he tended.

"I'm tryin' to say, I'm more used to seeing people look cold, like my dad," Arthur said. "There's no need for a kid like you to force himself into being nice around me."

He reached out and ruffled my hair. It was such a familiar gesture, such a friendly gesture, that my shoulders sank down away from my ears. Rather than see me as the firstborn prince, he was treating me as a normal kid three years younger than himself. It was a brand-new experience for me.

It seemed he really would help me protect the princess.

"Okay, then who teaches who first?" Arthur asked, bringing his sword up again.

But I wasn't thinking about swords just then. The warmth of Arthur's simple gesture still radiated through me. I didn't just have a confidant; I had a friend.

"Arthur," I said, taking care to address him directly. "I'm glad I met you." A faint smile ghosted across my lips.

"It's just one embarrassing line after another with you," Arthur said. "You're worse than Sir Clark."

But he laughed even as he spoke, and in that moment, I knew we'd forged a bond that would remain for the rest of our lives.

The Selfish Princess and the Trial

"**O**H, STALE. Are you training with Arthur again today?"

I'd just finished my lessons for the day when I ran into Stale in the hall, dressed in his usual practice gear.

"Yes. Arthur said this time of day works best for his schedule. You two should join us, if you have the time." Stale smiled at me and Tiara before hurrying for the practice room.

Ever since he and Arthur trained together yesterday, Stale was possessed with renewed passion. He spoke to Arthur like a comrade, a friend. He looked happier than ever when Tiara or I caught a glimpse of the two of them side by side. And the same went for Arthur. The timid boy who'd hid his face behind his hair perked up the moment he saw Stale.

"We just seem to get along," Stale had explained when I asked him what happened between them.

That wasn't much of an answer, and it left me feeling a little lonely. I also worried this was the rift that drove us apart, like in the game.

"Princess Pride!"

I turned to find Jack the guard rushing toward me. He was normally a quiet man, so it surprised me to see him in such a fluster.

When he stopped before me, he said, "Her Majesty has summoned you."

"I'm sorry to call you here so suddenly, my dear daughter."

We met in the throne room. Tiara tagged along, not wanting to leave my side. She seemed worried about letting me be on my own, but Mother didn't mind, so I figured I might as well take her with me.

Mother sat atop her elegant throne, the seat reserved for the highest authority in the kingdom. She was the very picture of dignity and grace as she looked down at her daughters. Father sat to her right, and Uncle Vest, the seneschal, stood to her left. Prime Minister Gilbert lingered at Father's side.

"It's no trouble, Mother. What is it that you needed?"

"I want to speak about what happened to the order," she said.

I flinched, struggling to maintain my composure. *There's no way she knows I went to the cliffs, right?*

"Are you aware that a man was taken into custody after the ambush?" Mother asked me.

Thank goodness. It's not about that. I stifled a sigh of relief.

"Yes, I know about that," I said honestly. I was the one who more or less took him into custody, after all.

"We believe that that man—or rather, his organization—is directly involved in the disappearance of our neighbor's royal order."

Prime Minister Gilbert filled in the details. "The plan was to have our neighbor, the kingdom of Anemone, welcome our new recruits into their land," he said. "Their knights would guide ours through the country. However, when their knights failed to arrive at the scheduled time, our knights' commander made an emergency expedition with a band of new recruits in tow. Well before they reached the border, a group of men ambushed them."

That was pretty much in line with what I remembered too. Mr. Carl had given me a similar explanation when we went to observe the order's training exercises. The kingdom of Anemone, though... Something about that name rang a bell. I knew we'd recently formed an alliance with them, so I might have read about their kingdom in a history book.

"The man we arrested tells us that he works for an organization that opposes our alliance. They took the Anemonian knights as prisoners, obtained information about our own order, and planned the ambush at the cliffs. They were aiming to take out both of our armies simultaneously."

In other words, it was all part of a larger plan.

"Unfortunately, the prisoner knew very little about the leaders of this organization he works for," Prime Minister Gilbert added.

This all made sense, but what did any of it have to do with me?

"Pride." Mother called my attention to her. "I heard from Albert that you've been studying our country's laws lately."

I snuck a glance at my father, Albert. He looked impassive as he waited for her to continue, but a strange little smile tugged at Mother's mouth. Then, she abruptly pointed toward one side of the room with the white, polished tip of her fingernail.

"As the next in line to the throne, you're to put this man on trial," she announced.

At her signal, the door behind me opened up for the second time. The guards dragged a man into the room. A gag covered his mouth, and rope bound his body. I recognized him immediately—Val, the man I'd forced to save me and Commander Roderick. Still, I wouldn't even know his name if it weren't for my memories of the game.

The guards shoved Val to his knees. When he spotted me, his eyes flew wide and he struggled and grunted, issuing a muffled cry of "Monster!"

"The offender's name is Val," Prime Minister Gilbert said. "He claims that the Anemonian knights he captured are alive and being detained somewhere far from the site of the ambush." He glared down at Val with frigid eyes. "However, he claims he's unable to explain the precise location in words. If we're to rescue these men, we'll need him to lead us there."

"So, my dear daughter, enlighten us," Mother said. "How do you intend to deal with this criminal?"

I see. She's testing my capacity as the future queen.

I took a deep breath. "First of all," I began, "the act of ambushing the order is a grave crime in itself. Appropriate punishments range from a life sentence to execution. Considering his actions may have affected our alliance with the kingdom of Anemone, I believe death to be an appropriate punishment."

Val's eyes went even wider, but this was merely the law.

"However, if he knows the whereabouts of the Anemonian order, then we can make use of a fealty contract."

Such contracts weren't an uncommon way to punish criminals, though they were unique to our kingdom. It was a useful way to get someone to confess the entire truth of any information they held. A fealty contract would force them to obey every order from their master for the rest of their life, which eliminated any threat of them breaking the law again.

"I can think of three ways to punish this man," I said. "First, we give up on finding the prisoners and sentence him to death. Second, we make him sign a fealty contract, rescue the captured knights, and then carry out his execution afterward. Third, we have him sign the fealty contract, rescue the captured knights, then release him, knowing he can no longer perpetrate any crimes."

I glanced at Val, who glared back at me with bloodshot eyes. The person I was in my previous life wouldn't be able to balance a life-or-death decision like this, but the part of me that was Pride coldly weighed the options. It was a stark reminder that I was still the ruthless, heinous queen from the game, no matter what I changed in this world.

At my side, Tiara squeezed my hand.

"Very well then, Pride," Mother said. "Choose which of those punishments this man will receive. I leave his judgment to you as the crown princess."

With such a heavy judgment before us, Mother sat there calmly, completely unruffled.

"The captured knights must be rescued before anything else," I reasoned. "Even though both of our kingdoms' new recruits couldn't complete their joint training, Anemone is still our ally. In fact, because our joint training fell through, we need to prove our allegiance by saving their knights now more than ever."

We couldn't abandon their knights—not if they were still alive. If we gave up as soon as our own knights were home safe, they'd see us as selfish and unreliable allies.

"And then..."

Would we execute Val after that? He'd certainly committed a horrible crime. Even if the cliffs hadn't come down, his ambush could have killed the commander and all those knights. The chaos would weaken our alliance with Anemone, which was surely his goal. Plus, both kingdoms would be left without knights. No doubt he deserved death for his transgressions, but...

I stepped forward, leaving a terrified Tiara behind as I approached Val and ordered the guards to remove his gag.

"If you speak out of turn, I'll have you executed right here and now," I warned him. "Answer my questions and say nothing more."

Please don't say anything about what happened at the cliffs, I prayed, then looked into his eyes.

"You're Val, is that right?"

Up close, I noticed new wounds all over his body. They must have tried to torture the information out of him. Yet he glared defiantly at me, the person who'd ruined his mission and gotten him captured. Seven years from now, he worked as Pride's underling, but in the game, he never got captured like this. Without my interference, he probably would have survived the cliff collapse thanks to his power and returned to the kingdom at some point in those next seven years. My memories of my previous life could very well mean his life ended decades before it should. Still, I felt no sympathy or guilt for that.

"Big Sister," Tiara whispered.

Even though I'd left her behind me, I regretted bringing her into this room at all now. *I should send her back to her room. No, she's the one who will become the true queen someday. She needs to see all of this, even if it's from behind me.*

Part of the queen's job was making hard choices.

Val had committed a grave crime. His group kidnapped the Anemonian knights and ambushed ours. Even if he led us to the missing knights, it would only be because we forced him to. Everywhere he went, he left a trail of victims behind. The Anemonian knights and their families were still suffering right now.

"Val, tell me which death sentence you prefer."

His eyes bulged; the man was downright bewildered. There was no reason to make him choose between life and death, as the answer was obvious—but I needed to hear something from him.

"If you sign a fealty contract, you'll never be able to commit another crime again," I said while he gaped. "You'll work an honest job, confined to this kingdom forever. Your life will be nothing like this one, even if it *is* a life. If someone harms you, you can never retaliate. No matter how hard someone strikes you, no matter how much they take from you, you can never so much as raise a hand. For you, it might be a fate worse than death, if you choose it."

It was true. A fealty contract did not provide any easy way out for Val. His darker complexion already made him stand out in our kingdom, and I wouldn't have been surprised if he had been treated as an outcast his entire life. These thoughts played out across his face as he deliberated.

"I don't wanna die," he said at last. "I'll sign that fealty contract or whatever you want. As long as..."

He grit his teeth, humiliation twisting his face.

I nodded. He wanted to live, no matter what.

"Very well. We'll have him sign a fealty contract, at which point we can release him."

The room fell silent. Val, Prime Minister Gilbert, Uncle Vest, Father, and Mother—everyone just stared at me. Finally, Mother smiled, offering me a nod.

"You've made your decision, Pride," she said.

Mother then reached out toward Uncle Vest. He retrieved a scroll and pen from his breast pocket, then handed them over to her.

"My dear daughter. You've just bestowed your judgment as the crown princess. Now you must be the one to execute the fealty contract."

Whenever a fealty contract went into effect, the queen took on the role of the "master." This prevented anyone from using such elements of power against Her Majesty. Mother herself had formed fealty contracts between herself and dozens of criminals, and now she wanted me to do the same with Val.

Mother presented the scroll to me. I didn't need to read it to know its contents. I would sign my name, and once Val followed suit, he would have to obey me for the rest of my life.

I took the pen and paper, but hesitated. Once I signed my name, I could never take it back. Even if he *was* a criminal, I was damning a human being to a life of servitude.

It was terrifying, to be honest. I was about to control some-one's entire life. The heinous queen Pride did the exact same thing to Stale. I... She even treated the entire population of Freesia, not just the love interests, as pawns for her benefit. My own crimes were so horrific, they made Val's look trivial in comparison, yet he'd be the one bound by this agreement.

With trembling hands, I gripped the pen and scribbled my name. I couldn't help fearing this was the beginning of my life as Pride, the evil queen. But if I didn't sign it, Mother would. She might execute him after that. I had to be the one to do this. Besides, this likely wouldn't be the last harsh, cruel decision I had to make. Queens sentenced criminals to death all the time.

Val wanted to live, despite his crime. He wanted to live here, in this kingdom. That was his wish. I wanted to grant him that grace.

I was going to commit unspeakable crimes in seven years, and they would be even worse than anything Val had done, but before then, I could still live as the heir to the throne in my kingdom. Eventually, I would be the one who deserved execution, but until then I could spend my days with the people I cared about.

I wanted Val to get that same chance.

I finished signing my name and passed the pen to the guard. He undid Val's restraints and handed him the pen. Val trembled even more than me as he signed the contract. The moment he finished, something shifted, as though my and Val's hearts beat in time.

Prime Minister Gilbert passed me another scroll. Val's punishment wasn't finished just yet. Next I had to read out the many terms of the contract for him to hear. A fealty contract could not be broken. The signer could not physically travel a certain distance away from their master without permission. They must obey their master's every order.

Then I added my own orders. Val could never commit a crime. He could never defy me or my family, nor could he lie to us, keep secrets, or treat us with anything but respect. He could never use violence, even in self-defense. He could never leave the kingdom without my permission. He could only live with the money he made from a real job.

I had to list out all these terms in detail. Simply telling Val he could never commit a crime wasn't enough if Val himself didn't see certain actions as "criminal." I had to explicitly forbid each crime: He couldn't steal. He couldn't claim anything he found on the ground as his own. He couldn't take money under false pretenses. He couldn't make deals that he knew would be disadvantageous to another party.

It was more exhausting than I expected. Though I simply read the list of items on the scroll, my throat, eyes, and mind wore down over time. The orders would bind Val as long as he could hear them, even if he wasn't processing each item. Thus, it fell to me to be careful about each and every word and not omit a single thing.

It took a long time to get through the entire list. But even when I finally reached the end, there was one more thing I had to add.

"I grant you temporary permission to leave the kingdom," I said. "I will also allow the royal order to give you commands. You must do everything in your power to safely assist the knights and make it back to Freesia. But your master is your priority. No matter what happens, you must stay with the knights and return to your master within seven days."

Hopefully, this would let Val leave the kingdom with our knights to rescue Anemone's knights and return to me without fail.

Val never said a word to me—no vow of hatred, nothing. But even when the guards took him away, and he was no longer bound by his earlier restraints, I could see him watching me with a look that told me there was something he wished he could say.

❧✳☙

"By the way, Pride, I heard our knights made it back to the castle safely."

It was the day after Val's trial. When Stale gave me that update, I sighed in relief.

After he left the throne room yesterday, Val and the knights went straight out to rescue the captured men from our

neighboring country. With Commander Roderick still healing, Vice Commander Clark had led the rescue mission. They
located the prisoners, escorted them home safely, and returned
to Freesia today. Our officials learned everything from one of
the soldiers capable of long-distance projections. This allowed
them to watch Val lead our knights to the prisoners and help
escort them home.

The captured knights had clearly suffered. Some had infected
wounds and soaring fevers. They could've come to our nation for
treatment, yet they all pleaded to go straight home to Anemone.
I was just thrilled to hear they made it back alive.

"I'm sure the commander is very pleased too," Stale said. He
smiled at me, seeming to sense my relief.

"All our injured troops won't be able to rest if they see their
gravely injured commander up and moving," the vice commander
had said.

Well, he was right, after all. Though Commander Roderick's
injuries were on the mend with the help of special powers, just to
be on the safe side, they decided on sending the vice commander
in his place.

"Pride, may I come with you when you interview the criminal?" Stale asked. I wanted to squirm away, but he fixed me with
a heavy gaze. Yesterday, he'd gone pale when he heard about the
trial from Tiara.

"Why didn't you call for me?" he'd said. "Did Prime Minister
Gilbert say anything to you? You signed a fealty contract with a
criminal?!"

I hadn't kept the information from him out of malice. I just didn't want to interrupt his practice with Arthur. But I found myself apologizing as Stale entreated me to invite him whenever I had to meet with Mother, Father, or Prime Minister Gilbert.

In light of that, I agreed to let Stale join me when I interviewed Val. It was kind of him to worry so much for my sake.

"Big Sister, may I join you as well?"

This time, the question came from Tiara, who was squeezing my hand and staring up at me. She'd been so scared of Val yesterday, but she was still worried about me enough to join. I was such a lucky big sister.

With my siblings in tow, I returned to the throne room to face Val again. He sat on his knees on the floor with guards standing over him. He flinched when he noticed us.

Don't worry. The fealty contract made it so he can't hurt us, I reminded myself. But the situation still made me nervous, so I told Stale and Tiara to stand behind me.

"Val, let me hear you speak," I said. "While we're here, throw around any insult you have for me. Tell me what you really want to say."

I stepped closer to Val. His dark brown eyes glared straight through me.

"Monster," he spat.

Val had witnessed my rampage on the battlefield. I wasn't surprised by him labeling me a monster, though I had to hold a hand out to keep Stale from reacting to it.

"You'll be released very soon," I told him. "Tell me how you plan to live in the outside world."

With the rescue mission complete, the knights would release Val from their custody. Thanks to the contract, he couldn't lie to me about his plans. He instead went quiet for a moment, then responded with a simple, "I haven't thought about it yet."

"I see." I closed my eyes, centering myself, then opened them to look at him. "Val, you're not allowed to discuss what happened at the cliffs or what I did that day with anyone else. I order you to keep all the information about what we did a secret. Finally, I have two more orders to give you, and they may be the very last."

Val furrowed his brow, tensing in anticipation. He couldn't disobey my commands.

"First," I said, "if you sense some kind of emergency, use your power to protect my beloved sister, Tiara."

"Pride, what are you—" Stale began, but I ignored him.

Val made a little noise of shock, but why wouldn't I use him for this purpose? He could use his special power to build tall, sturdy walls of dirt. It had protected the commander and me from the landslide; surely, it could protect Tiara from ordinary threats. In the game, Val protected Tiara from Pride several times. I needed to leverage that again, here and now, to make sure that when I became the evil, devious final boss, Tiara would still be safe. After all, she would be the one to rebuild the kingdom from the ground up once I wreaked my destined havoc—whether that was destroying the castle, as in some routes, or otherwise.

"This order takes the highest priority," I declared. "As long as you're following this order, as long as you're protecting Tiara, you can disobey any other command I've given you."

This command wasn't just for him. If I became so evil that I ordered him to harm Tiara, I needed him to disobey me. Val might not understand, but that didn't matter, as long as he complied.

"Finally, the second order..."

Val tensed all over again, preparing for another strange order.

"Val, if you find yourself in trouble, if you're in desperate and utter need of help, come and speak to me."

He blinked and leaned back a bit, as though my words had physically hit him. But once again, it didn't matter if he understood or not.

"Those are my orders. You're free to go, so begone from the castle."

Val rose in a daze, stumbling toward the door. He turned before he made it all the way to the exit.

"What's that supposed to mean?!" he snapped. A very natural question.

"Exactly what it sounds like," I said. "If you never find yourself in trouble, you'll never have to worry about it."

Val shook his head, but he accepted the order. Finally, he left the room, escorted by the guards toward the castle's front gates.

"Pride, why would you order something like that from a criminal?!" Stale demanded.

"Big Sister, why did you mention me? Aren't you the one to protect me?" Tiara said.

Stale and Tiara pelted me with questions the moment the throne room doors closed behind Val.

"Well, you're much more fragile than I am, Tiara," I said. "And what if that man gets into some kind of trouble his contract won't allow him to escape, even though he's finally free now?"

"Then that's what he deserves! He's a criminal!" Stale shouted, and I empathized with his feelings.

"Even so, now that he's free, he's just another one of my subjects," I said.

If he hadn't had information on the prisoners, we probably would have had to execute him. But now he could live as a normal citizen of the kingdom, despite his restrictions. And honestly, I wanted to help him do that, if he ever needed my help.

Stale didn't seem convinced. He sighed, shoulders slumping. "Very well. So be it. That side of you is why I..." He trailed off, but I caught him muttering under his breath. "I'll just have to keep an even closer eye out..."

Huh?

Was I already growing closer to becoming the wicked queen? Was Stale already suspicious of me now that I'd had Val swear fealty just like him? Queens had to sign fealty contracts all the time, but if my actions had put Stale on guard already, perhaps I wasn't as in control as I thought.

"Big Sister..." Tiara tugged on my hand. When I glanced over at her, tears shimmered in her eyes and her lips trembled. "Am I a burden to you?"

What?! I grabbed her tiny shoulders.

"Of course not! I love you very, very much, my little sister. Why do you think that?"

"You're going to be the queen, so no one deserves protection more than you," she said. "But you ordered that man to protect me because I'm so weak."

That wasn't my intention at all, but Tiara didn't understand. I knew from my past life that Tiara needed protection due to the events of the game, but now I'd upset her.

"I'm sorry, Tiara. You just mean so much to me. I want to know you're protected. I didn't mean to give you the wrong idea."

I pulled her into an embrace then and she fisted her tiny hands in my dress.

What should I do? First Stale and now Tiara. What if she thinks I secretly despise her? I squeezed Tiara hard. I knew from the game that she just wanted Pride to love her, but I'd already messed that up.

"I love you, Tiara," I said firmly. "We're family, and I care about you. You're my one and only sister. No matter what happens in the future, right now, I mean it, from the bottom of my heart. Please believe me."

Even if, seven years from now, I do something you can never forgive. Even if I hate you when that day comes, or you or the love interests hate me. I need to be sure you remember that right now, I truly love you.

Please never forget—there was a time when I loved you.

I hugged Tiara, as though I could press those thoughts into her very heart.

"Yes, Big Sister," she whispered, nodding against me.

Relief washed through me. I reached out for Stale, who'd been watching our exchange in polite silence, and pulled him close enough to join the hug as well. He stumbled into our embrace.

"I love you too, Stale. You're my one and only brother. Even if I lose all right to call myself the next queen, at the very least, I hope you'll always see me as your big sister, until the very end."

Stale's face flushed red, maybe because he was so close to Tiara. I just ignored it and held the two of them as close as I could.

When the time came for them to deliver my punishment, I hoped with everything in my heart that they would remember this moment.

"Ah! There they are, Big Sister!"

Tiara pointed off in the distance and tugged my hand gleefully. I followed her finger and spotted two familiar figures in the midst of a bout. Tiara and I rushed over to see them.

"Stale! Arthur!" I called out.

Stale and Arthur practiced in Stale's training room. Now that all that business with Val had concluded, Tiara and I could watch them fight today. They paused when I called out to them, and Arthur actually flinched. Stale waved, lowering his sword.

"We've been waiting for you two," Stale said. "Thank you for visiting us even though you're so busy."

I apologized for the interruption, but Stale just shook his head and told me they were about to take a break anyway. He tried to get Arthur's agreement, but Arthur had completely frozen up, eyes wide and flickering between me and Tiara.

"Prin—ide! Wh—! Stale! You!" he stuttered.

"Oh, sorry, I forgot to mention I invited the two of them to watch us," Stale said.

Just moments ago, Arthur had looked so calm and natural sparring with Stale. But the arrival of more members of the royal family had him so flustered, he could hardly speak. Well, Tiara *was* an especially beautiful girl.

"Tell me next time!" he roared at Stale.

"Sorry," Stale muttered with a shrug. He didn't look particularly remorseful.

At least Arthur spoke casually to Stale. It seemed they were getting along, even knowing each other less than a week.

"It's nice to see you practicing so hard, Arthur," I said. "I'm really happy that you agreed to be Stale's partner, so thank you for doing this. How are you feeling? You're not working too hard, are you?"

I knew he practiced with the commander of the knights, his father. Coming all the way to the castle had to cost him a lot of time and effort.

"N-no!" Arthur yelped, then took a step back. "I'm totally fine. My body's just fine. And it's helpin' me out a lot more than him, uh, Your Highness. I've only got my stu—my dad to practice with, and Stale, he teaches me all kinda new things."

Arthur stumbled over his words, clearly unsure how to address so many royals at once. His gaze flickered shyly to the ground, and his face was flushed, but a smile tugged at his lips when he mentioned Stale.

"Thank you," I said. "I hope you'll take good care of Stale for me. Tiara and I will be happy to see you every day, Arthur. Isn't that right?"

"E-every day?!" Arthur squeaked.

"Right, Elder Sister," Stale chimed in. "Please come visit us. Having you and Tiara watch us will be good motivation. Don't you agree, Arthur?"

He patted Arthur on the back, but Arthur was going redder by the moment. He opened his mouth, but no sound managed to come out.

"If it's too much of a burden..." I said, worried.

"Hell no, it's no burden, Your Highness!"

"That's a relief," I said. "Stale also seems to be enjoying himself ever since he began training with you. Tiara and I can never be that much fun for him."

Knowing what I did about the game, it was strange to see them becoming close. But I was just happy that Stale had a friend, and a boy near his age, at that.

Yet somehow, my comment flustered Stale. "That's not true!"

"It's not a bad thing," I said. "You both look so strong out here. It's so impressive watching you spar."

I smiled as I spoke, but the boys only looked more embarrassed, perhaps due to receiving so much praise in front of Tiara.

They were both going so red that steam could have burst from their ears.

"I'd like to see it again later, okay?" I said, and they managed to nod.

"Pride, please come back and watch us," Stale said. "I promise I'll get even stronger than I am now."

"Me too," Arthur added. "I'll definitely become a knight!"

The two of them placed their hands over their hearts, and Tiara smiled at my side. I grinned as well, but a dull ache held me back somewhat. I knew someday one of these two—or perhaps both of them together—would put an end to my wickedness.

"Do your best," I told them.

"I'll support you forever and ever, Stale and Arthur," Tiara said.

Stale, Tiara, and Arthur. How could I ask for better companions than these? Even if someday my actions drove us apart, at least for now, my heart burst with gratitude for their affection.

My world had gained such beautiful colors.

The Beauty of the Flowers

"**S**O THESE ARE SOUVENIRS for us? Pride? Tiara?" Stale said.

When Tiara and I entered his practice room that day, we carried in an assortment of baskets, so many that the maids had to help us. A simple observation that morning had turned into a shopping trip. At nearly seventeen, Stale was too old to join the outing. He had to stay behind and help Uncle Vest. He'd practiced with Arthur in the meantime, though he now wore his usual attire again.

Stale pushed his black-rimmed glasses up his nose and surveyed the baskets on the table before him. Arthur stood at his side, decked out in his knight's uniform, which he'd donned for practice despite having the day off. Tiara and I smiled at the boys' reactions, suspicious as if they'd been handed a jack-in-the-box.

"Can we open them?" Arthur asked.

Tiara and I nodded, and the boys lifted the lids off their baskets. They let out a little cry of surprise when they saw the flowers inside.

Tiara and I had gone to a local hill famous for its flowers to pick these. Stale and Arthur plucked a few from the baskets, looking at them curiously.

"You picked so many for us," Stale remarked.

He held small, jade-green flowers with many petals. They reminded me of cinerarias from my past life. They might have been a bit "cute" for someone like Stale, but I enjoyed the mature green color and glossy petals.

Arthur, meanwhile, held a handful of blue-and-white flowers. I thought the white matched his knight's garb, while the blue at the center resembled his eyes. The six large petals, nearly chained to one another in their design, reminded me of lilies back home.

"They're so pretty," Arthur said. "Did you choose these for us?"

"Yes!" Tiara said happily, jumping at Arthur's question. "Big Sister picked them all out, and she did such a wonderful job."

"I chose them based on their meanings in flower language and what I thought would suit you two," I said. "They represent things I've always felt describe you." The boys raised their eyebrows, clearly unfamiliar with flower language.

"Explain it to them, Big Sister," Tiara prompted.

"Well," I said, embarrassed to be put on the spot so suddenly, "Stale's flowers mean 'wisdom,' 'the fruits of hard labor,' and 'a bond stronger than blood.' Also..."

I rattled off the meanings, counting them on my fingers, but Stale stood more rigidly the longer I went on. He pressed his lips into a thin line and hardly moved. Was he even still breathing? I thought he might just die right there on the spot. He just watched me as I went through the list, which left me hesitant to explain the final meaning. I stood there, flustered, opening and closing my mouth as I gathered the courage to say it.

"'I hope to be worthy of you,'" I finally said. "That's the last one. I chose it because I want to be a proper queen worthy of a wonderful steward like you, and a proper sister too. Tiara feels the same, of course."

Even mentioning Tiara's devotion filled me with pride. I smiled to try to fend off the bashfulness coming on. But Stale still looked a bit stunned, face eerily blank as he stared at us. Was he upset?

Stale pressed the back of his hand against his mouth as heat crawled into his cheeks, his breathing quickened, and his glasses fogged. He almost seemed incapable of keeping himself together. It was as if he was reaching the dizzying heights of some grand emotion, although that seemed quite unlikely. If anything, I thought he might die right there on the spot. He bumped against Arthur beside him.

"Hey, what gives?" Arthur said, propping Stale up with one arm.

Stale just shook his head, still bright red from forehead to neck. I had no idea how to react to all this or what was wrong with him, so I just turned to Arthur's flowers instead.

"As for Arthur's..." I began.

Arthur's shoulders jerked as though he feared suffering the same fate as Stale. Color seeped into his cheeks as I continued.

"Your flower means 'heroic,' 'earnest,' 'strong and beautiful,' which are all perfect for you, right? And..."

Arthur grabbed the front of his uniform, holding it like he was clutching his own heart. He threw his other arm over his face to hide the flush rising to the tips of his ears, almost fearful in his attempt to conceal them. I just kept on describing the flowers, even while Tiara covered her mouth with her hands to keep from laughing and the boy's squirmy, puppylike reactions. This boy, too, appeared to be on death's doorstep for some unexplained reason. Still, I was too busy barreling through my embarrassment to pay it much mind.

"'I love the vow we made that day'...though that's a bit different from the original meaning," I concluded. "I wouldn't say it's inaccurate, though."

Arthur looked like he might implode. I knew the flower language was a bit much—some people even used it for wedding vows—but surely he knew I was referring to the vow he made seven years ago to become a knight.

Even so, he stood there shaking like a leaf, quivering down to the very tips of his fingers. He kept hiding his face from me; for a moment, I even thought I saw a glitter of tears in his eyes. Also, was it just me, or was he looking around for something with which to end his suffering?

Meanwhile, Stale's throat worked as he apparently tried over and over to swallow. Just what had I done to them with some simple flower language? I kept going regardless, trying not to smile at their obvious discomfort. Silence dragged on, like some kind of awkward live-TV mishap, and none of us seemed capable of making the next move.

"The flower languages are lovely, aren't they?" Tiara said, offering us all a reprieve.

Stale and Arthur managed to nod. "Thank you so much," they both said, voices hoarse.

"Well, anyway," I said, trying to change the subject, "Tiara made something wonderful. Isn't that right?"

At that, one of the maids at the back brought up another basket. Inside lay a dainty flower wreath woven out of colorful flowers. Stale and Arthur both cried out in awe.

"I didn't have enough time to make one for Big Sister," Tiara said shyly. "Would you two like to make one?" The boys froze, working through the implications of her invitation. Then they nodded, and Tiara beamed. "Please watch us, okay, Big Sister?" she said.

Tiara launched into her wreath-making class, directing while Stale and Arthur crafted in silence. I stepped back quietly, trying not to get in anyone's way as I joined the maids and guards at the back of the room. Besides, I knew how intense boys could get once they set about a task.

I contented myself just watching Tiara, who'd grown so much these past ten years. She, Stale, and Arthur looked so happy together; I dared not ruin their peace. Eventually, they stopped working, and Tiara clapped her hands together with a cheer.

"That's wonderful!"

"Are you done?! Let me see!" I said, rejoining them.

"They're very, very lovely!"

Arthur and Stale had returned to their normal hues, but as soon as they realized their work was done their faces flushed all over again. I got close enough to peer over their shoulders at the wreaths they'd made.

"How lovely indeed!" I said.

Tiara had done an excellent job teaching them and Stale and Arthur had taken to the task like naturals. Their wreaths, one jade and one white and blue, could even rival Tiara's.

"They're just wonderful!" I said. "You two—no, you three are so talented."

Arthur and Stale's wreaths were striking and stark, especially as the boys had only used one type of flower each. I swelled with pride at having picked out these flowers for them; clearly, I'd chosen correctly. I clasped my hands in front of my chest, resisting the urge to jump and cheer.

Arthur and Stale just held quiet. In fact, they bit at their lips, looking down to hide the bright color of their faces. I ignored it, much more interested in evaluating their fine work.

"Um..." Arthur said at last. He held his wreath out toward me, and Stale followed suit. My mouth fell open at the generous and sudden offer.

"Tiara said she couldn't make one for you.," Stale said. "So, if you'd like, you can have ours." His face went even redder as he spoke. Strain twisted his voice, and his eyes darted around as he said, "These represent our feelings for you."

Arthur nodded, too busy trying to keep the heat from his face to speak.

I gaped at the gifts. Here I was trying to explain flower language to the boys, but then they turned it right back around and used that same language to offer me such kind gifts. I never dreamed that such a simple gesture on my part would result in such precious presents.

"Are you sure?" I asked, a smile beginning to bloom on my face.

The boys nodded vigorously.

"Please have them," Stale insisted.

"We made them for you," Arthur said.

"Thank you. I'm so very, very happy. I'll cherish these forever!"

I beamed, reaching out for the wreaths. The boys' eyes went wide again, as though they were afraid of me or something. Did my face really threaten them so? Tiara interrupted before I could reach the wreaths.

"I think they'll both suit you very well," Tiara said. "So please let my big brother and Arthur place them on your head. I want to see you wear them as crowns."

Stale and Arthur immediately turned to each other in shock. Then, they snapped their heads around to gawk at Tiara in horror. Tiara just smiled sweetly at them. The usually eloquent Stale opened and closed his mouth like a goldfish. Arthur gripped his wreath with intense force. The two of them froze completely, so I gently bowed my head, hoping to help. For some reason, they jerked away when I did that—I could see it through the curves of my lashes. I let my wavy hair fall over my shoulders, keeping my head down.

Finally, Stale stepped up and carefully placed his wreath on my head. The emerald flowers accented my red hair, a bright, brilliant contrast. Stale moved so slowly and cautiously that it was almost like a coronation. I could just imagine him being there for that moment, an honor he himself might have pictured before, but really he should have been practicing on Tiara instead.

Arthur quickly followed and set his own wreath on top of the other. "P-pardon me," he mumbled.

Arthur's wreath was slightly bigger than my head, even including my hair, but when I lowered my head a little, it settled atop Stale's wreath and stayed there. The white and blue added to the splash of color. I raised my head again, now adorned with two flower crowns. I had to adjust them to get them to settle when I straightened.

"You look lovely!" Tiara told me.

I faced Stale and Arthur, waiting for their judgment as well. They watched me with their mouths hanging open and faces painted scarlet. I wasn't sure what they saw as I stood there in the flowers they'd set in my hair, each with its own sentimental meaning, but it seemed to fluster them.

"You do look lovely."

"They suit you."

"You look so pretty."

"It's very cute."

The boys babbled, words overlapping, and now it was my turn to be embarrassed. Having their attention on me left me shifting from foot to foot. I wasn't a cute, bubbly girl like Tiara or some dainty flower fairy; I was eighteen and doomed to become the evil final boss of this world. Flower crowns didn't suit me.

Not to mention that these particular flowers...

I reached for the baskets, still filled with flowers. I plucked one jade flower and one white flower free, then placed them in Stale and Arthur's hair, respectively. They flinched when my fingers brushed against the locks beside their ears.

"Pride..." Stale said.

The boys reached up to the flowers I'd stuck in their hair, then glanced at each other. I smiled, satisfied with my work.

"Yes. I knew it. These flowers suit you two more than anyone else in the world," I told them.

The jade flowers shone against Stale's black locks, while the blue-and-white flowers accented Arthur's silver hair.

"They really do suit you," Tiara added.

The boys just blinked at each other. How could flowers be so shocking? Then they started shaking and I worried I'd actually done something wrong. But those flowers looked so lovely on them. Stale, the poised boy who sometimes wore a cunning smile, actually looked cute with a flower in his hair. Arthur, the muscular boy with the handsome face, looked like a young maiden with petals caught in his long tresses.

Perhaps they had this same thought because they suddenly started laughing. Their faces flushed once again, though this time it was from mirth rather than embarrassment. I cocked my head, at a loss for words as they cracked up, barely able to manage a thank-you. I couldn't be that mad about seeing them so happy.

Plus, I liked knowing that the flowers in their hair matched the flowers in mine. I smiled, just watching the boys laugh, then Tiara tugged at my dress.

"They look very good on you," Tiara said, her gentle, golden eyes filled with a soft light as she smiled. Her head was the only one unadorned.

I reached into the basket, fetching one more crown for her. Tiara blinked at first, but her face lit up with happiness when I said, "But you look even better."

I relished standing there with Tiara, Stale, and Arthur, all wearing the same flowers as me. The maids and guards watched our moment with familial tenderness. For these few blessed moments, we had no worries, no cares. We laughed with perfect happiness, simply enjoying each other's company.

Our joyous little group symbolized the very peace of Freesia itself.

Bonus Side Story

"**S**TALE! Sorry I'm late."

I stood in the practice room, making my final preparations. I waved as Arthur jogged up to me. We'd been training together for a month already, but today was the first time Arthur had ever arrived so late.

"It's fine," I told him. "I was a bit late too. Did something happen to you, though?"

"When I told my mom I was goin' to a friend's place to train, she grabbed me and made me put on proper clothes," Arthur said between panting breaths. He bent over, hands on his knees.

Arthur only ever told his mom that he was "going to a friend's place," but she must have caught on eventually that I was no ordinary friend. I mean, how many people had a practice room in their home? It probably came as quite a shock. I could see why she'd make him change out of the clothes he worked the fields in.

"We have Mother's permission to train, so there's no problem there," I said. "Have you not told your mother that you're visiting the castle?"

"If I did, I'd have to tell her everything, including about the cliff collapse and all that," Arthur replied. "But I promised Dad I'd never say a word about any of it."

"I see." This whole thing would probably be quite alarming to Arthur's mother, especially if she had to learn of the cliff collapse at the same time. "I'm sorry that you and the commander have to keep secrets for us. Is it much of a burden for you two?"

"Huh? We're not doin' anything wrong. Dad's always hidin' stuff anyway. Besides..." Arthur stood up straight, staring down at me with a piercing gaze. He gave my shoulder a bump with his fist. "A kid like you shouldn't be so worried about someone else's family. I come here because I feel like it, y'know? Mom doesn't try to stop me from comin' either."

With that, Arthur picked up a practice sword and pointed it at me, prompting me to do the same.

"Then hurry up and become a knight already," I said. "We'll be able to live in the same castle that way, and it'll be less trouble to see each other."

I mirrored Arthur's pose. He plunged forward first, but I blocked the attack with a quick parry.

"Oh, that's right. My sisters told me they'll attend your entrance exam next year to support your efforts in joining the order."

"Huh?!" Arthur said. "Wait, hang on! You're really gonna make me take that exam next year?"

I ignored his outburst, thrusting my sword at his chest. He leapt out of the way.

"I told you, didn't I? I want you to become a knight as soon as possible. Don't worry, there's still plenty of time before then."

"No, there's not!" Arthur said, his voice slapping off the walls of the practice room.

It wasn't worth it to argue, so I just bit back a smile and threw myself into the bout. Later, when Pride and the others arrived to watch us train, the faintest hint of a smile slipped past my expressionless mask.

Afterword

IT'S VERY NICE to meet you. My name is Tenichi.

I'd like to thank you for purchasing *The Most Heretical Last Boss Queen: From Villainess to Savior*.

To my great honor, I managed to win Ichijinsha's very first Iris NEO fantasy award and was able to have my work published as a book. It still feels like a dream to me, even now. The fact that I made it this far is all thanks to the support I received from those who read the online version of my story.

I'm aware that the title is far too long, but the online version's title, *The Most Heretical Last Boss Queen Who Will Become the Source of Tragedy Will Devote Herself for the Sake of the People ~With the Princess's Powers and My Last Boss Cheats, I'll Save Whoever I Can~*, was even longer. Just as the name reveals, it's a story about a horrible, sinister queen who uses her many powers for the good of others. Not all otome games are like this one, but personally, I sure like the ones where most of the characters have tragic pasts. I wanted everyone to know that this story was about a final boss who saves the main characters in a darker otome game, so I ended up with a title that's way too long. Please feel free to call it "Last Boss Queen" or any other abbreviation you like.

I'd already decided how I wanted to end the story in the final chapters by the time I started uploading those first sections, but for this book version, the story only continues up to the point where Pride is thirteen years old, although she's eighteen in the new bonus chapter I wrote. I wanted people who were already familiar with the online version to be satisfied if they purchased this book too, so I put a ton of effort into writing new content, organizing the text, and filling in as much as I could. Of course, this book would have been great just with Suzunosuke-sama's illustrations alone.

I'd like to thank Suzunosuke-sensei for the truly, truly wonderful illustrations she made for this book. Her works of art are beautiful, adorable, and sublime. She brought the characters to life exactly how I imagined them, which made me so very happy. I looked them over many times, starting from the rough sketches, and they always filled me with joy. Thank you for granting this author hope with your godlike art skills.

Finally, I'd like to thank many people from the bottom of my heart—anyone who purchased this book, all of the web version readers who've stayed around for all this time, everyone at Ichijinsha, everyone who worked on the publication and novelization of this book, my editor, who treated me with so much care, Suzunosuke-sensei, and my family and friends, who always support me. I hope you can all experience even the tiniest amount of my gratitude for you.

And to my kindhearted readers, I hope to have the opportunity to see you all again someday.